C000263003

A
Work in
Progress

MATT HAYDOCK

Grosvenor House
Publishing Limited

The right of Matt Haydock to be identified as the author of this
work has been asserted in accordance with Section 78
of the Copyright, Designs and Patents Act 1988

The book cover is copyright to Matt Haydock

This book is published by
Grosvenor House Publishing Ltd
Link House
140 The Broadway, Tolworth, Surrey, KT6 7HT.
www.grosvenorhousepublishing.co.uk

This book is a work of fiction. Any resemblance to
people or events, past or present, is purely coincidental.

A CIP record for this book
is available from the British Library

ISBN 978-1-83975-652-8

To Alex

Preface

At some time in the future if my grandchildren ask, "What did you do in the Great Covid-19 Lockdown, Grandpa?" I shall simply pass them a copy of this book.

Even for those of us fortunate enough not to have caught it, it has been a strange time in all our lives. Unable to dine out with friends, theatres and cinemas closed, and travel beyond one's own locality forbidden. How to fill one's time constructively? I felt I had but two options – regale my wife, for hours on end, with tales of my childhood wanderings across the hills and mountains of Gwynedd, or write a novel. I sought my wife's guidance on this conundrum – and here's the novel!

So, what sort of novel is it? Well, to put it at its most succinct, it is a multi-threaded crime mystery containing the inevitable twists, with the longest of its threads stretching almost four hundred years. It is also the first in a trilogy.

Let me stress, regardless of whatever else it might be, this book is a total work of fiction. It is true that I have borrowed some names from people I have known, or places I have visited, but that is as far as it goes. Any resemblance between characters in the book and real people, whether alive or dead, is purely coincidental. And the same goes for the places whose names I have borrowed.

As any septuagenarian can tell you, ageing is not for the faint-hearted. However, I've found the whole writing process to be highly therapeutic and certainly much cheaper than counselling sessions. I can recommend it.

Acknowledgements

Before publishing this novel I had a few dozen copies of an earlier version printed and gave them to friends. It was an unconditional gift, with no obligation to provide critical feedback or, indeed, even read it. Fortunately, they did both. I will be eternally grateful for their extremely helpful comments and the sharp observational skills they deployed in spotting errors of various kinds. I hope my friends will forgive me for not listing and thanking them all individually here. However, there are two people who I feel should be singled out. Firstly, Dawn, who went to work on it, page by page, correcting and dissecting with her unappeasable and pitiless red pen. Secondly, I want to thank my wife, Alex, for providing boundless help and encouragement during the time I spent creating the book and, indeed, at all other times. Without her the book would never have appeared. All this said, however, I take full responsibility for it, so if it fails in its purpose, in any way, that is definitely down to me. Hopefully it won't.

Wednesday 30th August 1651. Four days before the Battle of Worcester in which Oliver Cromwell finally defeated King Charles II. And after which, the King fled abroad and Cromwell confirmed his control of the country.

The Reverend Shuttleworth inspected the sky. The daylight would soon fade, but the old priest decided there was just enough time to reach home before darkness fell, without having to increase pace. Not that it was his decision to make. It was a mild, dry, summer's evening and for some time he had been drifting in and out of a shallow sleep, with only a loose grip on the reins. But Gideon needed neither guidance nor encouragement as he pulled the old cart along the country track at a pace of his own choosing. It was a route the white shire had travelled with his master many times before, and he knew it well. Also travelling home was Adam, the priest's nine-year old adopted son, who lay sound asleep in the rear of the cart.

On just about any other day it would have been a most uneventful journey, Adam would have persisted in his slumber and the old priest would have continued to drift in and out of full consciousness, until Gideon delivered them safely home to their village of Prinsted. But today would be very different. In one of his more alert moments, the priest became aware of a noise of rising intensity and sensing it was coming from further back along the track, he straightened up and looked over his shoulder. Despite his far from perfect eyesight, he could make out a number of moving figures some distance behind and seemingly approaching at speed. As they came closer and more into focus, he could see that a heavy wagon, accompanied by a number of outriders, was fast bearing down upon him. Taking a much firmer grip on the reins he quickly directed Gideon off the track before bringing the cart to a halt.

Within seconds, the wagon, pulled by four horses and accompanied by four mounted outriders, raced past. There was no gesture of acknowledgement from anyone in the short convoy. Not even so much as a fleeting glance was exchanged.

The men were dressed almost identically and the old priest at once recognised their uniform. "Cromwell's men," he muttered to himself, as he watched the convoy disappear into the distance. Eventually, having first checked that nothing more was coming along to cause some further disturbance, he directed Gideon back onto the track to continue the journey home. Within little more than a minute a state of peaceful tranquillity was restored, with only the sound of Gideon's hooves clip-clopping on the ground and the rolling wheels of the cart to be heard. It didn't take long for the old man to resume his semi-conscious state, leaving Gideon once more in charge.

Despite the noise made by the wagon and its outriders as they rushed by, Adam had managed to remain soundly asleep, but suddenly, and at the same instant, both he and his father came to life and Gideon, without any instruction, came to a dead stop. All three had reacted to a series of loud bangs that had erupted a short distance ahead.

"What was that, father?" Adam called out, before hastily climbing up to sit next to the old man.

"'Tis the unholy sound of muskets and pistols, lad. And many of 'em," his father replied, putting an arm around the boy.

Whilst the din continued, the cart and its occupants remained silent and motionless. Eventually, a little while after the last shot was heard, the old man set Gideon moving slowly onwards once more, but just before coming to a bend in the track he again brought the cart to a halt. Reaching into a bag by his feet he pulled out a leather belt equipped with two holsters and a sheath, holding a short dagger. He fastened the belt tightly around his waist and placed a loaded pistol into each of its two holsters.

Shuttleworth stroked his son's head. "Wait here Adam, until I return. But if you hear any further commotion, you must turn the cart around and go as quickly as Gideon will take you to Widow Pugh's farm, one mile back along the road."

Adam was about to object, but his father silenced him with a finger placed over his lips. "No arguments lad. You must do as I say. Do you understand?" Adam lowered his head and nodded. The old man got down from the cart and gently patted Gideon before walking as quickly as his old legs would take him, towards the bend in the track, a short distance ahead.

As he rounded the bend he pulled one of the pistols from its holster and, keeping as close to the hedge as possible, continued to move forward, although more slowly than before. Fortunately, clouds had thickened on the western horizon and placed a shroud over the low lying sun, making the sky less bright and Shuttleworth just a little less visible. Eventually he reached a point from where he could see, some fifty paces ahead and stationary, the wagon and horses that had so recently raced past him. For a moment he stood in silence, straining to hear any unexpected sounds, before slowly venturing forwards once more. He didn't have to go much further before he had a clear view of the motionless bodies of several men lying around the track, directly ahead of him.

Heart pounding, he edged slowly forward, constantly looking around, until he stood alongside the covered wagon. Taking a fleeting glance inside, he saw that it contained several muskets together with two wooden chests. From this position he could also see several more lifeless bodies lying on and around the track.

The sight confronting the old priest was indeed one of horror, but it was not one with which he was entirely unfamiliar. In his younger days he had been a soldier in the service of King James, and on more than one occasion had a hand in creating such a scene as the one that now lay before him. But that was all in the distant past and he had hoped never to witness such things again. Some years before, he had found God and his own Salvation and turned his back on conflict, chaos and war. It was true that he might still be capable of violence, but it would only be as an act of defence and if no other option presented itself.

For several minutes he stood in silence, trying to understand what must have happened only a short while before. Some twenty paces in front of the wagon, a young tree was lying across the track and although this barrier would have been easy enough to move, the old man knew that it presented enough of an obstacle to have forced the wagon to stop. It was obvious that an ambush had taken place, but it was equally evident that matters had not gone well for the ambushers, or, indeed, for either side in the conflict. Clearly both sides had lost, and lost totally.

Cautiously he moved from body to body, but in no case could he detect any sign of life, until he approached the last of the fourteen bodies that he had counted. The heavily bloodied man was in a sitting position, his back settled against the trunk of a tree, his head down, resting on his chest. Although he could see that the man was grievously wounded, Shuttleworth sensed there was still a glimmer of life. Warily, he approached, unsure as to the kind of reception he might receive. And he was right to be wary, for as he knelt down, the wounded man raised his head, grabbed him with his left hand and with his right hand pushed the barrel of a pistol under his chin.

"Who are you?" The man demanded to know.

"I am the Reverend Richard Shuttleworth, vicar of the parish of Prinsted, and someone who wishes to help you," the old priest replied.

"God's whiskers!" exclaimed the wounded man. "Come to hear my confession have you priest?"

"If that is what you want. But whose confession will I be hearing?"

"I am Captain John Hadlington, loyal soldier of His Majesty King Charles. And I doubt either of us has time enough to hear the confessing of all my sins."

Hadlington coughed, spitting up blood, and in that moment the old priest disarmed him, placing his own pistol under Hadlington's chin.

The Captain stared at the priest. Though close to death, he still had a soldier's pride and felt shame having been disarmed by an elderly village priest. "A cunning move, especially for a priest," he said contemptuously.

Knowing that any threat had passed, Shuttleworth put his pistol back in its holster and sought to reassure Hadlington of his good intentions. "I haven't always been a priest. I, too, was once a soldier and sometimes a threat to other men, but through the Grace of Jesus Christ, I am no more. I served in the army of King James and now, like you, I am a loyal subject of his grandson, young King Charles. I wish to help you, to get you somewhere you can receive treatment for your wounds."

Hadlington smiled faintly. "I've been a soldier these twenty years and know well the stink of death. And we both know its filthy stench is all over me. There is nothing you can do for me ....but perhaps you can do something for His Majesty."

Knowing he had little time left, Hadlington decided he had no option but to trust the old priest, so explained what had happened. "Together with six of my men I left the main company of our troops to scout the local area. We knew a large body of Cromwell's men was somewhere in this region and my patrol was one of several sent out and tasked to find them and assess their strength. We stopped to rest here for a while, but barely had we settled when we heard the sounds of horses and a fast moving wagon coming our way. My men quickly placed a barrier across the road. We didn't know who was approaching, but if it were Cromwell's men, then we were prepared. On coming to the barrier they had no choice but to stop. The enterprise started well, with a single volley we cut down the wagon's driver and the four outriders. But my men were too hasty. Rushing towards the wagon without reloading their weapons, they were themselves cut down by musket and pistol fire from two heavily armed men hidden inside. The two men then leapt out to attack me with swords drawn. They fought like devils, but I eventually got the better of them." Hadlington raised a finger to point towards two bodies lying a few yards away, one of them with a sword through its torso. After spitting more blood, he continued. "The wagon contains two chests, each of which I forced open. This was no ordinary patrol. Those chests contain much treasure, and I believe I know from where it comes. For months past, Cromwell's men have raided throughout the north, plundering the homes and churches of those they suspect of loyalty to His Majesty. Having transported their loot south to the capital, Cromwell has used it to supply and pay his soldiers. By chance my patrol ambushed one of these transports. And a well-stocked one it would seem. No wonder they fought like devils to protect it." Again Hadlington spat. "As to my wounds - despite my twenty years of soldiering, today I forgot one most important rule - a man is not dead, until he is dead. As I stepped away from the wagon, I was shot in the belly, by him." Hadlington pointed to the body with a sword through its torso. "It seems I had not done such a good job of killing him the first time I ran him through. I put that right with my second attempt, although not before he'd done for me."

Hadlington was now exhausted and it was all he could do to keep his eyes open as he sat silently waiting for the priest's response.

Eventually Shuttleworth broke the silence. "And what would you have me do, Captain?"

Hadlington momentarily regained his strength. "Take the treasure and hide it. When Cromwell is finally defeated and King Charles safely restored to his throne, then you can declare it. Whatever you do, do not let it fall back into the hands of that son of a whore, Cromwell."

"Very well," said the old priest, "I shall do as you ask."

"Who is that?" exclaimed Hadlington, glancing over the priest's shoulder.

Shuttleworth grasped the handle of one of his pistols and turned to look, releasing his grip when he saw who it was. "I told you to stay with the cart, lad," he said abruptly.

Adam moved alongside his father. "I did wait a long time father, but I was afraid you might not come back."

Shuttleworth put his arm around his son and pulled him close, knowing that the scene he was witnessing would be extremely distressing for him.

"Your son is very young, priest," observed Hadlington.

"Adam is my adopted son," said the Reverend. "I have raised him alone since his parents both died from the fever when he was but a few months old."

Hadlington gave a gentle nod. "So, priest, no wife for you and no mother for the boy?"

"Quite so," Shuttleworth replied.

Hadlington focussed on Adam, "Tell me lad, does your father beat you?"

"Never, sir."

"Does he feed you well?"

"Always, sir."

"Then, you would say that your father is a good man, would you not?"

"My father is the best of men, sir," responded Adam, exchanging a smile with his father.

"I believe he may well be," said Hadlington, who, with some effort, reached into his pocket, pulled out a pouch and offered it to the boy.

Adam, at a reassuring nod from his father, stepped forward to accept it.

"That was presented to me by His Majesty, the first King Charles, after I had done him some small service," explained Hadlington. "But since I will have no further need of it, I give it to you, in the hope that you will treasure it as I have done."

Adam opened the pouch to see that it contained a large medallion. He thanked the Captain and promised to take good care of it, before putting it in his pocket.

"Now you both must go," said Hadlington. "Your only concern is the care of the treasure. There is nothing you can do for me ......except perhaps for one last service. Please return my pistol."

Shuttleworth had heard such requests before and knew well what it meant. "Are you sure?" he asked.

Hadlington held out his hand. "Never surer," he replied.

With a heavy sigh the priest handed him his pistol.

As Shuttleworth hurried back with Adam to where he had left Gideon and his cart, his brain was working harder than it had done for many a year, as he strained to create a plan of action. But the pair had gone less than fifty paces when the priest's concentration was interrupted by a single pistol shot.

Adam froze. "What was that father?"

The old man grabbed his son's arm to hurry him along, "'Twas the sound of a man gone to meet his maker, my son."

Shuttleworth decided that his best course of action would be to leave the ambush scene exactly as he had found it, except for one obvious detail - he would remove the treasure chests to a safe hiding place, a place that only he would know. In the morning, as the county awoke and people began going about their daily business, he knew that others would stumble across the scene of slaughter, ensuring that the dead would receive a Christian burial and the horses would be tended to. There was no need for him to concern himself further on such matters. The most immediate problem he faced was the transfer of the treasure chests from the wagon onto his cart. Fortunately, his cart was a few inches lower than the wagon, so through the use of horsepower he was able to drag the chests onto it, before covering them with a sheet. Temporarily removing the barrier that lay across the track, he replaced it once his cart had passed by. And finally, before leaving the scene, he said a short prayer for the souls of the dead.

THE PRESENT DAY

Day One - Saturday

Until just a few days ago, Rose had only ever driven on American highways, or the urban roads of the wealthiest and best maintained parts of American cities. Such roads could become congested at times, but at least they tended to be fairly straight and free from potholes, which, Rose had discovered, was almost invariably not the case with roads in Britain. And, as for British traffic roundabouts, well, just don't get her started!

Right now she was driving on a fairly narrow English country lane, one of those roads that she understood the least. And despite her seven years of driving experience, she had yet to fully come to terms with the concept of a speed limit. Sooner or later the inevitable was bound to happen. And it did. Rose took a bend rather faster than was advisable, or indeed legal, only to be confronted with a sight that is not entirely unusual on one of those English country lanes that she found so confusing - animals. In this case it was sheep, and quite a lot of them. Fortunately, although Rose might justifiably be considered to be a fairly aggressive driver, she has excellent reflexes, and in a split second had swerved off the road. Her quick reaction prevented her from hitting any of the sheep, but meant she crashed through a wooden fence, before coming to a jerking halt in an adjacent field.

It took several minutes for the last of the sheep to meander past. But there was a further problem, this time caused by something else that Rose felt she would never come to terms with - the British weather! It wasn't raining at that precise moment, but it had been, and quite heavily, on and off over the past few days. The ground she had swerved onto was so waterlogged and soft that her wheels could not get a grip. After several unsuccessful attempts to free herself she became resigned to the fact that she was stuck and in need of assistance. She took out her cell phone intending to call her sister who was at home just a couple of miles up the road. Frances, she felt sure, would call out the troops and she would be back on the road in no time.

Problems however, usually come in threes, and today was to be no exception. Rose's cell phone could detect no signal. She tried switching it off and back on, but that didn't help. She got out of her car, raised the phone high above her head, waved it around, but still no signal. So intent was she on trying to get a signal that she had paid no attention to the state of the ground she had stepped onto. However, she quickly became aware of it when she looked down to see her newly bought blue trousers splattered with mud. Muttering the occasional profanity, and with her frustration building, she looked around for any sign of help. That is when she noticed, about fifty yards away across the field, a lone figure standing motionless and facing away from her. She called out, but got no response. Walking towards the figure, Rose again called out, even louder this time, but still there was no reaction. Eventually, when she was barely ten paces away, the figure turned to face her. It was a tall, well built man in his forties, who had clearly suffered some severe trauma to the left side of his face, which was heavily scarred, and he wore a black patch over his left eye. He was dressed entirely in blue denim and had a shotgun tucked under his left arm.

Rose stopped dead in her tracks, but quickly collected herself, smiled at the man and pointed to her stranded car.

"I'm sorry to bother you, but as you can see I've had an accident. Unfortunately, I can't get a signal on my phone, so I was wondering if you had a phone that I might borrow for just a moment to make a call and get help."

She waited for a reply, but it never came. Without saying a word, the man simply turned away and slowly walked off. For a moment Rose watched him go, before calling him an "asshole" under her breath and walking back to her car, with frustration growing within her once more. It was then she noticed a chimney and the top of a roof, just visible behind a stone wall on the other side of the road, about thirty yards further on. Got to be worth a try, she thought. After all, the only other option was to walk the two miles to where her sister lived, but with the sky growing ever darker as the rain clouds thickened and threatened once more, this was not a very appealing proposition.

Rose walked up the road alongside the stone wall until she came to an opening, leading into a wide yard. To the left were three large outbuildings and to the right, a one storey stone cottage whose chimney and rooftop she had seen from the field. The front door of the cottage was slightly open, so, assuming someone must be at home, she knocked and called out. "Hello. Is anyone there?"

It was a voice from behind that responded, taking her by surprise. "Hello, yourself, can I help you?"

Rose turned to see a man wearing dirty overalls exiting from one of the outbuildings. He was dark haired, about six feet tall, with an athletic build. Rose thought he was probably in his late thirties and, well, quite handsome. He walked towards her whilst wiping his dirty, oily hands, on an equally dirty and oily rag.

Rose was a raven haired, dark eyed, stunningly beautiful woman and she knew it. She was aware of the effect that she could have on men. When a man came face to face with her for the first time, he would invariably give some form of noticeable reaction: speechlessness; gawping; and on occasions, even gibbering idiocy. She had seen the lot. But whatever the reaction, it invariably involved some display of awkward self-consciousness. This time, though, it was different. The stranger she was facing gave no particular reaction one way or the other. He was, in fact, the epitome of cool and simply smiled as he continued to wipe his hands on the dirty rag. Rose, on the other hand, was the one who began to feel self-conscious, a feeling to which she was entirely unaccustomed.

The man stopped several feet away and Rose returned his smile without speaking a word. Slowly his expression shifted to a more quizzical look and Rose realised she had been staring at him for far too long and was yet to respond to his question.

"Yes. Hello. Thank you," she eventually said, rather nervously. "I'm hoping that you can help me." Rose explained her predicament and her desire to phone her sister who lived a couple of miles down the road.

"Well I'm sure I can help you," said the man, gesturing for her to enter the cottage.

As the pair went through the front door and directly into what was obviously the sitting room, there was a flash of lightning followed almost immediately by a clap of thunder and the heavens opened.

"No mobile phone will work for at least half a mile in any direction from here," the man explained. "Apparently we're in a dead spot for communications because of the local topography. You'd have to go up into the village to get a strong signal, but there's a landline in my study you can use. It's through there." He pointed to one of the four doors that led off the sitting room.

Rose put out her hand. "Thank you so much. I'm Rose. Rose Harfield."

Instead of taking Rose's hand the man simply raised both of his own. Still holding his oily rag, he showed that neither of them was in a fit state to be shaken. "Brazelle, Chris Brazelle," he replied.

Rose smiled and pulled her hand away. "I'll take a rain check on the handshake then, Mr Brazelle."

"Good idea," said Brazelle, putting on another quizzical look. "Rose Harfield......and your sister lives a couple of miles up the road, you say. Would that be Harfield House, the Georgian mansion on the far side of the village?"

Rose nodded. "Yes, that's right. My family have lived there for a very long time, and I was born there. Do you know my sister, Frances Marshall?"

Brazelle shook his head. "No, I'm afraid I don't move in such elevated circles. Your family are considered to be the Lords and Ladies of the Manor around here, I understand."

"Well, maybe once I suppose," said Rose. "My ancestors used to own most of the land as well as just about everything in the village. But over the years quite a lot of it has been sold, so I don't think the title fits anymore, even if it did in the past."

Brazelle showed his oily palms again. "I need to wash my hands and get out of these dirty overalls and you need to make a phone call." He pushed open the door to his study, pointed to the telephone and was about to leave, when Rose asked, "What is this place called? I suppose it would help if I told my sister exactly where I am."

"Holford," replied Brazelle. "This area is called Holford and you're standing in Holford's Cottage. There's a sign by the gate, although it's a bit weather-beaten. But the name also appears on a road sign about twenty yards up the road towards the village, so it's fairly easy to find. Why don't you tell your sister to pick you up from here? It's pouring down and you'd get soaked if you walked back to your car."

"Thanks, I'll do that," replied Rose, disappearing into the study.

Some minutes later, Brazelle returned to the sitting room, having washed his hands and changed out of his overalls, and Rose reappeared from making her phone call. "I told my sister where I am and someone should be here to pick me up in a few minutes," she said. "It really is kind of you to help me out. Not like the guy I met in the field earlier."

"What guy was that?" asked Brazelle.

"There was some guy with a shotgun just standing in the field I crashed into. When I spoke to him he ignored me and walked off. I thought he was a bit scary and rude. But I also felt rather sorry for him, because he had a very heavily scarred face and a patch over his left eye. I don't suppose you…...."

Brazelle interrupted her. "Yes, I can see how that might have unnerved you a bit, especially just having had a car accident." He then changed the subject. "I hope you don't mind me mentioning it, but you said you were born here and yet you have a very obvious American accent."

Rose smiled and nodded. "Yes, that's right. I've been living in the States, mostly in New York, since just after my parents died when I was five years old, which makes it almost twenty years. I've been back here a couple of times for short visits, but I suppose I've grown up to think of the States as my home. Anyway, can I ask a question about you?"

"Yes. Sure. Go ahead."

There were numerous paintings in the room, either hanging on the walls, or simply propped up on the floor, whilst one, an unfinished painting of a church, was mounted on an easel. Rose waved her arm around the room. "Did you paint all these?"

Brazelle nodded.

"Then you're a very talented artist, Mr Brazelle. They're really lovely."

"I'm glad you like them and thanks for the compliment, but I never describe myself as an artist. I'm just someone who enjoys painting."

Rose smiled. "Well, whatever you call yourself, I think they're great. I only wish I could paint like that. You'd think I might be able to, because my father was a really skilled artist and my sister is pretty good too. But, for some reason, I seem to have missed out on the artistic gene."

"Ah yes, of course, you must be the daughter of Sir Cornelius Harfield," said Brazelle.

Rose nodded. "Are you familiar with my father's work?"

"A little. I've seen several of his paintings and I think they're quite outstanding. Your father, of course, was particularly keen on portrait painting, not something I've attempted much of myself. I've tended to stick to lanscapes and the occasional building, this sort of thing, for example." Brazelle pointed to the half finished painting of a church that stood on his easel. "That's a work in progress."

Rose turned to look. "Oddly enough, although I haven't been in or around it for years, I recognise it. It's the church in the village, isn't it? That's the church where my parents were married and where I was christened. I recognise it because I have a photograph of my parents on their wedding day with the church in the background. I have it on the wall of my apartment, so I see it practically every day."

Rose went silent and stared at the painting for a few moments, before eventually turning to face Brazelle. "I certainly owe you a favour for helping me out. Would you like to come up to Harfield House when you have some free time and take a look at my father's paintings? Over the years, a number have been sold or given away, but we still have quite a lot on display around the house."

"That's a very kind offer and I would very much like to take you up on it, sometime," replied Brazelle.

"Great," said Rose. "What about tomorrow afternoon?"

Brazelle was taken by surprise. He had assumed Rose's invitation to be one of those vague proposals that an acquaintance sometimes makes, but with no serious intention of following through on it. Now he realised that Rose was indeed very serious and decided he should give a gracious response. "Well, that sounds good to me." But then he hesitated. "Ah! No. Unfortunately I can't. Tomorrow's Sunday and I have something scheduled with a colleague. We won't be finished until around seven and by then we'll both be starving and need to eat. I'm afraid it's now my turn to take a rain check."

Disappointment spread over Rose's face, but then her smile returned. "Well that's okay. Why not come along after you've finished whatever it is you're doing and bring your colleague with you? You can both eat at Harfield House. I'll give you a tour and you can see some of father's paintings."

Again taken by surprise, Brazelle took a few moments to consider his response. "Well, if you're sure you don't mind, but what about your sister? Will she be okay with two strangers showing up in her home, and with very little warning?"

"Sure. Frankie is very relaxed about such things," replied Rose. "And she absolutely loves talking about father's paintings, especially to a fellow artist. But, in any case, Harfield House is as much mine as it is hers. When my father died he left it to both of us. It's just that my sister and her husband recently decided to live in it, but I didn't."

It suddenly started to dawn on Rose just how pushy she must have sounded. She had only just met Brazelle a few minutes ago and, for the second time, began to feel quite self-conscious. There was only one thing for it, she thought, she would confront the situation head on. "I'm sorry if I sound a bit pushy. It's just that I intend returning to the States very soon and I might not get another opportunity to show you my father's paintings. I would really like to do that, as a thank you for helping me out today."

"Well, I'm very grateful for your generous invitation and I have no doubt my colleague will be as well," said Brazelle.

"Absolutely perfect," confirmed Rose, "But would you mind if I ask a personal question?"

Brazelle smiled. "You can certainly ask. But until I hear it I can't promise you an answer."

"Well, I really love your quaint little English country cottage, and I just wondered how long you'd lived here."

Brazelle squinted. "Quaint? Isn't that a euphemism for odd?"

His smile told Rose that he wasn't serious.

"I think you know I didn't mean it that way. It's just that in the States you would never come across a cottage like this. It has a certain charm, an almost magical attraction. Well, for me at least."

"I know what you mean," responded Brazelle. "It holds a strong attraction for me as well, which is why I chose to live in it. But to answer your question, I moved in here three months ago on a six-month lease, whilst I complete a project that I'm involved with. Then I guess I'll have to move out and move on. Oddly enough though, the freeholder for the property is the Harfield Estate, so I guess that makes you my landlady."

"No way!" exclaimed Rose.

"Absolutely true," confirmed Brazelle. "And I'm told there are at least a couple of dozen other properties around here still owned by the Harfield Estate, including, by the way, the Prinsted village tavern, Cromwell's Treasure. So it looks like your family still are the Lords and Ladies of the Manor."

A car turned into the yard and Rose looked out of the window. "It's Damien, my brother-in-law."

Brazelle opened the front door, invited Damien in, and Rose performed the introductions. Damien was a tall, well dressed, man of about fifty years of age. Obviously a man of substance, thought Brazelle. But even if he hadn't been before he married into the Harfield family, he would be now. Brazelle could also tell there was clearly a close relationship between Rose and her brother in law - one resembling that between a father and his favourite daughter.

"Mr Brazelle has been really kind, Damien, helping me out in my hour of need," said Rose. "And as you can see, he's an artist, and a very talented one."

Brazelle corrected her, "I'm just a man who likes to paint."

Damien cast his eyes over some of the paintings. "You're too modest, Mr Brazelle. These are quite exceptional. Has my sister-in-law told you her late father was also an accomplished artist, Cornelius Harfield?"

"Yes, I did," said Rose. "And it turns out that Mr Brazelle is an admirer of father's work. So, as a thank you for helping me out today, I've invited him and one of his colleagues up to the House tomorrow evening, to take a look at some of his paintings."

If Damien thought that Rose's invitation to Brazelle, and someone she hadn't even met, was a bit precipitous, which he did, he didn't show it. "Splendid," he said. "I hope you find your visit enjoyable and, who knows, perhaps even inspirational. Unfortunately, I won't be there to welcome you myself, as I have to fly off tonight and I'll be away for a couple of days. But I'm sure my wife and sister-in-law will prove to be excellent hosts." He looked at his watch. "I think we should leave Mr Brazelle in peace now, Rose. You've taken up enough of his time already. Jonathan and Gareth are sorting out the recovery of your car. I assume you've left the keys in, like you always do, and like I'm always telling you not to do. Fortunately, the fence and the field you crashed into belong to the Harfield Estate, so at least we won't have any irate farmers to deal with after your little adventure."

Rose turned to Brazelle and gave him a grin and a slight shrug of the shoulders in response to Damien's sarcasm.

"Goodbye, Mr Brazelle," she said. "And thanks again for your help and shelter. I'll look forward to seeing you tomorrow, about seven."

"About seven," confirmed Brazelle. "I'm already looking forward to it."

Rose held out her hand. "I'll collect on that rain check now."

Brazelle took the hand that was offered, but Rose held on for several seconds longer than was necessary before letting go and running out to Damien's car.

"Why on earth did I do that?" thought Rose, as the car pulled away. Back in his cottage, Brazelle was thinking the same thing.

Day Two - Sunday

Harfield House is an elegant four-storey Georgian mansion, which, together with its extensive gardens, occupies a large plot of land on the northern edge of the village of Prinsted. The Harfield family first took possession of the site in the late seventeenth century and the existing mansion stands on the site of an earlier building dating back to that time. The previous property was demolished in the late eighteenth century, to make way for something more in keeping with the 'modern times'. A mortared stone wall, almost ten feet high, runs alongside the road some seventy yards in front of the House, ensuring its invisibility to all, except those privileged to enter through a pair of high metal gates that carry the Harfield family crest. French prisoners constructed the gates and the wall, which runs all the way around the House and its gardens, during the time of the Napoleonic Wars, so, perhaps not surprisingly, they are referred to locally as Napoleon's Wall and Napoleon's Gates.

A large retinue of resident servants once serviced the property, but nowadays, only three members of staff live-in: a married couple in their early sixties, Megan and Jonathan Richards; and, their thirty one year old son Gareth. Megan acts as housekeeper and head cook, overseeing a small team of non-resident domestic staff, whilst Jonathan heads up his own small team, taking care of property and grounds maintenance, as well as fulfilling the role of butler. Gareth supports his parents as needed being particularly proficient at ensuring the House is as up-to-date as possible in its technological development.

It was just after 7pm as Brazelle and his colleague approached Napoleon's Gates. Brazelle had driven past them numerous times, but could only ever remember seeing them closed. On this occasion, however, no doubt in anticipation of his expected visit, they were wide open, so the car, driven by his colleague, passed straight through.

The daylight was fading and it was raining quite heavily, but the House and the grounds in which it stood still presented a magnificent sight. Brazelle realised that generations of Harfields must have been people of good taste, as well as substantial means.

Despite parking the car as close to the house as possible, such were the weather conditions, both visitors were wet and dishevelled by the time they reached the front door.

In a property as grand as Harfield House it might well be the natural assumption that when the doorbell rang, it would be a butler or some other member of staff who would be the one to respond, but it was Rose, wearing a little black dress and a smile, who answered the door. "Welcome to Harfield House," she said, moving aside to allow her guests to enter into the grand entrance hall. Rose's smile, however, suddenly disappeared as she came face to face with Brazelle's colleague. "You're a woman!" she exclaimed.

Brazelle's colleague was indeed a woman. She was of similar age to Brazelle, quite tall, slim and attractive with long dark hair. Although somewhat taken aback by Rose's unexpected style of greeting, she nevertheless managed a smile and stretched out her hand towards Rose. "Yes that's right, Jenny Caulfield. I'm very pleased to meet you."

Rose took the hand that was offered and realised how ridiculous she must have appeared. "Oh, I am sorry.

I guess I just assumed you'd be a man. Let me help you get out of your wet coat. You're soaked."

Jenny removed her raincoat, prompting another expression of surprise from Rose. "You're a priest!"

Jenny touched the dog collar she was wearing and again smiled. "Yes, I'm the Prinsted Parish vicar. Are you okay with women priests?" The question was purely rhetorical and Jenny didn't wait for a response before continuing. "What an absolutely fabulous home you have."

"Thank you," said Rose, realising she had to pull herself together or her embarrassment would become unbearable. Once again she apologised for her outburst, but there was still one more surprise to come.

Brazelle had been standing just behind Jenny removing his own coat, but Jenny stepped to one side and Rose could see that he was also wearing a dog collar. "And you're a priest!" she exclaimed.

Brazelle nodded. "Yes. I suppose it would come as a bit of a surprise, bearing in mind the state I was in when we met yesterday."

Jonathan, in his butler's garb, arrived in the entrance hall and took possession of the guests' wet coats before immediately passing them to a young female servant who had also appeared.

"Can we start again?" asked Rose, having regained her composure and her smile.

"Sure thing," replied Jenny reassuringly. "But is there somewhere I could freshen up and sort out my hair? Priest or not, as you correctly pointed out, I am a woman."

"Yes, of course. You can come up to my room," replied Rose, before turning to Jonathan. "Take Mr Brazelle into the library and get him a drink would you, Jonathan, whilst I look after our other guest?"

Rose led Jenny towards the staircase, but momentarily turned back towards Brazelle. "We won't be long. Jonathan will look after you. Just let him know if you want anything."

On entering the library, Brazelle's eyes were immediately drawn to the large painting of a woman that hung over a rather grand fireplace, directly opposite the doorway.

"What can I get you, sir?" asked Jonathan.

"Whisky please, with just a single piece of ice."

Jonathan nodded and left the room, leaving the door slightly open.

Brazelle's first thought was that the woman in the portrait was Rose with much shorter hair. He moved nearer to take a closer look and was studying the picture so intently, he was unaware that a second person had entered the room.

"Beautiful, isn't she?" said a voice from behind. Brazelle immediately turned to find he was facing a tall, elegantly dressed blonde woman of around fifty years of age.

"Yes she is," he replied.

The woman stepped forward and held out her right hand. "I'm Frances Marshall, Rose's sister, and you must be Mr Brazelle." She pointed to his dog collar. "Or, should I call you Reverend Brazelle?"

"Call me whatever you feel most comfortable with," he replied, taking her hand.

Frances looked up at the portrait over the mantelpiece. "It isn't Rose, you know. It's her mother, Justine."

"Yes, I thought as much," responded Brazelle. "It did throw me for a moment. But then I realised it couldn't possibly be your sister and rather guessed that it must be her mother because of the incredible likeness. I noticed a small tattoo of what I think is a rose on the left upper arm and I'm fairly sure your sister doesn't have one."

Frances raised an eyebrow. "You're very observant. I don't know whether I'm more impressed that you spotted what is a very small tattoo of a rose in the portrait, or noticed that my sister doesn't have one."

Brazelle smiled. "Actually, I wouldn't have trusted my judgement on that one feature alone. I guessed that the signature in the bottom right hand corner is that of your father. And, if I'm right, then given that your father died twenty years ago, the picture couldn't possibly be a portrait of your sister."

"You are absolutely right Mr Brazelle. Justine acquired the tattoo, much to my father's disgust, as a kind of celebration of Rose's birth. Such was his irritation, he at first refused to include it in the portrait, but Justine insisted that he should and, although very much reluctantly, he eventually agreed. Really it was something of a compromise, because Justine's actual tattoo was quite a bit bigger than the one that my father included in the portrait." Frances smiled. "It was close to being the last picture he ever painted. He started it just after Rose had her second birthday and it took him quite a while to complete it. She was almost three by the time he declared it 'mission accomplished' and hung it up there, just two years before Justine died."

Jonathan entered the room carrying a small silver tray bearing two tumblers. Frances took the first tumbler before the second was offered to Brazelle. It contained rather more whisky than Brazelle was expecting and Frances could tell what he was thinking. "When it comes to whisky, Jonathan doesn't do anything by halves," she said. "It comes of having poured so many for my father in the past. Old habits die hard, eh, Jonathan?" Jonathan made no reply, but simply exchanged a faint smile with Frances, nodded and left the room.

Brazelle pointed at Justine's portrait. "Rose's mother must have been very young when she died?"

"Yes, she was. She'd only recently had her thirtieth birthday," replied Frances. "It was a tragic accident that happened almost twenty years ago. Justine was crossing over the stream that runs through the village. It was in full flood and the old wooden bridge she was crossing on was very slippery and barely above water level. Unfortunately, she slipped and fell, hit her head on one of the rocks and drowned. Sadly, it proved even more tragic. Understandably, it hit my father very hard. In fact it must have hit him even harder than we realised, because the day after Justine's funeral he took his own life."

Brazelle's eyes widened. "That must have been a series of quite devastating shocks for you, and for Rose."

"Yes it certainly was. And it was especially traumatic for Rose," responded Frances. "I was married to Damien when all this happened, but Rose was only just turned five and still an infant, so Damian and I acquired legal guardianship and took on the responsibility of bringing her up." Frances paused for a moment. "As I'm sure you will have guessed already, Mr Brazelle, Rose and I are, in fact, half sisters. Justine was my father's second wife. I'm the daughter of his first wife, Brigitte, who died when I was eighteen. My father and Justine first met about six years after my mother died when he was attending a conference with a lot of Italians, most of whom didn't speak English. My father's Italian was reasonable, but the people in charge insisted he had Justine along with him as his interpreter. She was totally fluent in Italian. They married a few months after they first met and Rose was born almost one year later. You will probably also have realised that Justine was much younger than my father. So, there you have it. A number of questions that would have almost certainly entered your mind at some point, already answered."

Frances changed the subject. "In order to better appreciate my father's approach to his art, it helps to learn something of our family history. And this room is probably the best one to start in. Why don't you take a look around and see what you think?"

Brazelle did as advised and took some time to look over the other paintings in the room. Bookcases covered the first six feet of all the walls, except the one with the fireplace and Justine's portrait. Between the top of the bookcases and the ceiling were a series of portraits running all the way round the room.

There were eleven pictures in total and each was the portrait of a man, although the first, the one in the far left hand corner of the room, was painted without a face. Judging by the changing style of dress in the pictures, Brazelle concluded that they were probably arranged around the room in chronological order, begining with the faceless portrait and ending with the portrait positioned in the corner to his far right.

He walked slowly around the room in order to take a closer look at each portrait in turn, beginning with the faceless portrait. Frances waited until he had concluded his tour before asking him what his conclusions were.

"Well, as far as the actual art is concerned, they are all very good. Indeed, truly excellent," Brazelle responded. "I see that the signatures on the last two and, oddly enough the very first one, more or less match that on the portrait of Rose's mother. I would guess that the other portraits were each painted sometime between the early eighteenth and mid twentieth centuries by different artists. Judging by the names and dates of the subjects of the portraits on the attached badges, I assume they are your ancestors, all the way back, to him." Brazelle pointed to the faceless portrait. "Why does he have no face?"

Frances saluted Brazelle by raising the tumbler she was holding. "Bravo Mr Brazelle! You are correct in every detail. They are my ancestors and my father did indeed paint the last two portraits and the first. He painted his father almost sixty years ago and his self-portrait about twenty years later. And the subject in the first portrait has no face for the very simple reason that nobody knows what he looked like. As far as the family is aware he had no portrait of himself created in his lifetime. He was a wealthy landowner and so it would have been extremely unusual, possibly uniquely so, that there should not have been at least one portrait of him created. The Harfield Estate has been in the hands of my family ever since his time, so if a portrait of him ever did exist, I'm sure we would know about it and almost certainly still possess it. My father always hoped that one day he'd be in a position to put a face in the portrait, so, despite having signed it, he always thought of it and frequently referred to it as still being, 'A work in progress'."

Brazelle pointed at the faceless portrait. "So, it was him, the man of the unknown face, who was the founder of the Harfield dynasty here in Prinsted?"

"Yes, that is Sir Richard, first Baronet Harfield, my nine times great grandfather, the man who first established the Harfield Estate in Prinsted and built the first Harfield House to stand on this site. And yet, despite his significant position in our family history, we know surprisingly little about him. What we do know is that he turned up in Prinsted in 1685, a short while after King Charles the Second died, having been an officer in the King's bodyguard. It was King Charles who, shortly before his death, created Richard the first Baronet Harfield and awarded him a substantial gratuity and pension for his services. There is a direct line from father to son, all the way round this room to my father, the 11th Baronet Harfield. And it looks like he'll also be the last, seeing as he only had two daughters, but no son."

Brazelle understood. "So all of your ancestors pictured here, including your father, held the title 'Sir' because they were hereditary baronets. Until now I had assumed your father was 'Sir' Cornelius because he'd been knighted."

"You're not the first person to make that assumption," said Frances. "It's a very common misunderstanding. My father received many honours and awards in his lifetime, but he was never knighted. My husband Damien, on the other hand, is a knight, and his title is not hereditary. But then Damien works in the Diplomatic Service where a knighthood tends to go with the job. The rank of baronet was introduced in England in the fourteenth century, so it's an ancient title. According to the historians, King James the First, Charles the Second's grandfather, holds the record for the number created by a single monarch. Apparently, he created a few hundred of them through selling the title to raise funds. His grandson, Charles, however, appears to have been rather more discriminating and we like to think that Sir Richard earned his title, rather than bought it."

"Do you know why Sir Richard chose Prinsted as the place to settle in his retirement from the military?" Brazelle asked.

Frances shook her head. "No, it's yet another mystery. Very little was written about Sir Richard in his lifetime, or indeed at any time. What we do know is that he was in his mid forties when he first arrived here, and he brought with him a much younger wife and an infant son. Other than the fact he'd been previously employed in the service of King Charles, we know little of his earlier life and certainly nothing of his origins."

"You have a fascinating family history. And mystery!" commented Brazelle, with obvious interest.

"Indeed we do," agreed Frances. "But then there is the greatest Harfield family mystery of all - the source of Sir Richard's wealth. He spent his first few years in Prinsted buying up considerable amounts of land and property, as well as building a substantial mansion on this site. Although he'd been granted a generous gratuity and pension by King Charles, that doesn't come close to accounting for the totality of his apparent wealth. One of the theories proposed, more than once over the years, is that his wife, who we believe was French, was a wealthy heiress and that it was her money he was using. But no real evidence has ever been put forward to support that idea, or indeed, any other theory. The truth is we just don't know how he came by such considerable wealth."

Frances would probably have continued with her tales of family history, but Rose and Jenny entered the room. Rose introduced Jenny to her sister before addressing Brazelle, "Jenny explained what you were doing before coming here this evening. I guess the dog collars, and the fact it's

Sunday, makes it fairly obvious. Anyway, I guess you're both starving. I didn't know what sorts of things you do or don't eat, so I asked Mrs Richards to put a varied selection in the dining room. You should be able to find something you like. Then I'll show you some more of the House and my father's work."

"Sounds great," said Jenny.

Rose smiled. "Well, if you'll please bear with me for just a few more minutes, I'll just check that everything's ready."

The sisters left the room, closing the door behind them. As soon as they were alone, Jenny whispered to Brazelle. "You know she's smitten, don't you?"

"What?"

"Smitten…. Rose….. She's smitten," repeated Jenny, this time a little louder.

Brazelle adopted a puzzled expression. "What do you mean …… smitten?"

Jenny prodded Brazelle in the chest. "With you! She's smitten with you. And about ten percent beyond totally, I'd say."

"Don't be ridiculous," objected Brazelle. "We only met yesterday and then only for a matter of minutes."

Jenny raised her right hand to silence Brazelle. "Trust me Chris. I know what I'm talking about. It only took a few minutes for me to fall for Gerald when we first met, you know. But don't you dare tell him, for goodness' sake, he's conceited enough already. Besides, what do you think we've been doing all this time since she took me up to her room? I'll tell you what mate - she's been giving me the third degree about you, that's what. She was bordering on the hostile until I told her I'd been happily married to the village doctor for the past twelve years. She asked all sorts of stuff about you. For Pete's sake, Chris, she even asked if I thought you were gay!"

Brazelle was about to respond when the door opened.

"Sir, Madam, if you would please follow me," said Jonathan, leading them to the dining room where Rose, Frances and the female staff member they had seen earlier were waiting.

Running down the centre of the room was a long, wide, dining table, which Jenny thought might be big enough to fit her entire congregation around, especially on a wet Sunday morning. On this occasion, however, it had just four places laid at one end. Along one side of the room was a second, much narrower, but equally long table on which were placed several large dishes and two hot buffet servers, piled with food.

"Mrs Richards has covered as many options as possible. If you want to know anything about the various dishes, just ask Layla." Rose pointed to the servant standing alongside, before giving a gesture of encouragement for them to help themselves.

There were a number of paintings hanging on the walls of the dining room, although unlike those in the library, not all were portraits. Brazelle took a look at each of them in turn, slowly working his way around the room and asking occasional questions. It was fortunate that Frances was on hand to answer his questions, he thought. She was clearly well informed about each of the paintings, whilst it was equally clear that Rose was not.

Once the meal ended, the group moved to the main drawing room where more paintings were on display. Although mostly the work of Sir Cornelius, a few had been painted by Frances. Brazelle was impressed by Frances' almost encyclopaedic knowledge concerning the numerous paintings in the House and how each fitted into the history of the Harfield family, but he now came to appreciate she also had real skill as an artist in her own right.

Throughout the evening, Frances had found herself warming to Brazelle and as he complimented her artwork in a way that she took to be sincere rather than simply polite, this feeling was reinforced. But there was another feeling she had experienced that evening, one about which she would later tell Rose. It was a feeling that she and Brazelle had met before, although she couldn't recall where or when. Having enjoyed the opportunity to talk about her family's art and its history, she thought it was time to find out a little more about her guests and decided to start with Jenny. "So, how did you and your husband find yourselves living and working in Prinsted?" she asked.

"Essentially because of Gerald, my husband," replied Jenny. "He was born and brought up here in Prinsted. His father was the village doctor before him and when his father retired a couple of years ago, Gerald took over his practice. Before that, he'd worked mainly in hospital Accident and Emergency departments, although, he'd also trained as a General Practitioner with the intention of eventually taking over from his father. He still likes to keep his hand in, in A&E even now, so a couple of times a month he takes on a shift at the City General. In fact that's where he is tonight. Its fairly exhausting work, but he still enjoys doing it - within limits!"

"I thought I recognised the name, Caulfield," said Frances. "So, your husband must be the son of Dr James Caulfield. I also seem to remember that the old vicar was the Reverend Raynworth. What happened to him?"

"You're right on both counts," responded Jenny. "Reverend Raynworth retired about three years ago and his place was taken by a Reverend Pickering. Then just over a year ago he left, and I applied for the post. It might have helped that Gerald's dad was a golfing chum of the Bishop, but I like to think I would have got the job anyway. Did you know Reverend Raynworth?"

"I knew him a long time ago," replied Frances. "But I stopped going to Prinsted Church after I got married. Damien is Catholic, albeit a rather lapsed one, and after we got married my church attendance sort of fizzled out. That's why you haven't seen me in your congregation despite the fact that Damien and I have been living back here at Harfield House for more than six months. I'm afraid we probably also rather neglected Rose's spiritual development as she was growing up, but perhaps one or the other of you two might be able to help with that?"

Jenny smiled at Rose. "We're always available to offer spiritual guidance, sometimes even when it's not asked for."

Rose decided to get the conversation moved on from the subject of her spiritual development and threw a question at Jenny. "What did you do before you became a priest?"

"I was a doctor like Gerald, a psychiatrist to be precise. In fact that's how we met. We were at Med School together."

"And what made you decide to give up medicine to become a priest?" asked Frances.

"I was a psychiatrist specialising in criminal deviance. I decided there were only so many psychopaths and serial killers I wanted to meet in a lifetime, and that I'd just about reached my limit." Jenny paused momentarily, "But more importantly, I got the call. I believe that if you don't get the call then you shouldn't go. But, if you do get the call, then you really have to respond. So I did. And five years ago I started training to be a Church of England priest. That's when I met Chris for the first time. We were on the same training programme and we've remained friends ever since."

Rose turned to Brazelle. "Jenny told me earlier that you and she were collaborating on some project. What sort of project is it? Or is it confidential?"

"No, there's nothing confidential about it," replied Brazelle. "The village church, St Catherine's, is being renovated and Jenny and I are involved in managing the progress of the work on behalf of the Diocese. The renovation started three months ago and should be completed in another two to three months, if all goes well. Obviously, Jenny is involved because she's the parish priest and it's her church. I'm involved, essentially, because of something I said to a Bishop whilst we were training five years ago. I told him I was interested in church architecture. A perfectly innocent confession to make you might think, but, what I didn't know at the time was that the Church of England hierarchy had decided that it needed more priests who were sufficiently knowledgeable about church buildings to be usefully commissioned to oversee projects such as this one. Consequently, the next thing I knew, I was sent on a short intensive training programme, a mixture of architecture, civil engineering and project management. Unwittingly, I'd made myself a hostage to fortune and a few years later, here I am. And I'm fortunate enough to have Jenny as my partner on the project."

"So, it was pure coincidence that two old friends ended up collaborating on the project," commented Frances.

"Yes that's right," replied Jenny. "St Catherine's was very fortunate to be given the money to carry out the work. It came as a most unexpected yet wonderful surprise when funding for the project was finally confirmed. There had been some provisional, exploratory work done on the building about six months earlier. Although a number of issues were identified, we were told that nothing sufficiently serious had been found that the Diocese, always claiming to be strapped for cash, felt warranted authorising any further expenditure. At the time we were extremely disappointed, as you might imagine, but then we heard a few months later that we were to get funding for the work after all. Apparently, the Diocese had been overruled by the Archbishop of Canterbury's office. We were told that a significant sum of money had been allocated to the project and that Chris had been appointed to be its overall manager. Unusual, some might say, but it gave St Catherine's what we wanted."

"What about you?" Frances asked Brazelle. "What did you do before becoming a priest?"

Before Brazelle could respond, Jenny interrupted. "Oh, you're wasting your time there, I'm afraid. We all tried to get Chris to open up when we were in training together, but without success. In the end we decided he must have been some sort of spy and signed the Official Secrets Act or something like that, so we gave up." She looked at her phone that had just beeped. "Oh, I am sorry, I'm afraid I'm going to have to leave. Gerald has just sent a message saying he's on his way home, shattered and hungry. I'd better go home and fix him some supper. It's really been a great evening. Thank you so much for inviting me along. I've enjoyed it immensely." Turning to Brazelle she added. "I'm sorry to break things up like this, Chris, but if you want a lift I'm afraid we're going to have to leave."

Rose looked at Brazelle, "I can give you a ride home. You haven't seen my father's studio yet. I was saving it to show you last. It's still just as he left it and I'm sure you'll find it interesting. And don't worry about this." Rose raised the glass she was holding. "I haven't touched a drop all night. This is strictly non alcoholic."

Brazelle was keen to see the inside of Sir Cornelius' studio, so accepted Rose's offer of a ride home, but accompanied Jenny to her car to retrieve his briefcase. Jenny took the opportunity to whisper a few reminders. "Don't forget you're coming to dinner tomorrow night. It should be interesting. And remember.....smitten!" Then, as an afterthought, in between giving Brazelle a wink and driving off, she added, "And I think the sister approves, but she's the type who'll let you know either way!"

Sir Cornelius' studio was at the very top of the House and, as Rose had said, was just as her father had left it on the day he died. Every so often Mrs Richards would go in, open the windows for a time and put a duster around, but nothing else. The decision to leave things untouched had essentially been taken by Rose. She was only five years old when her father died, but, as young as she was, she made one thing very clear - she did not want anyone to mess with 'Daddy's Things'. As a result, Frances gave the necessary instructions and nothing was changed.

The first thing that struck Brazelle on entering the studio was its sheer size. It was at least twice as big as any of the rooms that he had seen up to that point. The second thing that surprised him was that it looked more like a physics laboratory or engineering workshop than an artist's studio. There were various pieces of electronic equipment; two computers that clearly belonged to the later years of the last millennium; and, an array of four monitor screens which Brazelle guessed were part of a CCTV system. Around the walls there were a great many bookshelves, each holding a vast array of printed books plus a significant number of notebooks. And filling the spaces inbetween were numerous whiteboards, each carrying all manner of drawings and script, none of which was intelligible to Brazelle. The only obvious clues to the room's owner having an interest in art were four paintings hanging on the wall and two unfinished ones standing on easels in one corner. Brazelle had been inside quite a few artists' studios, but this one was like no other he had ever seen.

"I can tell it isn't what you were expecting, Mr Brazelle," said Frances.

"No it isn't," he replied. "I knew your father was a talented man with interests that went beyond his painting, but I didn't anticipate anything like this."

"Our father wasn't just a talented man, Mr Brazelle, he was a genius," asserted Frances. "He was capable of turning his mind to just about anything and was as much at home in the various disciplines of science and engineering as he was in the realm of art. He was an original and inventive thinker who registered numerous patents during his lifetime."

Brazelle was genuinely surprised. "I had no idea of the breadth and depth of his interests."

"You are not alone in that," said Frances. "Our father's genius was only matched by his modesty and his desire for privacy. He was adviser to many research groups and sat on a wide range of influential scientific committees, but he never sought public recognition or reward. If it had been his wish, he could have had a brilliant career in any of the world's top universities or research centres, but, as it was, he preferred to maintain his independence and determine his own priorities."

"And he was fortunate enough to have the resources to allow him to do just that," commented Brazelle.

"Yes," Frances replied. "And he never forgot how fortunate he was. Although it was his inborn desire to explore and understand that drove him, his greatest sense of fulfilment always came from discovering or inventing something that provided benefit to others."

Brazelle pointed at the monitor screens. "I assume these are connected to the CCTV security system?"

Frances nodded. "Yes, there are cameras outside and inside the house. Father used to spend a great deal of his time up here. In fact some nights he'd work so late that he'd just end up crashing out on that." She pointed to a day bed in the corner of the room. "There were times when he could get so caught up with one of his projects that he might not surface for a couple of days, but he had a well-stocked fridge and an en-suite, so he was pretty much self-sufficient, at least in the short term. He always liked to know what was going on, though, and because it's such a big house, he decided that CCTV was the best way of keeping himself informed. For security reasons there's a recorder connected to the system. Jonathan used to look after it in my father's day, but Gareth's our security boffin these days and the system is a lot more sophisticated."

Brazelle wandered around the room, watched in silence by the two sisters. Eventually, he found himself standing in front of a large oak desk on which lay three notebooks, all similar to those on the bookshelves. "Am I allowed to touch these?" he asked.

"They're father's notebooks. You can take a look at them, but please put them back where they were," replied Rose, still rather hesitant about allowing someone to touch 'Daddy's Things'.

Brazelle confirmed he understood the condition before picking up one of the notebooks. Most of the pages were covered with formulae, tightly written notes and hand drawn sketches, all quite unintelligible to him. However, there were odd pages on which was written some fairly mundane material, with even a quite ordinary shopping list appearing on one page. And every single entry was dated. Putting the notebook down exactly where he had found it, he picked up a second. It also contained a most varied collection of entries, ranging from extremely esoteric and quite unintelligible to the most prosaic. And, just like the first notebook, every single entry was clearly dated. Brazelle concluded that Sir Cornelius had been meticulous in recording almost every thought he ever had, regardless of whether it came from the depths of his considerable intellect or was simply some ephemeral, perhaps even fairly trivial, notion.

Replacing the second notebook just as he had found it, he turned his attention to the third. Judging by the dates of its entries it was the most recent of Sir Cornelius' notebooks - the last one in which he had ever written. Its contents appeared to be similar to those of the first two, except that a group of several pages immediately following the last dated entry had been roughly ripped out. It was a very small and, some would say, quite unimportant matter, but Brazelle found it quite surprising. Over the evening he had constructed a mental picture of Sir Cornelius, his personality, character and emotional make up. The image was of someone who was methodical and patient, who had a tidy mind and habits, and paid great attention to detail, perhaps even to the point of obsession. It was an image reinforced by what he had seen in the first two notebooks, so the idea that such a person would be capable of roughly, and seemingly impetuously, ripping out pages from one of his own notebooks didn't seem to fit. Most other people would have simply shrugged the matter off, but Brazelle was not one of those people. He quickly thumbed through several of the notebooks that were on the bookshelves, looking for evidence of other torn out pages, but found none. It appeared that the third notebook he had inspected was unique, a fact which Brazelle found intriguing. He was just beginning to think he had seen enough for one evening, but something caught his eye. It was a collection of tiny jars gathered together on one of the shelves and they all appeared to contain small amounts of hair. He picked one up to examine it more closely. "Do you know what these are?" he asked.

"Yes, as a matter of fact I do," replied Frances with a smile. "Like all true geniuses our father had occasional, although mercifully brief, lapses into mild eccentricity. What you have there is the evidence for one of those episodes. He got it into his head that it might be possible to determine something about the state of a person's health through examination of their hair. Over a period of time he took samples of his own hair as specimens for study and stored them in those jars. Whether or not he ever did anything with them I really don't know, but being the hoarder that he was he never discarded them, so there they remain."

Brazelle thought this was yet another intriguing fact, but, intriguing or not, it was getting late. It was time to thank his hosts and make his way home. He and the two sisters went downstairs and straight to the front door where, almost immediately, Layla appeared with Brazelle's coat and a coat for Rose.

Jonathan opened the front door and Brazelle took a step outside and looked up to the sky. "It's stopped raining, the wind has dropped, the sky has cleared and there's a full moon. It won't take me long to walk home. You really don't need to drive me, I'll be just fine."

"No. I made a promise and I intend to keep it," insisted Rose. And without waiting for Brazelle to say another word, she went out to her car, calling for him to follow.

Brazelle gave a nod of submission and put out his hand to Frances. "Thanks for everything. I've enjoyed every minute of my visit."

Frances took his hand with a smile. "It has been a most enjoyable evening for me too, and for Rose. I hope we meet again sometime......... Good night.......Chris." It was the sign that Jenny said would come. These psychiatrists, thought Brazelle, they're spooky.

The car pulled up outside Holford's Cottage and Brazelle once more thanked Rose for the evening at Harfield House and the ride home. As he went to get out of the car Rose touched him on the arm. "If it's dry in the morning I'm going for a run," she said. "Will it be okay if I drop in on you?"

"Yes. Sure. Please do," replied Brazelle, who then stood and watched as she turned her car around and drove out of the yard.

Back at Harfield House, Rose found Frances finishing off a bottle of wine in the drawing room. "What did you think of Mr Brazelle?" she asked.

"Well it was obvious to see what you thought of him, my darling. But I have to say I also thought he was very nice, and really quite perceptive. He would probably make a good detective or barrister, because he was quite forensic with his questioning. There was something else though, something which puzzles me about him. When I first came across him in the library and he turned to face me, I'm sure I detected a sign of recognition in his face, as if he knew me. It was as if he'd met me somewhere before and was surprised to come across me here. But he chose not to mention it."

"Maybe he'd seen you around in the village at sometime," said Rose. "Or perhaps you just imagined it."

"No, it was far more than a kind of, 'I've passed you in the street', look of recognition. And I'm sure I didn't just imagine it, because on a number of occasions during the evening I found myself staring him in the eyes and it sparked something in my brain. There were also odd things he said that gave me the occasional feeling of déjà vu. In fact by the time he left I was utterly convinced that I've met your Reverend Brazelle before, although, for the life of me, I can't remember where or when. And I'm also quite sure he knows it too."

Day Three - Monday

Overnight, the wind had dropped, the sky had cleared and, as the sun began to rise, so did the temperature. Ideal weather for jogging, thought Rose, as she ran out through Napoleon's Gates. In well under thirty minutes she had arrived at Holford's Cottage and the first thing she saw on entering the yard was Brazelle, standing by the open doors of one of the outbuildings and dressed in overalls, just as he had been at their first meeting two days earlier. He greeted her with a smile.

"What a change since yesterday," said Rose, pointing up and briefly looking at the sky. She walked towards Brazelle, glanced in through the open doors of the outbuilding behind him and immediately froze. "Wow!" she exclaimed. "What is that?"

"It's a Ferrari 360M Spider, with a few extra bespoke features," answered Brazelle, with just a hint of un-priestly pride.

It was a silver convertible with its roof down and Rose couldn't resist walking over to touch it. "It's magnificent. Is it yours?"

"Yes," replied Brazelle. "Every inch of it."

Rose adopted an expression of almost disbelief. "No offence, but where does a priest get the money to buy one of these?"

"I didn't buy it," replied Brazelle. "I won it."

"What, like in a lottery, or something?"

Brazelle shook his head. "No, in a poker game."

Rose pointed at the Ferrari. "What kind of priest plays poker with stakes as high as this?"

"I haven't always been a priest," said Brazelle. "I won it seven years ago, from a Lebanese guy, who had more money than luck."

Rose pointed to the dirty overalls Brazelle was wearing. "Is there something wrong with it? Have you been working on it?"

Brazelle laughed. "Good heavens, no, the Ferrari's in excellent shape. I've been working on that." He pointed to an old jeep in the corner of the building.

"Did you win that as well?" Rose asked, with a giggle.

"No, that one came with the property," said Brazelle. "But I've had to do quite a bit of work on it before I could use it. Anyway, I have to go over to Northope to pick up some stuff we need at the Church and was planning on going in the Ferrari. Would you like to come along?"

"Would I?" said Rose eagerly. "Is the Pope a Catholic?"

"Great. I'll just get out of these overalls and clean up. The Ferrari's open. You can sit in it while you're waiting, but in the passenger seat please. I know something about your driving!" Brazelle laughed, and Rose responded with an exaggerated frown.

Having chosen to ignore Brazelle's jibe, Rose was sitting in the driver's seat of the Ferrari when a man walked quickly passed the outbuilding's open doors in front of her. Although she got only a fleeting sideways glance, she recognised him instantly. Hurriedly getting out of the car and stepping into the yard, she was just in time to see him mount a wooden staircase running up the outside of the third outbuilding, before he disappeared through a door at the top. Rose was puzzled. It was the man she had seen in the field two days earlier. What on earth was he doing here?

Brazelle came out from his cottage just in time to see the man disappear through the door at the top of the staircase and guessed what Rose must be thinking. "His name's Max," he said, "and that's where he lives."

"You know him!" exclaimed Rose, turning to face Brazelle. "Why didn't you tell me when I mentioned him the other day?"

"Yes, I should probably have said something, but it seemed fairly pointless at the time. You were clearly shaken up by your crash and it never occurred to me that you would see him, or for that matter, me, ever again."

Rose was clearly irritated by Brazelle's sin of omission and it manifested itself through sarcasm. "So, how does he come to be living here? Did he come with the property? Or did you win HIM in a poker game as well?"

Brazelle got the message and put on a suitably contrite expression. "Neither. He came with me."

Rose dropped the sarcasm. "Is he a relative? Or..... does he work for you?"

Brazelle shook his head. "No, is the answer to both questions. There's a self contained studio flat up there and when I moved here, I let him have it."

"So he's a friend, then?" queried Rose.

Brazelle was hesitant in his response. "Well, yes, in a way, but it's a bit complicated. Look, he's a very private guy and wouldn't want me talking to you about him. That's probably why he didn't want to get involved with you the other day. He doesn't interact much with anyone, so don't take it personally. Like I said, I'm sorry I didn't mention that I knew him, but can we just leave it at that?"

"Okay," said Rose. "You really are full of surprises. But I guess it's none of my business. Anyway, what about the ride you promised me?"

The Ferrari roared out of the yard heading first into the centre of Prinsted before turning left towards Northope, a small market-town about three miles away. However, the couple had gone barely two hundred yards from the centre of the village when Rose let out a cry. "Stop!" she shouted, at the top of her voice.

Brazelle immediately hit the brakes and no sooner had the Ferrari come to a halt than Rose got out and walked quickly back along the road and into a children's playground. Brazelle sat for a moment, wondering what the fuss was about, before parking the Ferrari and following after her. When he caught up, she was sitting on one of the swings, staring silently into the distance. "Are you alright?" he asked.

"Yes, I'm okay. And I'm sorry about that," Rose replied. "For a moment I couldn't help myself. I saw this place and some memories came flooding back. My mother often brought me here and the last time was just the day before she died. It was the last time we did something together, just the two of us. I guess that's why I can recall it so vividly. I can remember what she gave me to eat and what we talked about. And I can even remember her going to speak to a man over there by the gate." For a moment Rose fell silent, but then grabbed Brazelle's arm tightly and stared into his face. "Chris, will you help me find out what really happened to my mother?"

It was the first time Rose had called Brazelle by his first name. In fact she hadn't actually called him by any name since their very first meeting. But far more importantly, he thought, what is this about her mother? He assumed she was referring to her mother's death which, as far as he knew, had been an accident. But, whatever the circumstances, why was she asking him?

Tears began to form in Rose's eyes and she continued to hold on to Brazelle's arm, waiting for his response.

Although still more than a little confused, Brazelle decided he had to break the silence. "I'm sorry about your mother, but my understanding is that she had an unfortunate accident and drowned in the stream that runs through the village. Or do you think there's more to it than that?"

"Yes, it's true that she drowned in the stream," said Rose, "but, I've always had the feeling that there's more to be explained."

"Your mother died a long time ago and I'm certain her death would have been investigated at the time," responded Brazelle. "But, even if there is more to be explained, I can't see how I can help."

"Perhaps you're right, but I'm not so sure," said Rose. "Last night I saw how you asked just the right questions and made your deductions. I was very impressed, and so was Frankie. She said your powers of observation were amazing and that you were forensic in the way you went about finding things out. She thought you'd make a good detective. So, will you help me?"

Brazelle was torn. If Rose had asked for his help on almost any other matter he would probably have said yes straightaway, but this was different. Was there really anything to find out? Would it just be simply a waste of his time? He had plenty of work to do on the Prinsted Church project, so could he afford to give time to what, very likely, would simply confirm what was already known? And anyway, was he really as astute as Rose seemed to be suggesting? But, on the other hand, it was Rose who was asking, someone he had known for barely forty-eight hours, but someone he was already finding it difficult to say no to. "Very well," he eventually said, "I'll see what I can find out. But I'll need your help. Firstly, you'll need to tell your family and the staff at Harfield House what it is you've asked me to do, so if I speak to them, they'll know it's with your approval. Will you do that?"

Rose dried her eyes and nodded. "I'll tell them as soon as I get back home."

"Good. That's where I'll take you as soon as we get back from Northope."

"So, how'd you get on with the little heiress?" Dr Gerald Caulfield immediately asked Brazelle, as he opened the front door of the Vicarage.

Jenny pushed Gerald aside. "None of your business," she said, before whispering into Brazelle's ear. "But you can tell me!"

"I have absolutely nothing to report," said Brazelle. "Well, nothing of the kind that either of you have in mind, although there is something that might interest you." Brazelle told them what had happened earlier that day, and how, in what he now considered to be possibly a rash moment, he had agreed to make enquiries into the death of Rose's mother.

"I don't find it particularly surprising that Rose reacted in this way, even after all these years," said Jenny. "The death of her mother was such a distressing event in her life, experienced when she was a very young child, and quickly followed by her father's suicide just a couple of weeks later. Then, as if that wasn't enough, she was almost immediately taken off to the States, away from all things familiar. She must have been completely traumatised. Ordeals like that leave their mark."

"I agree," said Gerald. "But, tell me Chris, what do you know about the death of Justine Harfield and its aftermath?"

"Only what Rose's sister told me. Just the bare bones, I guess," replied Brazelle. "Around twenty years ago she was found drowned in the stream that runs through the village. Apparently she was crossing on an old wooden bridge, when she slipped, hit her head, which presumably rendered her unconscious, fell into the stream and drowned. Then a couple of weeks later, Sir Cornelius, her grief stricken husband, killed himself."

Gerald nodded. "Well, you've certainly got the bare bones of the official story."

"Why 'the official story'?" asked Brazelle. "Is there an unofficial one?"

Gerald smiled and gave a slight shrug. "Well, it's not altogether uncommon, especially in situations such as this one, that some of the usual suspects, the conspiracy theorists that is, get to work. So yes, there were a few alternative stories going around. After all, Lady Justine was what might be called, Prinsted's First Lady, so, given the circumstances surrounding her death, I suppose it was fairly inevitable. Did she fall or was she pushed? Did she accidentally bump her head or was she hit? And if someone else was involved, who was it? And why did they do it? All the usual stuff. And probably all nonsense."

"Only, 'probably' nonsense?" queried Brazelle. "Do you think there might be some truth in any of it?"

Gerald took on a look of uncertainty. "I hesitate to give an unqualified 'yes' in response to your question, but there are some aspects that have never been fully explained. For example, Justine told the housekeeper she was walking down to the village post office to post a letter. Sure enough, one of the gardeners saw her turn left in the direction of the village as she went out through Napoleon's Gates. However, she never arrived at the post office and, in fact, never even went into the village. It was a warm sunny day and there were plenty of people out and about, but absolutely nobody saw her. There were quite a few people sitting out in the front garden of Cromwell's Treasure, for example, but not one of them clapped eyes on her. And believe me, if Justine Harfield passed you by, you would notice her! So she must have been coming back from the direction of the village, never having actually been there when she drowned. So what was all that about?"

Brazelle proposed a simple explanation. "Maybe she changed her mind about going the road way into the village and decided to walk on the path that runs alongside the stream. Perhaps she was actually on her way TO the village, when she was crossing the stream."

Gerald dismissed Brazelle's suggestion. "Nice try, but that doesn't fit either. Justine would have had to turn right out of Napoleon's Gates and pass a gang of road work men a short distance up the road. But not one of them saw her. So it looks like she was definitely on her way home."

Brazelle thought the matter could still be easily explained. "Maybe she changed her mind about posting her letter. I know there are a couple of other places between Harfield House and the village where she could have crossed the stream. Perhaps she did just that and was returning home along the streamside pathway never having gone into the village."

"Well, it certainly looks like you've accounted for the facts as I've given them to you so far," agreed Gerald. "But there is still one matter that needs to be cleared up. What happened to her letter? The housekeeper says she saw Lady Justine put an envelope into her handbag just before she left the House, so we must assume that it definitely existed. But, when her handbag was found, there was no letter in it."

"Could it have come out of her handbag during her fall? Then been simply washed away in the stream?" asked Brazelle.

Gerald shook his head. "No chance. She must have dropped the handbag before she fell into the stream, because it was found on the bridge, still zipped up and full of all sorts of stuff, but no letter. As you know, between Harfield House and the Village Post Office there is nowhere else she could have posted her letter."

"You really do know a lot about this case," commented Brazelle.

Gerald laughed. "Ah, so it's 'a case' now is it? I was at home on vacation at the end of my first year at Med School when it happened. I remember so much about it because it was the most shocking event to have occurred in the village for years. And, of course, my dad was very much involved. He was one of the first people called to the scene and the one who certified her dead. Afterwards, he visited Sir Cornelius several times to check he was okay. They'd known each other for years and dad was quite fond of him. He was very shocked and extremely saddened when Sir Cornelius killed himself."

Gerald had been moving into something of a slouch, but suddenly straightened himself up. "Look! There's someone who knows a heck of a lot more about this case than me. Probably more than anyone else does either. He's one of those people I was telling you about - you know - the conspiracy theorists. But this chap's different to the others, he actually knows what he's talking about. He was the village policeman at the time, so very much in the thick of it. Although he retired several years ago, he's never really let it go. He's a patient of mine and if you do intend to take this further then he's probably the one you should talk to first. Would you like me to see if I can set up a meeting?"

When, earlier that day, Rose had asked him to help her investigate the death of her mother, Brazelle's first thought was that she was deluding herself and that there was probably nothing to be found out beyond that which was already accepted as the truth. Having just listened to Gerald, however, he wasn't so sure, so accepted his offer.

"Excellent," said Gerald. "I'll get it sorted first thing in the morning, but for now, let's get down to some serious drinking!"

As Brazelle later walked home from yet another rather boozy evening at the Vicarage he pondered on the evils of drink. He wasn't what any reasonable person would call a heavy drinker, but, so often during an evening with Gerald Caulfield he would drink rather more than he had intended. That evening had been one of those occasions. But, even an occasional over indulgence in alcohol, as Brazelle well knew, was heavily frowned upon by the Church and quite frequently preached against from the pulpit by many of his peers. As far as he was concerned, however, the sin of hypocrisy was much worse and he had vowed never to give a sermon on the subject. But, how did Dr Gerald Caulfield deal with HIS conscience? He wondered. There must have been numerous times when he advised one of his patients to moderate their drinking for the good of their health, before he himself went home and immediately reached for the whisky bottle. Brazelle did not dwell for too long on the matter, self-righteousness and condemnation were not his way. He simply resolved to make sure he drank less the next time, as he had also done on more than a few occasions before. But not only had it been a boozy evening it had also been a long day, so within barely a minute of his head touching the pillow, Brazelle had fallen into a deep sleep.

Day Four - Tuesday

Brazelle would probably have slept until well after dawn if it hadn't been for the loud knocking on his front door. Awaking to a bedroom in total darkness, he switched on the light and looked at the clock. It was 2 a.m. He put on his dressing gown, but before answering the door, glanced through the window. A figure illuminated by the porch light was instantly identifiable. At this time of night, he thought, what on earth is she up to.

Brazelle opened the door to a smiling Rose, but she dropped the smile when she saw the dressing gown. "Oh, I've woken you, haven't I?" she said.

"Well, it is two in the morning."

Rose pointed to the illuminated study window. "Yes, but I saw the light on in your study and thought you might still be awake."

Brazelle nodded. "Ah. Yes. I must have forgotten to switch the light off. Anyway, I'm awake now, so you might as well come in."

"I couldn't sleep and decided I might as well go for a jog. It's only been a few days since I came over from the States and I'm still a bit jet lagged," Rose explained.

Brazelle frowned. "Don't you think it's rather unusual and just a bit dangerous to be jogging along a dark country lane at this time of night?"

Rose held up a headlamp she had been wearing. "Well, I've got this." Then pointing to her high visibility top, "and this. Anyway, there's a full moon in a cloudless sky, so it's not as dark as you might think and there's nothing on the road. I didn't see a single person or vehicle on my way here."

"Was it your plan to call here when you set off?" Brazelle asked.

"It might sound silly, but I don't really know what I intended to do, but when I saw your light on I thought I'd come and say, Hi." Rose raised her right hand and rather limply said, "Hi.......but now I realise it wasn't such a good idea. I'm sorry I woke you. You will forgive me won't you?"

"Yes, I'll forgive you. I'm more concerned about you running along a dark country lane in the middle of the night, full moon or not. Unfortunately, I was at the Vicarage earlier, imbibing rather too copiously with Gerald Caulfield, Jenny's husband, and a man with hollow legs. So I'm not really in a fit state to drive you home. I'll get dressed and walk you back. I'm afraid it's the best I can offer. Whilst I get ready feel free to go in the kitchen and help yourself to anything you want." Pointing to the bathroom door he added: "or whatever else you might need."

"There is an alternative," said Rose. "As long as you don't mind, that is. I could just stay here on the sofa until the morning. Then you can go back to bed and I won't be any more trouble. I promise you won't hear a peep out of me and in the morning I'll be gone. What do you say?" Rose put on her helpless kitten expression.

Brazelle paused for a moment, giving due consideration to Rose's proposal. "Okay. But it's on one condition. You must promise that you won't go for any more late night jogs down dark country lanes."

"It's a deal," replied Rose, "but just one more thing - any chance of a blanket?"

Brazelle gave Rose a blanket and, thinking he might just have been mugged, went back to bed.

When he woke for the second time, Brazelle was shocked and annoyed to discover it was almost eight-thirty. He felt even worse as he remembered his uninvited guest, but gave a sigh of relief when, on entering the sitting room, he found only a neatly folded blanket on the sofa. Assuming that Rose must already have left he began to focus on getting ready for the day, but something caught his attention. He sniffed the air. It was definitely the smell of frying bacon and apparently coming from the kitchen.

"Good morning," said a smiling Rose, as Brazelle opened the kitchen door. "I thought I might have to wake you. Breakfast is almost ready. How do you like your eggs?"

Taken by surprise, Brazelle gave an instinctive, rather than a thoughtful, response. "However they come, thanks," he heard himself say.

"Great," said Rose. "All ready in five minutes."

Brazelle gave a faint smile, closed the kitchen door and returned to the sitting room where, almost immediately, he became aware of the sound of gentle tapping on the window. Turning to see what it was, he was horrified to see Gerald returning his gaze and giving him a friendly wave. Although realising he had little option but to open the front door, Brazelle still thought, even at the risk of appearing rude, he could prevent Gerald from actually entering. "Good morning Gerald, what brings you around so early in the morning?" he said, doing his best to block the doorway.

"Early?" queried Gerald, looking at his watch whilst at the same time pushing past Brazelle. "It's not far off nine o'clock and some of us have already done almost a full shift."

Brazelle remembered Gerald's hollow legs and the fact that whatever happened the night before, he still rose with the lark in the morning. And, of course, as a busy G.P. well used to visiting his patients' homes, but never having any time to waste, he had acquired the habit of not waiting for an invitation before entering into any property.

Gerald thrust a piece of paper at Brazelle. "This is the address of that ex-policeman I was telling you about. I popped round there first thing this morning, told him what you'd like to talk to him about and he was really keen. His name is Frank Weston, but there's something you should know before you meet him. I couldn't mention it last night because I needed his permission first. Frank's a dying man and probably only has a few weeks left at most. This case has been a bit of an obsession with him and he was concerned that when he dies it will be the end of it, so he's really glad there's someone else who'll pick it up."

"Sounds like a bit of a heavy load," said Brazelle.

Gerald nodded. "It is! And I have no idea what you intend to do, but you'd definitely be bringing some solace to a dying man if you at least let him think you're going to take it on. And he's my patient, so you'd be doing me a favour as well. You can turn up at his place anytime, he never goes anywhere, but given his state of health, I wouldn't leave it too long."

"Okay, I'll do what I can. I'll go round later this morning. Thanks for this." Brazelle waved the paper he had just been handed whilst at the same time doing his best to usher Gerald back through the front door.

Gerald was almost over the threshold, but stopped to sniff the air. "Smells like you've got something good on the go in the kitchen. I'll leave you in peace to get on with it."

Another second and Brazelle would have been able to close the front door and been home and dry, but the kitchen door opened, just in time for Gerald to catch a glimpse of Rose carrying a tray. Brazelle realised the game was up and stepped aside, allowing Gerald to re-enter.

"Hello," said Gerald, before casting Brazelle a knowing glance.

"Hi," responded Rose, with a smile.

Brazelle introduced Gerald and was about to introduce Rose, but Gerald interrupted. "I know who this is. It's uncanny. You are the spitting image of your mother. And it's an absolute pleasure to meet you."

Rose took Gerald's hand. "And I'm so glad to meet you. Jenny told me so much about you. It was really great meeting her the other evening. She's such a lovely person."

Gerald was yet to stop smiling and to take his eyes off Rose. "Well, believe me Jenny thinks the same about you.

She really enjoyed spending time with you and your sister and still hasn't stopped talking about it." Gerald suddenly raised the index finger of his left hand. "I've got an idea. Why don't the two of you come over to the Vicarage and have dinner with Jenny and me. Unfortunately, it can't be tonight because I'm working, but how about tomorrow night?"

"That sounds great," Rose replied eagerly.

"Assuming my liver can cope twice in one week," commented Brazelle.

"Just because I lead you to the river you don't have to drown," responded Gerald. "So that's settled then. We'll see you both tomorrow, about seven?"

Rose moved towards the kitchen door. "Thanks for the invite. I shall really look forward to it. Now, I'd better get the rest of the breakfast things."

Once Rose had left the room, Gerald, wearing a broad smile, whispered to Brazelle. "What was it you said? Oh yes, I remember, 'Nothing of interest to report'."

Brazelle frowned. "I don't suppose there's any point in saying that it isn't what it looks like, is there?"

Gerald shook his head. "No, absolutely none whatsoever, old boy. I look forward to seeing you both tomorrow." He winked at Brazelle and went out through the front door.

If only Rose had stayed in the kitchen just a couple of seconds more, thought Brazelle. Just a couple of seconds more!

Rose returned from the kitchen with a second tray and Brazelle turned his attention to the food. It looked and smelled very good, but where had it all come from? He didn't want to sound ungrateful, but his curiosity got the better of him. "This looks great, but you didn't find much of this in my kitchen, did you?"

Rose shook her head. "No. I was up early, so ran down to the village store. I thought making breakfast was the least I could do after I woke you and then imposed even more on you last night. You are okay with that aren't you? You did say I could go in the kitchen and help myself to anything I wanted."

Brazelle smiled. "Yes, I'm very okay with it and I'm very grateful. You can do it anytime." Have I really been mugged? He thought. Well perhaps it wasn't that bad.

It was a couple of hours later that morning when Brazelle rang Frank Weston's doorbell. He had come alone, having decided not to tell Rose about the purpose of Gerald's unexpected visit. The door was opened by a large and particularly unattractive woman of about sixty years of age. She greeted Brazelle with a near toothless smile. "You must be Mr Brazil," she said. "I'm Jocasta, Frank's wife. Pleased to meet you. Frank's in the front room and looking forward to seeing you."

Apart from carrying what Brazelle thought to be a somewhat ill fitting name, Jocasta also spoke with a strong accent that he found impossible to place, although, thankfully, just about understandable.

In the front room, Weston was sitting, or, more correctly half lying, in a reclining chair, behind which were two large cylinders providing him with a constant supply of oxygen. Even if Brazelle had not been forewarned about Weston's state of health, he would have instantly realised that he was looking at a very sick man.

"This is Mr Brazil, Frank," said Jocasta. Brazelle stepped forward with his right hand extended. Weston took the hand, but said nothing, simply raising his left hand slightly as a gesture of greeting.

"Would you like a cup of tea, Mr Brazil?" asked Jocasta. "I was just getting one for Frank."

"That would be very nice, thank you, Mrs Weston. Just a splash of milk and no sugar, please." Brazelle had decided there was little point in attempting to correct her about his name.

"Right you are dear, I'll go and get that sorted and leave you two to have your chat." Jocasta left the room and closed the door behind her.

"I'll give her the correct version of your name after you've gone," said Weston with a faint smile, before adjusting his seat and moving to a slightly more upright position. "Dr Caulfield tells me you're a friend of the Harfield family and that you've taken an interest in Lady Justine's death. Why's that then?"

"Well, I'd describe myself more as an acquaintance of the Harfields than a friend. And I find myself taking an interest in the death of Lady Justine because, Rose Harfield, her daughter, asked me to," replied Brazelle.

"Yes, that's what the Doctor told me. He came to see me early this morning, which he does a few times a week, normally, to see if I'm still here, and today he told me about you. Then he phoned a bit later to tell me you were coming to see me and that he'd met Lady Justine's daughter round at your place having breakfast." Weston paused, having become rather breathless.

A bit too much information thought Brazelle.

Having caught his breath, Weston continued. "Doctor Caulfield also told me that Rose is the spitting image of her mother. So, I can well understand why you've decided to do what she asked. If she's anything like her mother, what man could say no to her? Lady Justine was the most beautiful woman I've ever clapped eyes on...."

Weston fell silent in what seemed like mid sentence as Jocasta entered with a tray, which she laid down on the table. Brazelle said nothing, but simply gestured his thanks with a smile and a polite nod as Jocasta passed him his tea before leaving the room once more, closing the door behind her.

"......... except for the wife, of course," said Weston, finishing his sentence.

"I understand," said Brazelle, choosing a form of words, which whilst inoffensive, was not stained with hypocrisy.

"Well, let's get down to business, shall we, Mr Brazelle. Pass me that box will you?" Weston pointed to a cardboard box sitting on the table. "This box contains everything I've gathered together about this case over the past twenty years." Weston removed two A4 size notebooks from the box. "These notebooks contain reports of all the interviews I've done, all the physical evidence I've seen and all of my musings on the case. And from all of this, one thing is clear. Lady Justine's death was not an accident caused by her simply slipping on a wet wooden bridge. Someone helped her on her way to the great hereafter. I'm convinced of it. A lot of the evidence may be circumstantial, but it's there nonetheless. For a start there's the mystery of the missing envelope. Did Dr Caulfield tell you about that?"

Brazelle nodded. "Yes he did. And he told me that you were the first person to realise that things didn't add up."

"That's right," confirmed Weston. "Me and old Dr Caulfield were the first people called, after the body was found. Lady Justine's handbag was still lying on the bridge where she must have dropped it, so I had a look through. Of course I didn't know anything about an envelope at that point. I didn't find out about that until I spoke to the housekeeper. After I'd spoken to the gardener and quite a few other folk in the village, including the postmistress and a gang of men doing road repairs, I realised she must never have gone into the village. So, I was left with the mystery of what happened to the envelope. I rummaged through her handbag a few times, but I never found it."

"What was in the handbag?" asked Brazelle.

"I can see what you might be thinking," said Weston. "Well, there was no sign of it being a robbery. Her handbag contained a purse with about three hundred pounds in cash and a couple of bankcards. And there was just the sort of stuff you'd expect to find in a young woman's handbag, make up, lipstick and so on. And there was a small notebook with all sorts of things scribbled in it. Oh.... and three keys - one that looked just like a house door key and a key ring with two smaller keys on it. That's just about it. I took pictures of everything, including what was written in her notebook. You'll find it all in the box. The pathologist confirmed there were no injuries suggesting any kind of struggle and Lady Justine still had her rings on when the body was found. Her engagement ring alone was reckoned to be worth at least forty thousand pounds. So, why would a robber not take that?"

"What about a mobile phone?" Brazelle asked.

Weston smiled and shook his head. "You have to remember this all happened twenty years ago when mobile phones were far less common than they are today. But you live around here these days, so you'll know how poor the phone signal is. Take it from me - if you think it's bad now, well, it was nonexistent twenty years ago. So it was pointless carrying a brick-like mobile phone around with you, even if you owned one. Anyway, a few days after Lady Justine's death I took the handbag up to Harfield House and Sir Cornelius and his daughter, Frances, had a look through. They said, as far as they could tell, nothing was missing. I remember Sir Cornelius' only comment was about the three keys. He said he'd never seen any of them before and wondered what they were for."

Having seemingly satisfied Brazelle's curiosity about the handbag, Weston turned his attention back to the contents of his box. He took out a large envelope from which he pulled a photograph of two men and handed it to Brazelle. "Do you recognise the man on the left?" he asked.

Brazelle studied the photograph. Although the man on the left looked vaguely familiar, it was the red-haired man on the right whom he instantly recognised and whose appearance in the photograph shocked him, although he didn't mention this to Weston. "I can't say I can put a name to the face. "Who is he?" Brazelle asked.

"Andrew Carpenter, or Sir Andrew Carpenter as he is these days," answered Weston. "Now do you recognise him?"

Brazelle nodded. "Yes I do, the Commissioner of the Metropolitan Police, who has rather less hair these days than he does in the photograph. So, where does he fit into the case?"

"He turned up here in Prinsted two days after Lady Justine's body was found. He was a Chief Inspector with the Met in those days and was supposedly sent here to assist us local police with our investigations."

"Was there anything unusual about that?" asked Brazelle. "Given the circumstances of her death it would be quite normal to have an investigation involving the police, surely. And given the fact that she was married to a wealthy member of the British Establishment I suppose it wouldn't be unusual to find that the Met got involved, even this far north of London."

"Well yes, that's all fair enough," responded Weston. "But it wasn't quite as simple as that. At that time Carpenter wasn't just a run of the mill detective from the Met. He was with Special Branch. Why was Special Branch involved, and why all the secrecy? It was me who took that photograph, but I had to take it without the two of them knowing about it. 'No photographs!' was almost the first thing Carpenter said when he turned up - red rag to a bull that was!"

"How do you know he was with Special Branch?" asked Brazelle, "Did he tell you?"

Weston gently shook his head. "No, he didn't. He just introduced himself as Detective Chief Inspector Carpenter and flashed his warrant card. After that he only spoke to ask questions. Remember I was just the local village copper, nobody of any importance. I didn't find out he was with Special Branch until some years later when he was beginning to make a name for himself. I read an article about him in the Police Gazette. At the time of Lady Justine's death, all he told me was that he'd been sent by the Met to assist with the investigation."

"And did he assist?" asked Brazelle.

Weston again shook his head. "Hardly! He just spent a couple of hours asking lots of questions. Then the two of them went to the morgue to look at the body and speak to the pathologist. After that, they just cleared off and I never heard from either of them again."

"And what about the other person in the photograph, the red-haired man?" asked Brazelle.

"Well, that was just as odd," replied Weston. "I wasn't even told his name. He arrived with Carpenter and I don't remember seeing him speak to another soul. Occasionally he'd scribble some notes and every now and again whisper something in Carpenter's ear. Then Carpenter would ask a question. It was like he was the one in charge. You know, as if he was the ventriloquist and Carpenter was his dummy. Weird! But there was something else about him - he gave me the absolute willies. He struck me as being a pretty unsavoury character. It's an occupational hazard of being a copper, occasionally coming across people like him, but they're usually the ones you're locking up."

Weston went silent for several minutes as Brazelle rummaged through the box. In addition to the notebooks and the photograph of the two men it contained numerous press cuttings and a second envelope containing photographs and photocopies. There was also a small plastic bag containing several spherical balls slightly less than two centimetres in diameter and they appeared to be made from lead.

Brazelle held up the plastic bag. "What have these to do with the case?" he asked.

"Damned if I know," responded Weston. "Perhaps nothing at all. I found them lying half buried in the mud around the bridge a couple of days after Lady Justine's death. They look to me like old lead musket balls and they could have been lying around there for ages, I suppose."

Brazelle nodded his agreement. "I'm pretty sure you're right, they do look like old musket balls, although they don't look like they've ever been fired."

The pair chatted for several more minutes until Jocasta re-entered the room and said it was time for Weston to take his medication and have a nap.

Brazelle realised it was time to leave. "I'll make my farewells. Thank you very much for your time. It's been extremely interesting and helpful. Just one last thing though - I wonder if I could borrow the box for a couple of days, so I can study the contents, especially your notebooks? And, with your permission, I'd like to make a copy of some of what you've got in there?"

Weston smiled. "Oh, I can do better than that. The box and everything in it is yours. I'm never going to do anything with it now. One of the greatest regrets of my life is that I couldn't get justice for Lady Justine, but perhaps you will. If you have any questions after you've had a chance to go through the box, just ask, but for obvious reasons, don't leave it too long. Please pass on my best wishes to Miss Harfield." Then, after pausing to catch his breath, he added, "Good bye Mr BRAZELLE," giving emphasis to his visitor's name for the benefit of his wife.

After leaving Frank Weston, Brazelle drove straight to Prinsted Church. Although it was barely seventy-two hours since he first met Rose Harfield he had come to realise that his relationship with her was beginning to seriously interfere with his work. He knew he had some catching up to do, so, on arrival at the Church, he went straight into conference with Fred Simpson, the supervisor of the team working on its repairs. Once he had assured himself that the current phase of work was up to date and within budget, he spent the rest of the day working on plans for the next phase. It was very late when he arrived back at Holford and he was so tired that he crashed out on his bed, still fully clothed.

Day Five - Wednesday

It was still dark when Brazelle was awakened by knocking on the front door. He had no idea what the time was because his bedside clock and wristwatch were both strangely missing. And he was surprised to find he was wearing pyjamas, having no memory of getting changed. Putting on his dressing gown, he went into the sitting room and switched on the light before opening the front door. Given what had happened just the night before, he was not surprised to find who it was. Without saying a word, she moved past him, walked over to the fireplace and placed a key ring with two small keys attached and a third, separate, larger key, onto the mantelpiece. Brazelle wanted to say something but found he couldn't speak. And it began to dawn on him that her hair was shorter, she had on the same dress that Justine was wearing in her portrait and there was a tattoo of a rose on her left upper arm. The sound of knocking on the front door returned.

It was broad daylight when knocking on the front door woke Brazelle. He looked over at his bedside clock. It was eight o'clock. And he was still fully dressed from the night before. With no need for a dressing gown he went straight into the sitting room, opened the front door and was not surprised to find Rose standing on his doorstep.

"Good, you're dressed," she said. "I was beginning to think that I might be waking you again. I've knocked a couple of times."

Brazelle said nothing, but simply stood aside to let her in.

Rose held up a shopping bag. "I've brought breakfast. I saw how much you enjoyed it yesterday. You said…. and I quote, 'You can do it anytime'. So here I am! I felt sure you wouldn't be sleeping late again after what you said yesterday."

The day before, Brazelle had used the phrase 'You can do it anytime,' more as a figure of speech rather than as something to be taken literally, but he let it pass and said nothing.

Rose noticed that Brazelle appeared to have his mind elsewhere. "Are you alright?" she asked. "Is something the matter?"

Brazelle shook his head. "No, everything's fine," he replied, although rather unconvincingly. He walked over to the mantelpiece and ran his hand over it, finding only dust.

Thinking his behaviour rather strange, Rose repeated her question. "Are you sure you're alright?"

Brazelle had begun to get himself back together. "Sorry if I seemed a little odd. I had something on my mind when you arrived and I needed to finish thinking it through, but I'm okay now."

Rose gave a sigh of relief. "Well I'm glad about that. I was beginning to think I might have assumed too much and that I was imposing."

"No, its fine, you haven't assumed too much." Brazelle, pointed to the shopping bag Rose was holding. "You're welcome, whether you come bearing gifts or not. I had a long day yesterday, crashed out sometime after midnight, still in these clothes, and then had an extremely vivid and weird dream. I was still having the dream when you woke me. It had me confused a little, I guess."

"So I did wake you," said Rose, dropping her smile. "Sorry."

Brazelle tried to reassure her. "There really isn't anything for you to be sorry about. I certainly hadn't intended to sleep this late, but I crashed out before having a chance to set my alarm, so you actually did me a favour. Anyway, now I'm up I need to go and get showered and changed. You make yourself at home and I'll be as quick as I can."

Rose regained her smile. "Okay. I'll make a start in the kitchen."

Returning to the sitting room a few minutes later, Brazelle immediately became aware of voices in the kitchen and went to investigate.

"Good morning Chris," said Gerald, greeting him with a smile and a wink. "Rose was good enough to let me in and has invited me to join the two of you for breakfast. I've been helping out with the culinary activities." To emphasise the nature of his involvement Gerald waved the spatula he was holding before passing it to Rose. "Do you mind if I leave you to cope on your own again, Rose, whilst I have a quick word with Chris?"

Rose shook her head. "No I don't mind, you carry on. It'll all be ready in five minutes."

Gerald followed Brazelle into the sitting room shutting the kitchen door behind him. "I came to give you some bad news Chris," he whispered. "Frank Weston passed away in his sleep last night. I've just been to see his wife and she told me how pleased he was that you went to see him yesterday. So, regardless of the motivation for your visit, it was a good deed that you did. And from your point of view, it seems you got to him just in time. Jocasta also told me that Frank passed over all of his research on the case to you. I haven't mentioned any of this to Rose, by the way. I didn't know what, if anything, you'd told her."

"Thanks for coming to tell me," said Brazelle. "I'm sorry to hear about Frank, but, having seen the condition he was in yesterday, I can't say it's come as much of a shock. And thanks for not saying anything to Rose. I haven't told her anything about Frank Weston, or what he gave me, and for the time being I intend to keep it that way."

Gerald nodded his understanding. "Did you find what Frank told you, helpful?"

"Yes, I certainly did. What you told me the other day left me intrigued, but Frank convinced me there was very definitely more to this case than the official version of events would have anyone believe. Whilst there still remains the strong possibility that Justine's death was, after all, just another tragic accident, the circumstances surrounding her death certainly don't seem to add up."

"So you're picking up where Frank left off and going to investigate the case yourself then, are you?" asked Gerald.

Brazelle nodded. "Yes, I am. And I've already decided where I'm going to start."

The conversation might have continued but the kitchen door opened and Rose appeared with a tray of food.

Brazelle spent the rest of the day at Prinsted Church until returning to Holford to get ready for his second evening of the week at the Vicarage, this time with Rose. Earlier that day they had tossed a coin to decide which one of them would drive and Brazelle lost, so Rose was to be the driver. As he waited for her to arrive, he passed the time by reading some of Weston's notes. Apart from one of the gardeners who simply exchanged a good morning with Justine as she walked out through Napoleon's Gates, Megan Richards, the Harfields' housekeeper, was the last person known to have spoken to her on the day she died and Brazelle decided to start by reading a statement that Weston had taken from her.

Lady Justine had been reading the newspaper in the drawing room with Rose playing around her, before she came into the kitchen and asked me to look after Rose, whilst she walked into the village and posted a letter. I said I'd get one of the staff to post it for her, but she insisted on doing it herself. It was highly unusual for Lady Justine to go anywhere without taking Rose with her. The two were next to inseparable. When Rose was born, Sir Cornelius had wanted to employ a nanny, but Lady Justine wouldn't hear of it. She said she wanted to be a full time mother to Rose. Especially on such a lovely day, I was very surprised that she didn't intend to take Rose with her. Rose herself was not at all happy about it, but Lady Justine was adamant. It meant I had to stop doing anything else and concentrate on distracting Rose, which wasn't easy given her upset state. Then Lady Justine left and I never saw her alive again.

Weston had listed a number of questions he had asked Mrs Richards and two of these in particular took Brazelle's interest. He had first asked if Mrs Richards had actually seen Lady Justine carry a letter out of the house and Mrs

Richards confirmed that she had seen her put an envelope in her handbag, just before she left. Remembering what Gerald had said about the significance of the disappearing letter, this question seemed to Brazelle to have been quite relevant, but he was puzzled about the reason for the second question. Weston had asked which newspaper Justine had been reading in the drawing room just before going to post the letter. Mrs Richards said it was the same local paper she read every day, The Morning Chronicle. Weston's interest in the subject had clearly persisted, because when rummaging through Weston's box, Brazelle found a copy of The Morning Chronicle from the day of Justine's death. He was still puzzling over the matter when the sound of a car horn told him that Rose had arrived.

The Caulfields were invariably excellent hosts and the occasion of Rose's first visit to the Vicarage was no exception. Gerald told a number of his humorous medical anecdotes, all of which Brazelle and Jenny had heard before and not, in most cases, just the once. But they were all new to Rose and her laughter made it clear that she enjoyed them at least as much as Brazelle and Jenny had, when, at some time in the distant past, they had heard them for the first time.

But there were two sides to Gerald Caulfield. There was the jocular, highly sociable individual who was always good fun to be around, but there was also the highly skilled and serious medical professional, with a quick mind and sharp intellect. Every now and again, even on social occasions when his more frivolous side tended to dominate, his serious side might make a sudden appearance and, as both Brazelle and Jenny left the room for a moment, it did. "Tell me Rose: what do you remember of your mother?" he suddenly asked.

Rose was momentarily thrown by the question, which took her completely by surprise, but she quickly recovered. "More than some people think I do. Why do you ask?"

"Chris told me you've asked him to investigate the circumstances of your mother's death, and I want to see if I can help. I knew your mother, or, perhaps to put it more accurately, I was acquainted with her. And like you clearly do, I've always had serious doubts about the official story concerning her death and the circumstances surrounding it. My father was one of the first people on the scene when your mother's body was discovered and both he and I have maintained a great deal of interest in the matter. I've already shared with Chris all that I know and can remember."

"Did you ever speak to my mother?" Rose asked.

Gerald nodded. "Yes, on several occasions. But it was only ever to say good morning, good afternoon, or something like that when we passed each other in the village. They were only ever brief moments, but I can still remember most of the occasions when our paths crossed. And there's one thing in particular that I remember - I never saw her out without you."

Rose smiled. "I wasn't out with her on the day she died, but I can remember very clearly the last time that I did go out with her. When I was in the car with Chris the other day we passed the place where she took me. That's when the memory of it came back and overwhelmed me, and I asked Chris if he would help me to find out what happened to her. Maybe I was too hasty. Given the state I was in he probably felt sympathetic and, being the kind person that he is, felt he had to agree. After all, I've only known him a few days and it's a bit of a burden isn't it? Do you think I should tell him that I won't hold him to it?"

"No I don't," Gerald said emphatically. "Chris told me what happened the other day and perhaps at the time he did feel obliged to agree, but not anymore. Knowing what he knows now, I think he's become interested enough to investigate regardless of you having asked him, although the fact that you did, just makes him even more inclined to help. As you may already have come to realise, he's quite a complex character. Despite having known him for several years, there remain depths I have yet to fathom, but there is one thing I have learnt - when Chris Brazelle makes a commitment he is relentless and in some ways quite ruthless, about seeing it through. I doubt you could have chosen anyone better."

Rose was surprised by Gerald's choice of words. "Ruthless?" she queried. "But surely you mean that in a nice way."

Gerald laughed. "Well, maybe, some of the time."

Brazelle and Jenny came back into the room and Gerald asked what they had been doing. "Not plotting my doom, were you?"

"Good Lord, no, you organised that yourself ages ago," replied Jenny. "Chris was just briefing me on what needs to happen at Church over the next couple of days. Apparently, the workmen have discovered a void in one of the walls."

"And we need to find out why it's there and whether it's in some way contributing to the damp problem, that part of the Church suffers from," added Brazelle. "We'll need to open it up in order to investigate. It could take a couple of days, but we'll keep the disruption to a minimum and get it sorted as quickly as possible. I thought I'd better tell Jenny tonight because I want the men to get started on it first thing in the morning."

"Do you think the void's been there ever since the Church was built?" asked Gerald. "You might find something interesting in there, perhaps even the legendary Cromwell's Treasure."

"Well, the Church predates Cromwell by a few hundred years, so who knows?" said Jenny. "But, a thought occurs to me. If there is anything of value in there, who does it belong to?"

Before Gerald could demonstrate his knowledge of the 1996 Treasure Act by answering his wife's question, Rose interrupted. "What's Cromwell's Treasure?" she asked.

"Yet another very good question," said Gerald. "And as someone who, like me, was born in Prinsted it is your birthright to know the answer. Let me explain..."

It was now Jenny's turn to interrupt. "A good time for me to go and make some coffee, I think. I've heard this story a few times before!"

Gerald waited until Jenny left the room before starting his explanation. "It all started just about the time the English Civil War finally ended in 1651. About three miles north of here, a farmer came across what looked like the aftermath of an ambush of a group of Cromwell's troops by some of the King's soldiers. There were more than a dozen dead bodies lying around, together with a wagon and some horses, but no sign of any survivors. The farmer hot footed it to the nearest village to report what he'd seen and a group of villagers went out to retrieve the bodies and collect the wagon and horses and so on. The news quickly spread around the district and within a few days a detachment of Cromwell's troops arrived, lined up all the villagers and demanded to know where the contents of the wagon were. Despite being threatened, the villagers were adamant that the wagon had been empty when they found it, except for a few weapons that they'd left untouched. Soon afterwards, reinforcements arrived and searched every building in the village. But they found nothing, so began to widen their search, eventually taking in the whole of the district for miles around. They shifted between making threats and offering rewards, but got absolutely nowhere. To begin with, none of Cromwell's men said what it was that they were looking for, although it was obvious it had to be something valuable, judging by all the trouble they were taking. But then one night in the village tavern, one of the Roundhead officers had a bit too much to drink and he let slip that they were looking for two treasure chests belonging to Cromwell himself. And so the legend of Cromwell's Treasure was born, although, of course, nobody really knows if the officer was telling the truth or if his drink was doing the talking for him. After a couple of weeks, the troops left, but every so often they'd return and carry out some more searches in the village. Over time, their visits became less frequent, until eventually they stopped altogether."

"And where does Prinsted fit into all this, exactly?" asked Rose.

"Well," said Gerald, "Prinsted was the village at the heart of it, where it all started. And the tavern here in Prinsted was where the Roundhead officer first talked of Cromwell's Treasure. It was probably the most exciting thing that had ever happened in the village. So, for good or ill, the villagers made it their own bit of history. What you might call their unique selling point, so to speak. That's how, after the monarchy was restored, the village tavern came to be named 'Cromwell's Treasure'. Previously, it had always been known simply as the Prinsted Tavern."

Rose's imagination was caught. "Was any treasure ever found?"

Gerald gave a shrug. "Who knows? But if it was, then whoever found it kept it very quiet, because nobody's ever heard about it, that's for sure. Good bit of folklore though, isn't it? It gave Prinsted its fifteen minutes of fame and many of the locals have been dining out on it ever since. When strangers visit the village they invariably ask how the tavern came by its unusual name, which is a lead in for any of the locals who happen to be within earshot to open up and tell their own particular version of the story."

"That's so very interesting. I didn't know any of that," said Rose. "So isn't it odd that I never asked anyone how the tavern got its name."

Gerald shook his head. "No, it's not odd at all. It's in your blood. Consciously you weren't aware, but your subconscious knew the answer, so there was no need for you to ask the question."

"Mumbo jumbo," interjected Brazelle. "Rose didn't ask anyone about the tavern's name because she's got more important things to think about."

Gerald gave a shrug. "Maybe, and perhaps on this particular matter you're right, but take it from me, my point about the subconscious knowing things of which the conscious is unaware is totally valid and, if an opportunity arises, I shall try and prove it to you."

Jenny came back into the room carrying a tray. "Right, that's enough village folklore for now. I have far more important questions to ask. Like who wants milk and sugar in their coffee?"

The conversation might have moved on to other matters, but Rose's curiosity had not yet been satisfied and she had another question for Gerald. "You said that the subconscious can know things of which the conscious mind is unaware, but how can you know that? I suppose I'm asking, how do you tap into someone's subconscious in order to find out what it knows that the conscious mind doesn't?"

"Another very good question," responded Gerald. "I'll attempt to explain. There are two sorts of things you know without consciously being aware. Firstly, there are things that you once knew, but have long since forgotten......except that you haven't. They've simply been stored away in some part of your brain to which you don't have immediate access, your subconscious. Secondly, there are things stored in your subconscious that you were never actually consciously aware of, things that you sensed subliminally. Your brain is constantly absorbing new information through the senses and whilst much of it might well be discarded, a great deal of it is not. Sometimes you might make a conscious effort to try and retain some of this information, keeping it more or less available for immediate recall, perhaps if you're about to sit an exam, for example. At other times your brain subconsciously makes the decision, choosing whether to discard or retain and, if it opts for retention, where to store it. You can be pretty sure that your emotional state at the time will influence this decision making process. Of the information that is retained, quite a lot will end up in the deep recesses of your mind and be unavailable for immediate recall. Occasionally though, something might happen that leads to you gaining partial conscious access, maybe causing a feeling such as déjà vu. On other occasions, you might have an experience that is so traumatic or profound, that it causes a memory stored in the subconscious to be transferred into the conscious. You might then recollect something that you were previously unaware that you knew. And there is a technique for accessing subconscious memories that has been around a long time and is still being used, and that is hypnosis."

"But there are a few problems with it," interjected Jenny. "With many people it doesn't work and, worse still, with some people it can create false memories that can be very hard to shift."

Gerald nodded his agreement. "That is true, but whether or not it works, and works correctly, is determined more by the skill of the hypnotist, rather than the identity of the subject. And it's not just a matter of skill, there are ethical issues to be considered as well."

"Are either of you two skilled at it?" Rose asked.

"We've both been involved with it in the past," replied Jenny. "But I haven't been, or wanted to be, since I gave up medicine. Gerald, though, still dabbles."

"I wouldn't call it dabbling, darling," objected Gerald. "You make it sound like some form of witchcraft."

"Perhaps it is," interjected Brazelle, who until that point had been listening in silence. "But, I have a question for you, Gerald. Suppose there was an event that occurred when I was a five year old child, not one that could be described as traumatic, but one that had affected me enough to have left a clear mark on my conscious memory, could hypnosis help me uncover even more details about that event?"

Before Gerald had time to answer, Rose interrupted. "You're thinking about me, aren't you, Chris?"

"Yes," said Brazelle. "But my question is hypothetical."

"Well, Chris," responded Gerald, "hypothetical or not, and regardless of whether it relates to you, or to Rose, the answer to your question is the same, and it is......... perhaps. But what is this event you're referring to and why is it so important?"

"It's the last time my mother took me to the children's playground on the edge of the village," said Rose.

"And for Rose that gives it importance of itself, but it may also have significance because of something that happened," said Brazelle, before turning to Rose. "Do you remember you told me that a man appeared and your mother went over to the gate to speak to him?"

Rose nodded. "Yes I remember, but why might that be important?"

"It might not be," replied Brazelle, "but if it's possible to find out anything more about the man, I would like to do that. I'm puzzled as to why he would want to speak to your mother."

"Perhaps he was lost and was simply asking the way," suggested Jenny.

"I did consider that as a possibility," said Brazelle. "But there's a prominent road sign with clear directions right outside the playground and it looked to me like it had been there for a lot longer than the past twenty years, so why would anyone need to ask for directions?"

"Well, it's entirely up to Rose," said Gerald. "I'm prepared to give it a try, but it must be her choice."

Rose readily agreed. "Chris has very kindly said he will make enqiries, so, if he thinks there is the slightest chance it might help, I'll do it."

"Okay," said Gerald. "I hope to finish seeing patients tomorrow by six o'clock. If you come over to the surgery then we'll see what we can find out."

"I'll be there," confirmed Rose. "Thanks for offering to do this. I know how busy you must be."

Gerald smiled. "Good. Now that's settled, I have a question I would like to ask you, Rose. Jenny tells me that you were only planning to be over here for a few more days before returning to the States. Is that still your plan, or are you now thinking of staying here for a bit longer?"

"That's none of your business Gerald," interrupted Jenny.

Rose smiled. "That's okay, I don't mind answering. The truth is I'm not sure yet just when I'll be going back. The reason I came over in the first place was because it's my twenty-fifth birthday next week and there's rather an important family event planned. My father arranged that when he died, his entire estate would be placed in a trust. Since his death the trust has made payments to maintain Harfield House and to provide a regular income for Frankie and me, but, on my twenty-fifth birthday, a week today, the trust will be dissolved and the family solicitors are coming to Harfield House to announce my father's instructions and explain what happens next. I guess I'll decide what I'm going to do after that."

"I'm sure you'll make the right decision," said Gerald. "But I'm also sure I speak for all three of us here, when I say I hope you decide to stay, at least for a bit longer."

"I'll certainly give that some thought," replied Rose. "But I don't think I can stay any longer tonight, though. Although it feels like a long time, because so much has happened, it's not even a week since I arrived from the States and I still haven't got into a regular sleep pattern. It's been a great evening and I've really enjoyed spending time with you all. I hope we can get together again real soon at Harfield House."

"And I have an early start in the morning," added Brazelle. "So, I shall have to leave too, especially since I'm hoping for a ride home.

Rose pulled up in the yard outside Holford's Cottage. "I know you're going to be busy tomorrow, Chris," she said, "but will it be okay if I come round after my session with Gerald? I can tell you what, if anything, we discovered."

"Yes, I'd like that. But there's one condition."

"Which is?"

"That you don't eat before you come, so you can experience the full benefits of my culinary skills."

"It's a deal," said Rose, before driving off.

Day Six - Thursday

Brazelle arrived at the Church early, just before Fred Simpson, the work supervisor, although he didn't stay very long. After spending a short time discussing the work plan for the day, including the opening up of the recently discovered void, he gave a promise to return later and then left. Soon after, he was on a train heading to London, on his way to New Scotland Yard to meet with Sir Andrew Carpenter, the Commissioner of the Metropolitan Police Service.

The nature of Sir Andrew's job meant he frequently spent a substantial part of his working day away from his office. However, Brazelle knew he was due to hold a press conference at New Scotland Yard at noon and, despite having made no appointment, he felt sure the Commissioner could be persuaded to meet with him for a few minutes, either one side or the other of this planned event, although he wasn't relying on his own powers of persuasion to make this happen.

Sir Andrew Carpenter was the quintessential journeyman police officer, yet he had somehow managed to rise, some might say 'without trace', to occupy the highest office in the British police service. He was a man who, in so many ways, epitomised the very concept of 'average'. He was of average height and average build; his golf handicap was mediocre; and, he would almost certainly have shown up as being of just about median intelligence and ability, if compared with his fellow graduates of his rather undistinguished alma mater. His whole career, in fact, had been quite remarkable by its lack of distinction. Indeed, it was only once Sir Andrew had achieved the status of Commissioner of the Met that most people, even those who probably should have known, became aware of his existence. So, how did he do it? Very early in his career, and probably without even consciously realising it, Sir Andrew had stumbled across the fundamental precepts of one route to achieving a successful career in the public sector. It was a route that many before him had taken with varying degrees of success, so he had some examples to learn from. The first rule is to stay away from anything remotely controversial with its potential risk of alienation, which, even if it involves only small groups, can have a very undesirable effect on one's career. Secondly, at all stages of one's career, one must quickly identify the centres of power and influence and make sure to agree with them, as a matter of principle. And when those centres of power and influence change, together with their associated dogma, as from time to time they most assuredly will, it is essential that agreement with them is maintained - as a matter of 'modified' principle. And thirdly, and most importantly, accept blame and responsibility for nothing, but claim credit for everything, although only after doing due diligence to ensure that nothing can come back to bite you.

On arrival at New Scotland Yard Brazelle joined a short queue at the public reception desk and, when it became his turn, simply asked to see Sir Andrew. He was immediately told, as he was already certain that he would be, that Sir Andrew was a very busy man and that any request to meet with him should be sent to his office in writing. Alternatively, the receptionist enquired, could the matter be dealt with by some other police officer? Did it really have to be the Commissioner himself? Once the receptionist had finished explaining the protocol, he voiced his hope that Brazelle would have a nice day and immediately turned his attention to the next person in the queue. Nothing he was told came as a surprise to Brazelle, so he simply thanked the receptionist and, after making a quick phone call, took a seat in the reception area and waited.

Upstairs in his office, Sir Andrew was making final adjustments to his press conference statement when his PA, Mrs McAllister, came uninvited into the room. "I'm sorry to disturb you sir," she said, "but apparently there's a Reverend Brazelle, a Church of England priest, who would like to see you for a few minutes. He's waiting downstairs in the public reception area."

Sir Andrew put his pen down and raised his head with a puzzled look on his face. "I don't want to sound rude Grace, but are you feeling alright?"

"Absolutely, sir," Mrs McAllister replied nervously.

"Then why on earth have you come to tell me this? For goodness sake, Grace, you know the drill at least as well as I do. Instruct reception to tell Reverend Brazelle to put whatever he has to say in writing and send him on his way. If I gave just two minutes of my time to every member of the public who demanded to see me personally I'd need eight, twentyfive hour days in the week. Shut the door on the way out would you."

Sir Andrew picked up his pen once more, but, before he could return to tinkering with his statement, Mrs McAllister, hesitantly, interrupted him for a second time. "Yes sir, that is what I would normally do, but the request hasn't come directly from the Reverend himself. It's come from someone else on his behalf."

Sir Andrew looked up. "Alright, and this had better be good, from who?"

"The Chief of the General Staff," replied Mrs McAllister.

Sir Andrew took on a look of disbelief. "What? Is this genuine? It's not one of those silly wind-ups, is it?"

"It's definitely genuine sir," replied Mrs McAllister. "I rang the MOD and checked it out. It's genuine alright." Then referring to her notebook, she added, "General Michael's PA said he'd consider it a personal favour if you'd give Reverend Brazelle just a few minutes of your very valuable time."

Sir Andrew put down his pen for the second time and wiped his hands over his forehead. "Why on earth, would the head of the British Army be interested in whether or not I give five minutes to some Church of England priest?" He thought aloud, before addressing Mrs McAllister directly. "Very well, tell the reverend gentleman he can have five minutes and then let General Michael's PA know that I've agreed to see him."

Mrs McAllister opened the office door and was about to leave, but Sir Andrew called after her. "Before I see him, ask Inspector Jenkins to step in for a moment, would you?"

Inspector Ifor Jenkins was, at six and a half feet tall, an imposing figure of a man and an energetic, resourceful and highly ambitious police officer. If he had been born two generations earlier he would probably have gone to work in one of the coalmines that were dotted around the South Wales valley where he was born and any local rugby team would have been pleased to have him in their squad. But things had changed. He had been the first of his family to receive a university education and on graduation had identified a career in the police service as an appropriate vehicle for his skills and talents. Given his imposing physical presence, reasonably agile mind and political nous, not to mention his normal cool headedness and slightly above average level of all round general cynicism, it was probably not such a bad choice.

Once enlisted, just like Sir Andrew before him, he had quickly identified the advantage of being as close as possible to the centre of power. Through dedication to that objective and more than just a little good luck, he had managed to establish himself as Sir Andrew's go-to officer of choice, when any potentially sensitive matter needed to be dealt with.

As Sir Andrew waited for Inspector Jenkins to appear he decided it was pointless trying to tinker any further with his press conference statement, since his ability to mentally focus had, for the moment, been lost. Fortunately, he didn't have to wait long before Jenkins, having only given the faintest of knocks on Sir Andrew's office door, barged into the room. "Mrs McAllister said you wanted to see me urgently, sir."

"Yes, Jenkins, I want you to check someone out for me," said Sir Andrew.

Jenkins produced a notebook and pen from his pocket. "In connection with what, sir?"

"In connection with finding out, who the hell he is." replied Sir Andrew somewhat tetchily. "He'll be in the anteroom in a minute, so you can take a look at him there. Grace will give you his name and anything else she might know about him. Apparently he's a Church of England priest, so you might want to start with their HR department. And he also seems to have some very high up friends at the MOD, so you'll need to take a sounding there as well." Jenkins was about to speak, but Sir Andrew raised a hand to silence him. "Don't bother asking me any questions. I've just given you the sum total of what I know about this chap. And I haven't the faintest idea why he seems so determined to see me. So, off you go, and report back to me a.s.a.p."

Jenkins finished scribbling in his notebook and exited as hurriedly as he had entered.

A few minutes later Sir Andrew's office door opened once again. "Reverend Brazelle," announced Mrs McAllister.

Brazelle stepped forward with his hand outstretched. Sir Andrew put up his hand, but kept his elbow on the desk and remained seated, forcing Brazelle to reach out over the desk before he could shake his hand. He gestured to Brazelle to take a seat and gave a gentle nod to Mrs McAllister, as a sign for her to leave the room.

"Thank you for agreeing to see me at such short notice, Sir Andrew, I know you are a very busy man," said Brazelle.

"You're absolutely right there, so let's cut to the chase shall we?" responded Sir Andrew pompously.

Brazelle said nothing in reply, but handed over the photograph that he had been given by Weston. It had an immediate and obvious effect and Sir Andrew spent several seconds looking at it in silence before asking how Brazelle came to have it.

"Does that matter?" asked Brazelle. "I assume you recognise yourself and know where and when it must have been taken?"

Sir Andrew nodded. "Yes, I know. Just what is this about?"

Brazelle realised he had touched a nerve. The superciliousness with which Sir Andrew had initially greeted him had vanished and been replaced with a look of slight unease. Brazelle took his time before eventually answering his question. "The daughter of the woman whose death you were involved in investigating when that picture was taken has asked me to help her in carrying out her own investigation. She was only an infant when her mother died and had no understanding of the circumstances, knowing only that she had suddenly lost the person she depended upon and loved the most. Now, as an adult, she wants to achieve her own understanding of those circumstances and I believe you may be able to help her to do that."

"It was all a very long time ago, I don't think I can help," responded Sir Andrew, putting down the photograph and still sounding slightly unsettled. "As I recall, I was sent from the Met to see if any assistance was required, presumably because of who her husband was. But, it was quickly identified as a clear case of accidental death. It was all very routine stuff."

Brazelle shook his head as a sign he was rejecting what he had just been told. "But it wasn't, was it, Sir Andrew? It wasn't just routine stuff. Frank Weston, the village constable who took that photograph without your knowledge, spent the next twenty years continuing his own investigation. One thing he later discovered was, at the time of your appearance in Prinsted, you were an officer in Special Branch. That fact alone suggested to him, as it does to me, that your presence there was highly unlikely to be simply, routine. Why would Special Branch be involved? But, Weston would have thought your presence was even more curious, and even less likely to be anything approaching routine, had he known what I now know. At the time, you weren't just a member of Special Branch, but you were, in fact, on secondment to the Security Service, MI5."

Sir Andrew reached for the glass of water that was on his desk and took a mouthful. "How do you know all this?"

"I don't think that matters," said Brazelle. "But I think we've established that your presence in Prinsted couldn't possibly be described as simply, routine. Why was MI5 interested in what appeared to be the accidental death of the wife of a wealthy, but very minor peer of the realm? I will be very grateful if you would help me answer that question? And I think it might help if you start by telling me about the part played in all of this by the red-haired man standing next to you in the photograph?"

Beginning to regain his composure, Sir Andrew took another sip of water. It had been a long time since he had allowed anyone to talk to him in the way that Brazelle was doing and he decided to bring it to an end. "I think I've heard enough, Mr Brazelle. You've had your five minutes. Whatever you think you know about the circumstances of this affair, the reality is that there was an investigation, followed by an inquest, conclusions were drawn and the matter was then closed, twenty years ago. I'm sorry that Lady Justine's daughter was left without a mother at such a young age, but perhaps your time and energy would be better spent helping her come to terms with her loss, rather than encouraging her to continue on a wild goose chase.

And now if you'll excuse me, I have other pressing matters to attend to. I'm sorry I can't be more helpful." Sir Andrew rose from his seat.

Brazelle responded, but remained seated. "But you have been helpful Sir Andrew. I would like to have learned more from you, but you've essentially confirmed most, if not all, of what I thought I knew. And now I certainly have enough to take to the press. It may have happened twenty years ago, but it has all the elements of a tale that the media love. The mysterious death of a beautiful young woman, married to a much older, titled and wealthy man - a man who then, in what appears to be a state of deep depression, takes his own life. Then the icing on the cake - the involvement of players from secret agencies in the form of an ambitious police officer seconded to MI5, who now holds the most senior police rank in the land, and a red-haired assassin, who comes from who knows where."

Sir Andrew fell back into his chair. "You can't take any of this to the press! And what the hell is this about a red-haired assassin?"

"Oh, you didn't know?" said Brazelle rhetorically, already knowing the answer to his own question. "And yes, I certainly can and will take it to the press, unless you and I can come to an understanding."

Sir Andrew was indignant. "You certainly are the weirdest cleric I've ever come across. You turn up without an appointment, apparently pulling strings to get me to see you. Then you come out with things about me that are classified and claim I've been associating with an assassin. And now, to top it all off, you're trying to blackmail me."

Brazelle made no reply, but stood up, retrieved Weston's photograph and moved towards the door.

"Just a moment," called out Sir Andrew, having dropped his air of indignation. "What kind of understanding were you hoping for?"

Brazelle smiled and returned to his seat. "Blackmail, as you well know, Commissioner, involves the intention of one party to gain a benefit at the expense of another. I have no such intention. I believe we can each gain a benefit without cost to the other."

Sir Andrew nodded faintly. "Go on."

"Any police officer worth their salt would have quickly seen that there were circumstances surrounding the death of Lady Justine that required further investigation. I believe that you, just like Frank Weston, also came to that conclusion and that under normal circumstances you would have done just that. But, you weren't the one making the decisions, were you Sir Andrew? Your red-haired companion was the one in charge, someone about whom you knew nothing, probably not even his name, but a man about who you had serious reservations. Once he'd achieved his objectives, of which you knew nothing, he called a halt to the matter and you both withdrew. You've probably never met him since and been grateful for it. But, for you, the matter has never been closed, has it? My guess is that you, just like Frank Weston, have had this case gnawing away at your conscience, on and off ever since. Working together there is the possibility of resolving the matter and providing a benefit to both of us, bringing closure for Lady Justine's daughter and also for you. If you were seen to be investigating the matter it would quickly become public knowledge and questions would be asked.

On the other hand, if I do the investigating, nobody will care very much at all."

"And how do I know that I can trust you? We've only just met and I know nothing about you. Although you seem to know quite a lot about me," observed Sir Andrew.

"But I assume you trust the man who asked you to meet with me. If you were to call him now, while I'm here, I have no doubt that he will vouch for me, although I'm quite certain he'll tell you nothing more."

Sir Andrew thought for a moment before responding. "That won't be necessary. But, if I agree to go along with you, perhaps the first understanding we can come to is that all talk of going to the press, or any other public outlet, ceases immediately and we agree that whatever passes between us, stays just between us."

"Agreed," said Brazelle. "And the second understanding must be that our interest in each other begins and ends with this particular matter. Beyond what it is necessary to know with regard to this case, I intend to take no further interest in you and you must take none in me. Is that also agreed?"

Sir Andrew hesitated for a moment. He had just sent Jenkins to do exactly what Brazelle was now demanding that he must agree not to do. But surely, he thought, the commitment he would be entering into could only be for the future, not the past. He could not undo that which had already been done, so, having rationalised the problem away, at least to his own satisfaction, he gave his agreement.

Brazelle felt a minor concern over Sir Andrew's hesitation, but decided he must let the matter pass. Sir Andrew would have to leave soon and Brazelle was still to hear his story. "Until now I've done most of the talking. I know you have another engagement shortly, but perhaps you could briefly tell me about your visit to Prinsted and, in particular, where the red-haired man fitted in."

Sir Andrew took another sip of water. "To be honest, I'm not sure where he fitted in, except that he was the one put in charge. And apart from his striking red hair and the fact I didn't like the man, the only other thing about him that I can immediately recall is that he had……"

Brazelle interrupted and finished Sir Andrew's sentence. "….particularly large feet."

"Yes……..that's right…..he had particularly large feet," echoed Sir Andrew, who stared at Brazelle for a moment, before continuing with his narrative. "I was told by my MI5 senior that a woman the Security Service had an interest in had been killed and that her death, which would inevitably be investigated by the local police, still needed to be inquired into confidentially by the Security Service itself. From what was already known, he said it appeared that her death was, most likely, the result of an unfortunate accident, but that the Service wanted to make its own assessment before coming to a final conclusion. I was told I was being assigned to the case because I had experience of such investigations and, as a senior warranted police officer, I was able to ask questions of just about anyone without raising suspicion. I was told I must make no reference to the Security Service or Special Branch and that as far as anyone was to know, I was a Met officer sent to offer my assistance in investigating a potentially suspicious death. It was presented as all very routine stuff. However, I was also informed that I would not be the one in charge. That's when I was first introduced to the red-haired man and told

I must take my instructions from him. He called himself John Smith, but if that really was his name then I'm the Pope's uncle. After he introduced himself at our first meeting he hardly spoke again except to tell me what questions he wanted answering, or to give other instructions. From the outset I took a dislike to him and thought he probably had more in common with some of the people I'd arrested rather than any of the other MI5 people I'd come across. In Prinsted I spoke to at least a dozen people, including the village policeman you mentioned, and the village doctor who'd been the first medic on the scene and the one who first declared the woman dead. We visited the scene of death and also went to the morgue to look at the body. There'd already been a post mortem by the time we got there. The pathologist gave us a verbal report on her findings and confirmed that she'd found nothing to make her think it was anything other than an accidental death. There was a gash to the side of the head, almost certainly caused by hitting a rock when she fell, rendering Lady Justine unconscious. There was a bloody mark found on one of the rocks that rose above the water level and it was presumed that it was there where she hit her head. There was also a small bruise on her forehead, probably caused by her head banging into something after she'd entered the water. The cause of death was given as drowning. After talking with the pathologist we returned to London, I handed my notebook over to John Smith, or whatever his name really was, and I never saw him, or my notebook, ever again. There was an inquest, of course, and a verdict of accidental death was recorded. As far as I recall, MI5 then considered the case closed and nothing more was ever said about the matter. That's just about all I can tell you that you probably don't already know. I assume you know about the missing envelope and all the other odd aspects of the case. The village policeman was the one who told me about these, so I presume he's told you as well."

Brazelle nodded. "Yes he did. Did you ask anyone why MI5 had an interest in Lady Justine?"

"As I'm sure you're aware Mr Brazelle, MI5 is not an open organisation. I worked for them on a strictly need-to-know basis. I assumed that if I needed to know something then I would be told without having to ask. I had been given specific instructions not to mention any aspect of the episode to anyone else, either inside or outside of the Service. Even my senior, who was the one who'd given me the assignment in the first place, never mentioned the case again. But tell me about John Smith. I thought he was certainly a nasty piece of work, but it never occurred to me that he was an assassin. Just how do you know this?"

"I know what he is because our paths have crossed in the past," answered Brazelle. "I know him by the name Orlando, but can tell you little else, except to confirm your conclusion that he is a nasty piece of work. I find his involvement in this case really quite puzzling. I'm sure a man like Orlando would never be employed by MI5, so I can only conclude that the investigation you were carrying out when you went to Prinsted was not an MI5 operation. My guess is that you were loaned out to some other clandestine agency without your knowledge, a much darker agency and one that had occasional need of Orlando's specialist skills. You were probably assigned to the operation, not just for the reasons you were given at the time, but also because you were fairly inexperienced in the ways in which the spooks sometimes work, so, would take what you were told at face value, as you appear to have done."

"You refer to Orlando in the present tense. Does that mean you think he's still alive?" asked Sir Andrew.

Brazelle gave a shrug. "I know he was still alive just over five years ago, but beyond that I don't know. If it's true that only the good die young, then Orlando certainly is still alive. And where people like him are concerned, I've found it's always best to assume the worst."

There was a knock on the door and Mrs McAllister entered the room. "Sorry to disturb you, Sir Andrew, but they're calling for you downstairs at the press conference. What would you like me to tell them?"

Sir Andrew rose from his seat. "Tell them I'll be down in just two minutes," he said, before addressing Brazelle. "Regrettably I must call a halt to our meeting. Time, tide and the British media wait for no man. And, quite frankly, I need some time to take all this in. With a little more time I might be able to recall some further details of the event. Perhaps I could contact you in a few days time. Will that be acceptable?"

Brazelle stood up and held out his hand. "That will be perfectly acceptable. I will await your call."

Sir Andrew stepped forward to shake Brazelle's hand, this time not requiring him to lean over a desk.

After finishing his press conference, Sir Andrew returned to his office. Very soon afterwards Inspector Jenkins arrived looking rather downbeat, a far cry from his usual ebullient self. "I'm afraid I've got a lot less to report than I would have hoped for, sir. I started with the Church of England HR people. It seems Reverend Brazelle is a Peculiar."

"I think I'd already come to that conclusion," interrupted Sir Andrew.

"No, not peculiar in the way I imagine you're probably thinking sir," continued Jenkins. "Apparently, 'Peculiar' is a technical term used in the Church. If Brazelle is the priest of a parish, although nobody I spoke to seemed to know whether he is or not, it would have to be what they call a Peculiar, because his line management lies outside the Church's normal hierarchical structure. Although he's only a fairly junior priest, it seems he reports directly to the Archbishop of Canterbury."

"I assume, therefore, that you got on to the Archbishop's office," said Sir Andrew with his impatience still obvious.

"Yes I did, but sadly they couldn't make the situation any clearer. Brazelle's file is held in a cabinet to which only the Archbishop has access. Unfortunately, the Archbishop's on Retreat somewhere in the wilds of Canada, combining a bit of prayerful contemplation of the soul with a spot of bear stalking, and isn't expected back for the best part of a fortnight. Meanwhile, the office's instructions are: No interruptions unless it's The Second Coming."

"Couldn't you try an old fashioned copper's bluff?" asked Sir Andrew, "the threat of a warrant or something?"

"I've tried that one already, sir. It won't work. Apparently, under some ancient law that dates back to Henry the Eighth, the only power that can order the Archbishop's personal files to be opened, without the Archbishop's explicit consent, is the Monarch, as Head of the Church." Then sensing and rather enjoying Sir Andrew's obvious frustration, Jenkins added mischievously, "shall I get on to the Palace, sir?"

Sir Andrew was clearly not amused. "Don't push your luck Jenkins. You can cut the sarcasm. What about the MOD? How did you get on there?"

Jenkins put on a glum expression. "Not much better, I'm sorry to say, sir. I started at General Michael's office, but got passed around quite a lot until I ended up talking to a Major Daniel Coyte-Sherman." At that point, Jenkins referred to his notebook. "And Coyte-Sherman said, 'Why don't you expletive stick to handing out expletive parking tickets and stop expletive asking expletive questions about expletive matters that are well above your expletive pay grade. Now just expletive off you expletive Welsh expletive'. At that point I asked him to stop swearing and Coyte-Sherman said, 'Expletive, expletive, expletive, expletive, and hung up on me." Jenkins put his notebook back in his pocket.

Sir Andrew looked puzzled. "And that's all he had to say?"

"Well, I might have missed out the odd 'expletive' sir, but other than that - Yes."

Sir Andrew leaned back in his chair. "So, Jenkins, it appears we know no more about Reverend Brazelle now than we did before."

"Well, we do know that whatever it is that he's been involved with, it's somewhere above my pay grade, sir."

For a fleeting moment Sir Andrew managed a faint smile. "I'm afraid that doesn't narrow the field much Jenkins." He then reverted to a more serious face. "I'd hoped for a short cut, but it appears we'll just have to resort to more painstaking techniques. Assign a couple of your crew to give you a hand and see what you can come up with on Reverend Brazelle using the usual methods. And while you're about it, see what you can come up with on some unsavoury chap who, to some people at least, is known by the name, Orlando. He's about my age and has striking red hair. Oh yes, and particularly big feet."

Jenkins summarised his instructions in his notebook. "And if my crew ask what it's about, what shall I tell them sir?"

Sir Andrew smiled. "Tell them it's above their 'expletive' pay grade."

Jenkins got the point. "Understood, sir, will that be all?"

"Yes that's it," replied Sir Andrew, before quickly changing his mind. "No, wait. There is something else you can do. I want you to Google me, Jenkins."

Jenkins thought he must have misheard. "Google you, sir?"

"Yes, that's right, Jenkins, I want you to Google me," confirmed Sir Andrew. "I want you to find out what I've been doing for the past twenty years."

On arriving back at Prinsted Church, Brazelle went straight into discussion with Fred Simpson who confirmed that the void had been opened up, but nothing of interest had been found and there were certainly no issues of concern. In fact, the only thing he thought worth mentioning was a mismatch of mortar he had spotted in one part of the partition wall, where the associated stonework had been laid in a far clumsier style, suggesting the void had been partially opened up at least once in the past and then resealed.

Inside the Church, Jenny was carrying out her own examination of the void and was so deep in thought, she only became aware of Brazelle's presence when he was just a few feet away and called out her name. She turned with a start.

Brazelle apologised for startling her. "Sorry, I made you jump, but I'll give a penny for your thoughts."

Jenny gave a facial shrug. "I'm not sure they're worth that much. All I can definitely say is that the partition wall must have been constructed a long time after the Church was built. It goes over part of a memorial stone that has a date of sixteen hundred and twenty and the Church is much older than that. Why on earth would anyone go to the bother of creating it? It simply partitions off a niche in the Church wall and appears to have served no useful purpose."

"I guess we know what the purpose of the niche was originally. It's more or less identical to the others dotted around the Church," observed Brazelle, as he pointed to a couple of other niches housing small statues, standing on plinths. "Years ago, I guess there would have been a varied collection of icons and probably some 'holy relics' on display, no doubt. So, your question is a good one, why would anyone bother to partition this one off? And surely the most likely answer to that question has to be...........”

Jenny completed Brazelle's sentence...........“because, they had something to hide.”

Brazelle agreed, but not without reservations. “On the other hand, I doubt that the sudden appearance of a new partition wall enclosing a niche in the Church would have gone unnoticed. I'm sure there would have been at least a few people asking questions about it, especially if it was created around the time of the disappearance of the legendary Cromwell's Treasure.”

Jenny disagreed. “Not necessarily. Looking around the Church, you can see some large tapestries hanging on the walls. In the past there would have been even more and some may well have covered over niches. In fact the tapestry over there covers one.” Jenny pointed to a tapestry hanging on the other side of the Church.

“Well, well!” said Brazelle, “I've been in and out of this Church hundreds of times and thought I knew the place inside out, but I never knew that.” He walked over to the tapestry and pulled it away from the wall slightly, only to find there was no niche. Rather perplexed by the contrast between what he had just been told and what he had now seen, Brazelle turned to face Jenny and saw she was laughing.

“Do you get my point?” she asked.

Brazelle stared at her with a puzzled look, but after a few seconds it changed to a smile, and he went back to join her. “I get it,” he said, “but I'm not sure you should tell lies in a church to make your point.”

"Lies are intended to deceive, but what I said was intended to enlighten," replied Jenny. "Although you know this Church better than practically anyone else, apart from me, you had no idea what lay behind that tapestry. And if YOU don't know, then what chance would anyone else have. Perhaps this niche had been covered with a tapestry before the partition was constructed and then it was simply put back after the partition was built. Or, maybe a tapestry was hung up for the first time after the partition was constructed. Either way, the result would have been the same. Nobody would have been any the wiser."

Brazelle was not yet convinced. "And what about the curious parishioner who took a peep and thought - 'Where did that bit of wall come from? It wasn't there last week'!"

"Oh come on Chris, you're pushing the bounds of credibility aren't you?" objected Jenny. "Most people have far more important things to be curious about than what lies behind a tapestry in the Parish Church, especially if it had been there for as long as they could remember. Anyway, maybe the parish priest put out an edict that nobody should touch the Church tapestries on pain of excommunication." She laughed.

"Now it's your turn to go too far," said Brazelle. "But I get your point. We're left with the definite possibility that this niche might have been sealed off to create a hiding place. Perhaps.........even a hiding place for the legendary Cromwell's Treasure.........assuming it ever existed in the first place. But it's definitely empty now. I think I'll sleep on it and take a closer look at it in the morning, when the light's better."

"I'll do the same," added Jenny. "Perhaps I should run a competition in next month's Parish Magazine to see who can come up with the best suggestion for why it was sealed off."

Brazelle was far from being what might reasonably be called a good chef. However, over the years he had concentrated on improving his skill at preparing a small selection of dishes to a better than simply satisfactory standard. Tonight he would be preparing one of these for Rose, although with a slight modification. It was to be chilli con carne, but since Rose did not eat red meat, Brazelle was, for the first time, attempting it with just vegetables and no carne. So, more correctly, it was chilli sans carne. He had also chosen a bottle of Malbec to go with it, but having noticed that Rose was an exceptionally light drinker, he assumed he would be drinking most of it himself.

Rose arrived shortly before seven and was clearly eager to tell Brazelle about the results of her hypnosis session with Gerald. "Before we started, Gerald warned me that I might be disappointed with the results and that I might even come up with a false memory, just like Jenny warned last night. But something seemed to work and I did recall a couple of things that I'm convinced are true memories."

"And these are?" prompted Brazelle.

"Well firstly, you remember I said that my mother went over to the gate to talk to a man? Under hypnosis, I remembered he waved to catch her attention and that she handed him something. It was a small packet or an envelope. The man was quite a distance away from me, so I never got a very good look at him, but I remembered he had red hair." Rose was clearly pleased at having recalled these details. "So, what do you think?" she asked.

Brazelle gave the matter a moment's thought before replying. "I'd say there's a very good chance your recollections are accurate and, if they are, they suggest that the meeting between your mother and the man with red hair was not coincidental, but prearranged. There are a number of possible reasons for that and most of them are entirely innocent. You told me that the playground was a place where your mother often took you, so it could have been a convenient place to complete some business. For example, your mother might have been arranging some kind of surprise for your father and wanted to make arrangements away from Harfield House, in order to keep it secret. I think we need more information before letting our imaginations run away with us, but it's a good start. Let's leave it for a while and in the meantime you can see what you think about my culinary expertise."

Not long after dinner, Rose, who was still not fully recovered from jet lag, fell asleep on the sofa in the sitting room. After making a fairly half-hearted attempt to wake her, Brazelle simply covered her with a blanket and retired to bed himself. It had been a long day and he fell asleep almost as soon as his head touched the pillow.

Day Seven - Friday

The sun was still some minutes off rising when Brazelle woke and went to check on Rose. Entering the sitting room he found only a neatly folded blanket on the sofa, but, glancing to his left, he saw the door to the study was slightly open and the light was on. He went to investigate and found Rose poring over some papers on his desk.

"What are you doing?" he asked.

Rose, startled, immediately turned to face him. "Oh, I woke, and came in here to see if I could find a book I might read. I didn't think you'd mind."

Brazelle gave a reassuring smile. "No, I don't mind and I'm sorry I startled you. What is it that's taken your interest?"

Rose picked up one of the sheets from the desk and handed it to Brazelle. It was a hand drawn sketch of a circular object about ten centimetres in diameter bearing the image of a man's head with a crown above, together with several other smaller images and some Latin script. "It's this. What exactly is it?" she asked.

"It's a drawing of what some people would call a medallion, but what the experts might be more likely to call a phalera," answered Brazelle. "The Romans are thought to be the first people to have created them, but that one comes from a much later period. They were awards, like medals. The Romans sometimes presented them to individual soldiers for gallantry, or for a particular act of service to the state or the emperor, but more usually they were awarded to groups of soldiers, such as a whole Legion, for winning a particular battle, or mounting a successful campaign. The Legion would then attach it to its Standard and, over time, gather quite a collection. They're what you might think of as precursors to modern medals and also to the battle honours that are emblazoned on a military unit's colours."

Rose pointed to the sketch now being held by Brazelle. "Do you know very much about this particular one?"

Brazelle nodded. "Yes, as a matter of fact I do. It was one of six awarded by King Charles the First to members of his personal bodyguard for saving his life, in some cases, on more than one occasion. They were all slightly different, although they all had the head of the King as their most prominent feature and each had the name of the recipient engraved around the edge. The whereabouts of only five of the six is known, one is owned privately and the other four are in museums." Brazelle handed the sketch back to Rose. "That's a sketch of the one that's missing."

"Did you draw it?" asked Rose.

"Yes. I copied it from another sketch that was drawn by someone who I believe actually saw it. It does have a fascinating history attached to it, but why are you so interested in it?"

"Because I have it," Rose replied.

After what Rose had told him, Brazelle was eager to see the phalera, but decided he must first make a visit to the Church. He got there just after Fred Simpson and his work team had arrived and was soon joined by Jenny. It was his intention to examine every inch of the newly uncovered niche and he had brought along a powerful torch and a magnifying glass to assist him. Jenny thought this was a bit over the top and said so.

"I thought you were interested in finding out who partitioned off the niche and why they did it," said Brazelle.

"Yes, I am," replied Jenny. "I'm curious, but not obsessed about it. I was hoping we might find something of interest hidden away inside, but sadly we haven't. My guess is we'll probably never find out who created it and why. We might come up with one or two theories, but it all happened a very long time ago and we'll probably never know for sure. But I'll put a piece in the Parish Magazine, like I said, and see if anyone can throw some light on the matter."

Brazelle waved his torch. "Well, talking of throwing some light on the matter, that's just what I plan on doing." He switched on his torch and crawled inside the niche on his hands and knees. Despite the upbeat attitude he displayed to Jenny, in reality, he held out little hope of finding anything of interest, so he was pleasantly surprised when he thought that he just might have done. It wasn't much to look at, but it was enough for Brazelle to think it worth showing to Jenny.

Jenny was rather disparaging. "I wouldn't have thought that was much to get excited about...... a button!"

Brazelle only partially agreed. "Well it may not be much to look at, but I'm pretty sure it didn't get there on its own."

Brazelle next showed the button to Fred Simpson, but he denied all knowledge of it and confirmed that the buttons on the company issued overalls worn by him and his men were all of a different colour and size.

In his determination to establish the provenance of the button, Brazelle decided to play a hunch and drove over to the office of the Northope building company that had carried out the survey of the Church a few months earlier. After showing the button to the company's manager, Brazelle was introduced to another member of staff and went off to speak to him in private. Very soon afterwards, he had learned not only where the button had come from, but also how it had found its way into the void. Feeling very satisfied he had played the right hunch he drove over to Harfield House.

Rose had given Brazelle a code for the automated security system that controlled the opening and closing of Napoleon's Gates, so, on arrival, he was able to simply enter the code and, with a feeling of great privilege, drive straight through. Rose greeted him at the front door, led him into the library and handed him the phalera. Brazelle examined it with the aid of his magnifying glass, paying particular attention to its edge, in order to identify the name of its original owner. It read, 'Captain John Hadlington', which was the name Brazelle was expecting to see. Declaring it to be genuine, he asked Rose how she came to possess it.

"Gareth gave it to me just before we moved to the States. I was only five, but I can still remember. Both my parents had died and I was being taken away from my home. It was a very miserable time in my life and I guess he took pity on me. He said it was his most precious possession, but I could have it and it would be a secret between us.

Every time I felt like crying, he said I should hold it and it would make me feel better. You're the only other person who knows I've got it. I've never told anyone else about it."

"And did it work? Did it make you feel better?" Brazelle asked.

"Well, I did get it out from time to time, like he said, but I can't really remember if it made me feel any better. Perhaps it did a little. For quite a long time after my parents died I would have fretful fits. They came over me in waves. I can't say that I ever felt especially happy, but perhaps it stopped me from feeling even worse."

"You're very fond of Gareth, aren't you?"

"Yes, I am. We were more or less brought up together, until I moved to the States. He was like a big brother, always very patient with me and he taught me things. Mrs Richards says, even when I was an infant, I was one of only a very few people he would communicate with. Everyone in the family is fond of Gareth. My father more or less treated him as a son and, because of his special needs, spent a lot of money getting him the best support possible to help with his development - support that Mrs Richards and Jonathan would never have been able to afford."

"Do you know where Gareth got the phalera?" Brazelle asked. "And apart from what he told you when he gave it to you, did he ever say anything else about it at anytime?"

"No, he never told me where he got it and I don't remember speaking to him about it since the day he gave it to me. Perhaps you should ask him about it."

"I intend to," said Brazelle, "but not just yet. You're very lucky to have a friend like Gareth, that phalera is solid gold and worth a small fortune. The scrap value alone would be a few thousand pounds, but as a rare historic artefact it's worth many times that. It needs to be insured and kept in a safe place. Where have you been keeping it until now?"

Rose giggled. "I've kept it with some other odd bits and pieces in an old shoe box under my bed."

Brazelle smiled. "Probably best if you find somewhere more secure to keep it."

Rose assured him that she would and asked how he knew so much about it.

Brazelle gave her what he thought was the best response possible for the time being. "I can't tell you that at the moment, it's a complicated matter, but your phalera is another step forward towards achieving a resolution. I'm hoping I'll be able to work everything out soon. And when that time comes, I promise you'll be one of the very first to know. However, one thing I can tell you with certainty is that I have to go back to work right now. But I have a day off tomorrow and since the weather forecast is good, I was wondering if you'd like to come with me for a drive and we could go somewhere interesting to have lunch."

"Oh, I hope you know that I would if I could, but Damien's away for the weekend and I've promised Frankie I'll go into the city with her tomorrow and do some shopping. I've spent so little time with her since I came back to the UK. She would be ever so disappointed and I'd feel terrible if I let her down. You do understand don't you? Can I see you sometime on Sunday, in between your other commitments?"

Brazelle smiled and nodded reassuringly. "Of course, I understand. On Sunday I should finish my morning commitments and be back home to change by twelve-thirty at the latest. If you come round and meet me then we can go somewhere for lunch, or come to Church in the morning and I'll see you there."

Rose was hesitant in her response. "I think for the moment I'd rather meet you at Holford. Is that okay?"

"Yes, of course. You must do what you feel is right. I'll meet you at Holford at twelve-thirty and, who knows, I might even let you get behind the wheel of the Ferrari."

"That sounds great," said Rose excitedly. "But I'm free tonight as well."

Brazelle frowned. "Unfortunately, it's now my turn to say I can't make it. I have a couple of work commitments that will take me well into the evening. We even have a visit from the Bishop to contend with and he always turns up late and stays too long. I think it must be a clause in his job description. So it will have to be Sunday. I shall look forward to it."

"And so will I," said Rose, before doing something she had never done before. She leaned forward and kissed Brazelle on the lips.

Brazelle had hoped to say goodbye to the Bishop by ten at the latest, but, as he had earlier predicted to Rose, the Bishop turned up late and stayed longer than planned, so it was gone eleven before he was able to head home. Fortunately, despite being extremely tired, he was fully alert as he turned into Holford's yard where, slamming on his brakes, he just managed to avoid hitting a black Range Rover with blacked out windows, parked facing him, just inside the yard entrance. Having come to a stop, other instincts immediately took over. He switched the lights of the jeep onto full beam, put the gear stick into reverse whilst keeping his foot on the clutch pedal and gave three short bursts on his horn. With his engine running, he sat and waited until a man he recognised stepped out of the Range Rover, at which point he shut down his jeep and went to greet his unexpected visitor. "I hope you haven't been waiting long, Sir Andrew," he said.

Sir Andrew shook the hand that was offered. "You took your time deciding whether or not to get out of your car, Mr Brazelle. Did you feel under threat?"

Brazelle, pointed up to where Max was standing at the entrance to his studio, holding his double-barrelled shotgun. "Well if I was, I certainly wasn't the only one."

Sir Andrew turned to look up at Max. "Does he have a licence for that shotgun?"

Brazelle gave a shrug. "I don't know. He's a Glaswegian with a bad attitude, why don't you go and ask him?" Having given the all-clear sign to Max, he gestured to Sir Andrew to follow him into the cottage.

Sir Andrew shook his head. "You really are the weirdest cleric I've ever come across."

"Well, in that case you've still a lot more to meet," responded Brazelle, adding, "I imagined you'd turn up at some point, but thought you might call first."

"What, just like you did when you came to see me the other day?" responded Sir Andrew, before casting an eye over some of Brazelle's paintings. "It's easy to guess what your hobby might be."

"Fair comment," said Brazelle who, keen to move things along, chose to ignore Sir Andrew's reference to his artwork. "Anyway, just how long have you been waiting? And how did you know I was going to be here?"

"I've been here about half an hour and would have waited a bit longer if necessary," replied Sir Andrew. "I guessed you'd turn up eventually, I contacted the Diocesan office earlier today and they told me you had a meeting planned with the Bishop and that it was due to finish around 9pm. I've been at a meeting of senior police officers in Birmingham, so decided to give my driver the night off, make a slight detour and take the opportunity of dropping in on you on my way back to London. I've remembered a couple more details about my previous trip to Prinsted. Given the nature of our business, I didn't think you'd mind that it's rather late."

"No, I don't mind," said Brazelle. "But why did you contact the Diocesan office? We made an agreement that you wouldn't take any interest in me."

"I contacted the Diocese to ask what your business here in Prinsted is. You already know what my job is. That seems fair to me. In fact the nature of our agreement was the first thing I wanted to get clear, before we discuss anything else."

"Very well.......go on.......I'm listening," responded Brazelle, with a hint of suspicion evident in his voice

"Just before we met the other day and therefore before you and I entered into any form of agreement, I asked one of Wales' finest, Inspector Ifor Jenkins, a man who hopes to have my job one day, to check you out. He contacted the Church of England and then the Army, both organisations with which you appear to have a close relationship, but he came back with precisely nothing, apart from a foul-mouthed earful from a Major Daniel Coyte-Sherman."

Brazelle became more relaxed and smiled. "I already know about that. I got a couple of calls to let me know. It didn't concern me because, as you say, it happened before we made our agreement. Is there anything else?"

"Yes, I asked Jenkins to check out Orlando, but he came back with nothing there either. Orlando has no police record and neither does he make an appearance on any other official database that Jenkins accessed. Well, at least not under that name. It seems he's just as much of a ghost as you are.........And then I asked Jenkins to check me out."

"Check YOU out?" interrupted Brazelle with a look of surprise.

"That's right. I wanted him to find out what was publicly available about me, and it turns out there's a hell of a lot. In just a couple of hours on the internet he found out almost everything there is to know, right down to my shoe size, although, I have to say, not all of it is correct. That's what comes of being a public figure, I suppose, it's not easy to keep anything secret. Well, maybe not easy, but perhaps not impossible either, because there were a few things that he didn't turn up, like my work with MI5, or my connection to the Harfield case, for example. But then you found out about these from private sources didn't you, Mr Brazelle? Have you grasped my point yet?"

Brazelle nodded. "Yes, I believe I have. You think that the second clause of our agreement is a bit one sided, don't you?"

"Not a BIT one sided Mr Brazelle, I'd say TOTALLY one sided," answered Sir Andrew. "You clearly did your homework on me before we met. Anyway, you needn't worry, although I got Jenkins and a couple of his crew to try some more traditional police methods to check you out, they still came up with the same result as before - absolutely nothing. It's as if you never actually existed, until the day you entered training to become a priest."

"So you've breached the second clause of our agreement," asserted Brazelle.

"Although I may not have kept exactly to the letter of our agreement, I believe I've certainly kept to its spirit," replied Sir Andrew. "But, in any case the result is the same, I know nothing more about you now than I did at the time we made our agreement and I've now stood down Jenkins and his crew. I wouldn't be human, let alone a policeman, if I didn't wonder just who and what you were. But, despite being Head of the Met and having privileged access to all kinds of information, I've been unable to answer those questions, so I've now decided to close the file. You must certainly have some very powerful friends to assist you in erasing your past in the way that you seem to have done. Having said that however, you will know as well as I do, that it's impossible to extinguish one's history entirely. I'm sure that somewhere there will be clues and links to your previous life. Let's hope, for your sake, the wrong people don't find them."

Brazelle was clearly irritated. "Your curiosity is one thing and quite understandable, although taking action over it is something else......... However, you didn't need to have told me any of that. I'll take it as the confession of a repentant man driven by conscience........and grant absolution........on this one occasion. Are you sure we now understand one another, Sir Andrew? And you agree that from now on we both stick to the letter of our agreement, aswell as its spirit?"

Sir Andrew nodded. "Yes, I understand...... and agree."

Brazelle's mood eased. "Very well, so what is it that you've remembered?"

"Two incidents that I believe have relevance. Since you seem to know Orlando much better than I do, you will know that he is a man who displays no emotion. He is a real cold fish and someone who would almost certainly score very high on the psychopath scale. But when we visited the morgue and the pathologist pulled back the sheet covering Lady Justine's body, I definitely detected a brief sign of emotion. It was so short lived, I'm sure most people would have missed it, but as an experienced detective I was well used to picking up on unspoken hints from body language and other non-verbal clues. I'm quite sure it wasn't just the sight of a dead body that caused Orlando's reaction. Although it didn't strike me at the time, putting it into the context of what I now know, I believe he already knew Lady Justine. And there was an incident that took place just after Orlando decided he'd seen enough and we were leaving Prinsted to return to London. He suddenly decided he needed a pee. I was the one driving and he began giving directions that took us off the route we were planning on taking and straight to a children's playground where there was a public toilet. I asked him how he knew about the toilets. He said he didn't know and that finding them was just good luck, but I'm quite certain he was lying. It's pretty obvious to me that he'd been there before, but, for whatever reason, didn't want to admit to it."

"I think you're correct in both your conclusions," said Brazelle. "In fact I would go further and say I'm quite certain that you're right. Orlando and Justine had met on at least one occasion at the playground you visited. But I'd like to ask you a few questions about your dealings with MI5 on this case, Sir Andrew. Firstly, who in MI5 did you ever discuss this case with and what precise instructions were you given regarding its confidentiality? Secondly, when you did have discussions with anyone, where did they take place? And in particular, where and when were you first introduced to Orlando?"

Sir Andrew took a moment to consider his response. "I only ever discussed the case with my senior, the person who gave me the assignment. And as for confidentiality, I was given the very clear instruction that I was never to mention any aspect of the case with anyone, ever, not even another member of the Service. There was nothing unusual about that instruction. Ever since the Philby affair, both MI5 and MI6 have tried to maintain cell structures, so if a leak did appear it didn't drain the whole pond, so to speak. The only thing that was unusual and out of the ordinary was that all discussions took place at my senior's London flat and not at MI5 HQ. The first discussion happened when my senior asked me to join him for a drink at his flat and he told me what he wanted me to do. That's also when I met Orlando for the first time. The only other discussion

I ever had about the case also took place at my senior's flat, the day after our visit to Prinsted, but Orlando wasn't present on that occasion. At our second meeting, my senior said that MI5 had learnt what it wanted to know, reminded me about the strict level of confidentiality put on the matter and said the case was now closed. Since that second meeting I've never spoken about the case, or even heard mention of it, until you turned up in my office two days ago."

Brazelle gave a nod signifying his understanding. "As I told you the other day, in my view, Orlando was not a man who MI5 would ever consider employing, and I believe you essentially agreed with me. I suggested that for the purpose of carrying out this assignment you must have been loaned out to some other agency, one much darker than MI5. For want of a name, we'll call them 'The Agency' shall we? So Sir Andrew, just how good a copper are you?"

Sir Andrew put his head down and clasped his hands together. He remained in that position for several seconds, before eventually clearing his throat and sitting upright once more. "I've always had a feeling of unease about this whole affair and now I'm beginning to understand why. I was duped wasn't I? I was working for the other side, whoever the other side was?"

"I'd say that's the most obvious conclusion," said Brazelle.

Sir Andrew posed the inevitable question. "But why use me?"

"For the same reasons that any service, either friend or foe, would have chosen you," answered Brazelle. "For the reasons I listed two days ago. But there was an extra benefit from the point of view of The Agency - you were transitory – you were at MI5 on temporary secondment. Not long after the completion of the operation, you would be gone, reducing significantly the chance that any of this would come out. It's clear to me that as far as The Agency was concerned, Lady Justine's death was entirely unexpected and they were interested in finding out exactly what had happened to her. To do this, they needed to move fast and you were instantly available. Had they involved someone else, perhaps someone who wasn't a genuine police officer, then an extra and unnecessary risk would have been introduced. That would have increased the chances of failure and introduced the possibility of all sorts of things unravelling. That's why you were chosen for the job. You were the ideal candidate, or, to use the American parlance, Sir Andrew, you were 'the perfect patsy'."

Sir Andrew was still somewhat dazed. "What about the disappearing letter and Lady Justine's non-appearance at the post office? Orlando showed no interest in these matters. Why was that? And why was a man like Orlando chosen for the job?"

"All easily explained," replied Brazelle. "Orlando was chosen because he knew Lady Justine and could identify the body. The Agency wanted to be sure that it really was her who had died. As for the disappearing letter and the non-appearance at the post office, Orlando already knew the answers to those apparent riddles. Justine had, either met him before she reached the village and given him the envelope, or, put it at some prearranged drop point from where he could recover it. There was no need for her to go all the way into the village, so she crossed the stream at one of the other bridges that exist between Harfield House and the village and was crossing back, on her way home, when she fell off the bridge and drowned. But the identification of Justine's body wasn't Orlando's only reason for being there. Do you remember when we spoke in your office, not only did I tell you that he is an assassin, but also that he is a specialist?"

Sir Andrew nodded. "I remember, so what is his specialism?"

"He is what is often referred to as a 'Cloaked Assassin'. He specialises in killing people in ways that make it look like suicide or an accident, although that doesn't preclude him from occasionally putting a bullet in someone's head. In the case of the death of Lady Justine I believe he was playing the part of poacher turned gamekeeper. He was there to cast an eye over the situation, so he could advise The Agency whether or not, in his expert opinion, her death really had been an accident."

"I'm a senior police officer, so I've come across the term 'Cloaked Assassin' before," said Sir Andrew, "although, assuming you're right about Orlando, as far as I know he's the only one I've ever actually met. But what conclusion do you think he came to about Lady Justine's death?"

Brazelle shook his head. "I haven't figured that out yet. There are a few more questions I need answers to, before I'm going to hazard a guess."

"Have you any ideas about the nature of the relationship between Lady Justine and Orlando?" asked Sir Andrew. "Why would she be giving him an envelope and, just as importantly, what do you think was in it?"

"I don't know what was in the envelope, but I'd guess it was something she'd taken from her husband without his knowledge. Sir Cornelius was a brilliant scientist and engineer, involved in all sorts of projects, many of them highly classified. He had access to a great deal of highly confidential and secret material, just the sort of stuff that an organisation such as The Agency would be interested in. They would either use it themselves, or sell it to someone else who would, depending upon whether they were a state sponsored organisation or freelance. With Orlando involved I'd assume it was the latter."

"And what is your theory as to Lady Justine's motivation for betraying her husband and being a spy?" asked Sir Andrew.

"You're a highly experienced policeman, so you'll be aware what the training manuals have to say about those who get involved in espionage. They do it for one of four reasons: money, or some other reward; ideology; a sense of grandeur fuelled by either a feeling of self importance, or bravado; or, they're under duress. In Justine's case I think it was most likely the last of these, and that she was being blackmailed. That would explain why The Agency wanted to be sure she really was dead and hadn't simply faked her own death in order to escape their clutches. I'll bet she had no idea what kind of organisation she was passing secrets to and that Orlando was one of only a very small number of its members she ever had contact with. I have no doubt that had she ever shown signs of becoming a threat to the organisation or outlived her usefulness, Orlando would have done his worst and she would have been killed. But there's one very big question I must ask you before we go any further, Sir Andrew...........Who was your senior, the MI5 officer who gave you the assignment and the person who duped you?"

Sir Andrew took a deep breath. "Sir Ted Gant," he said.

A look of astonishment covered Brazelle's face and he sat back in his chair.

There was a long silent pause, before Sir Andrew spoke again. "He was just plain 'Mr' Ted Gant in those days, a middle ranking MI5 officer in his mid thirties. But a couple of years after my secondment ended he transferred to MI6 and, nowadays of course, he has a knighthood and is Deputy Director of that Service. What's more, he's the favourite to take over as Director of MI6 when Sir John Phelps retires early next year."

An even longer pause followed, before Brazelle eventually broke the silence. "And the whole thing reeks of plausible deniability on the part of Sir Ted Gant, doesn't it? If you go to the Prime Minister and tell him what you've told me, Gant simply denies it and where does that leave you? There's a lot of evidence that compromises you, but none whatsoever that points to him. It was you who went to Prinsted and, with Gant's denial, it would appear that you went without authority and told lies about being sent by the Met. Worse still, you were there in the company of a murderer. Although there are very few of us, I'm not the only person alive who knew Orlando for what he was and could identify him in the photograph that Frank Weston took. If you tried to use it as support for your story it could just as easily, in fact even more easily, be used against you. If you made a move against Gant now, he would have you plucked, stuffed and in the oven before Christmas."

Sir Andrew looked totally downbeat. "You're right, of course, but how do you know I'm not lying? I could have made all of this up and be deceiving you, couldn't I?"

"That's a very good question. And don't think it hasn't crossed my mind," replied Brazelle. "However, unless you're the world's worst policeman, you will have a strong suspicion that at some point in my life I must have come across some very bad people." Brazelle paused, and Sir Andrew nodded. "Well, your suspicions are correct. I have, and I've decided that you're not one of them."

Sir Andrew gave what Brazelle thought to be a sigh of relief and a faint smile.

Brazelle continued. "Of course there remains the slimmest possibility that Gant was himself duped, by someone higher up in the ranks of the Service, but that really is incredible. He was an experienced MI5 officer and would have immediately smelled a rat if he were asked to involve himself with a man like Orlando, especially if required to do it in his own home and in complete secrecy."

Sir Andrew nodded in agreement.

"We need a plan of action aimed at forcing Gant into exposing himself as a traitor and exonerating you," said Brazelle. "And if, after all, and against all the odds, I am wrong about his guilt, then that should also be determined."

Brazelle stood up, stretched out his arms and yawned. "But now, Sir Andrew, I'm going to bed. I'm absolutely shattered. We both need to sleep on this and work out what we do next. And perhaps you could find out what you can about the late Lady Justine. I understand her maiden name was Hellyer."

"I'll put Jenkins onto it first thing in the morning, but right now though, I need time to fully absorb all this. I'll get back to you on Monday. In the meantime take this." Sir Andrew handed Brazelle a small card with a phone number printed on it. "It's my confidential direct line and it's available twenty four hours a day. When you get through, the operator will simply ask, 'Who is it?' And you must give the password that's written on the back of the card. The password is unique to you, so they'll be able to identify you immediately. If I'm available they'll put you through straight away, but if I'm not, they'll let me know you called and I'll get back to you a.s.a.p. That card carries highly privileged information, known to only a very limited number of people, so please memorise what's on it and then destroy it. Remember, when you call, give the password exactly as it is on that card. If you deviate by just one syllable the operator will just hang up on you."

Brazelle waited until Sir Andrew drove off before turning over the card and reading the password he had been assigned. He rolled his eyes and sighed.

Day Eight - Saturday

Brazelle woke just after seven and by eight o'clock had drawn up a list of tasks he aimed to complete by the end of the day. Saturday was the one day in the week when he was not regularly involved in some kind of activity at the Church, so he could commit it fully to whatever he chose. He was just about to get into his jeep and set off to start working through his list when Rose drove into the yard.

"What are you doing here?" he asked. "I thought you were going shopping with your sister."

"I am," replied Rose. "But Frankie and I went out for dinner last night, after you rejected me, and we got home late. She's slept late and only just started getting ready, so I thought I'd just pop round to see you. I've got something for you. That's okay, isn't it?"

"Of course, it's okay. I'm always pleased to see you," responded Brazelle. "And, by the way, I didn't reject you, as you put it. I told you I had a number of commitments last night, including dealing with a visit from the Bishop."

Rose smiled. "Yes, I know. I'm only joking. We passed here last night on our way home and saw a car parked in the yard. Did it belong to the Bishop? He must have stayed very late."

Brazelle shook his head. "No, it wasn't the Bishop's car. I met him at the Church. And you probably wouldn't believe me if I did tell you whose car it was."

"You never know, I might," said Rose. "But surely there are subtler ways to tell me to mind my own business."

Brazelle smiled and gave a shrug of the shoulders. "Anyway, have you got time to come in and have some tea?"

"No, I'd like to, but I'd better not. Frankie doesn't mind being late herself and keeping other people waiting, but she's a grouch when people do it to her. I just wanted to see you and give you this." She leaned over and kissed him on the lips. "That's it. I'm going now. See you twelve thirty tomorrow."

Brazelle's first port of call was the bridge from which Justine had fallen and drowned. Although it was a central feature of the investigation he had agreed to undertake, it was only today that he had got around to visiting it for the first time, and he took several minutes giving it a thorough inspection. It seemed likely that some of the timbers had been replaced at some time during the past twenty years, but Brazelle concluded the structure was most probably just as it had been at the time of Justine's death. Although the weather was dry and sunny at the time of his visit, there had been a fair amount of rain during the previous week and the stream level was quite high. Another couple of inches, he thought, and it would be washing over the bridge timbers, making them extremely slippery. Never having visited the bridge before, he had been unaware of its exact location in relation to Harfield House. He could now see that it stood to the east of the House and its grounds, and that the stream ran alongside and fairly close to Napoleon's Wall. He also discovered there was a door in the Wall, quite close by the bridge. It was an old oak door that would originally have been opened with a key, but the keyhole had been covered over and access was now controlled by a digital code lock.

Standing on the bridge, Brazelle had an uninterrupted view of the top three floors of the House, but there was also something else that caught his eye and took his interest. Within the House grounds, roughly midway between the House and Napoleon's Wall, there stood a solitary prominent tree with a relatively large tree house attached to it. He took out his binoculars to get a better look and quickly realised there was someone moving around inside. For several minutes he focussed on the tree house until eventually his patience paid off and he managed to identify who it was.

Brazelle's second visit of the day was to Harfield House. On arrival at Napoleon's Gates he got that same feeling of privilege he had experienced the day before, as he once again entered the code that Rose had provided and they opened before him.

Mrs Richards opened the front door and was about to inform Brazelle that none of the family was at home, but he interrupted her to say that he was already aware, and that it was she who he had come to see. She led the way through into the kitchen, where she normally based herself during her working day.

The modern and well equipped kitchen had been created in a spacious extension on the ground floor at the back of the House. Its location came as a surprise to Brazelle. "I was rather expecting that in a house as old and as grand as this one, the kitchen would be down in the basement," he said

Mrs Richards smiled. "Oh, there is one down there alright, but it hasn't been in use for years. This extension was added about seventy years ago by Sir Cornelius' parents, although it's been updated quite a few times since then.

The basement has just been used for storage since this was built and it hasn't been cleared out in years. Sir Cornelius was such a hoarder, there's no knowing what's to be found down there."

"I assume Rose told you that I might want to speak to you, and why," said Brazelle.

Mrs Richards nodded. "Yes, she told all of us that we must help you in any way that we can. But can I just say, although I've known Miss Rose since she was born and think the world of her, and you're very kind to offer to help, I really think you're wasting your time. Lady Justine's death was a tragic accident, a terrible loss to us all, especially Miss Rose, but I think the matter really should be laid to rest."

Brazelle begged to disagree. "That's not what Rose thinks and, quite frankly, having already made some preliminary enquiries, I've come to have some serious concerns myself. There are many unanswered questions surrounding the events that day and although it's perfectly possible that the answers will eventually be found to be quite simple and straightforward, I've committed myself to try and find out what they are, if only to put Rose's mind at rest. Now, I know you must have told the story many times before and I'm sure there are elements that you might find upsetting, but please take a few minutes to tell me what you remember of that day."

Mrs Richards gave a gentle nod and cleared her throat. "Lady Justine had been in the drawing room with Miss Rose before bringing her into the kitchen and asking if I'd look after her whilst she popped into the village to post a letter. I said I could get one of the staff to post the letter for her, but she said she wanted to do it herself, although she didn't say why."

Brazelle interrupted. "Was any of this unusual? Not taking Rose with her and leaving her with you to look after? Or, going to post a letter herself?"

Mrs Richards' eyes opened wider. "Oh, it was all very unusual, but I'd noticed that Lady Justine had appeared a little agitated and been behaving rather out of character, ever since returning from taking Miss Rose to the playground the day before. In the past she'd asked me to keep an eye on Miss Rose from time to time, whilst she took a phone call, or something like that, but she'd never asked me to look after her whilst she left the house before. She always took Miss Rose with her everywhere. And I don't ever remember her making a special visit to the post office to post a letter before, either. The staff are always coming and going, so if there's anything to post I ask one of them to pop it down to the post office. Actually, not much post did go from the house though. Lady Justine didn't send much and most of Sir Cornelius' post was sent by a specialist courier service because such a lot of it was highly confidential. Anyway, after she left Miss Rose with me, Lady Justine left the house and sadly none of us ever saw her alive again."

"And what happened then, after Lady Justine left the house and you were alone with Rose?" asked Brazelle.

Mrs Richards was puzzled. "Do you think that might be important?"

"I don't know," replied Brazelle. "Perhaps not, but I'd like to hear it anyway, so please, go on."

"Very well," replied a still puzzled looking Mrs Richards. "Miss Rose was upset because her mother had gone out without her and so I had to distract her. I kept her in the kitchen here with me and found a colouring book and some crayons and started to draw with her. After a while I found I could pull away a bit and get on with some chores whilst she carried on drawing."

Brazelle again interrupted. "But you stayed in the kitchen all the time, both of you, did you?"

"Yes, of course. It would never be a good idea to leave a five year old alone in a kitchen," replied Mrs Richards.

Brazelle noticed that Mrs Richards bit her lower lip after giving her answer and her cheeks coloured slightly. She was clearly a woman who wasn't used to telling lies and he decided to challenge her on what she had just said. "So you never left her alone? Not even for a second?"

Mrs Richards again bit her lower lip and her cheeks coloured up even more. "Actually, there was a moment when I did leave her alone. I heard the sound of breaking glass coming from the corridor outside and, instinctively I suppose, I went out to see what the commotion was. One of the cleaners had dropped some glasses, so I gave her a hand to clear up the mess, but only the bigger pieces. Then I left her to clear up the rest on her own. I was gone from the kitchen for less than two minutes."

Brazelle sensed that Mrs Richards was yet to completely unburden herself. There was clearly more to tell and he wanted to hear it. "So what happened then? What did you find when you returned to the kitchen?"

Mrs Richards put her head down before responding and when she did it was with a breaking voice. "Is any of this really necessary, Reverend? Surely, none of this will shed any light on what happened to Lady Justine, will it?

Nobody's asked me these questions before. Nobody's been interested to know what happened after Lady Justine left the house?"

"Well, I'm interested," responded Brazelle. "And until I hear it, I can't decide whether it's relevant or not. Please go on. Tell me what happened after you returned to the kitchen."

Mrs Richards raised her head and Brazelle could see tears were forming in the corners of her eyes. "Miss Rose was gone," she said.

Brazelle said nothing, but got off his stool, picked up a clean glass, half filled it with water and passed it to Mrs Richards who, after taking a sip and drying her eyes, regained her composure and continued. "There are only three doors out of the kitchen. One leads out through the corridor where I was clearing up the broken glass, so I knew she couldn't have come out that way. The second leads into the utility area, but I couldn't find her in there, so I knew she must have gone out through the third door, the one that leads out of the House. I'd been in and out all morning, so I'd left it unlocked with the key in the lock on the inside, but Lady Justine must have taken it, because after she left I realised it wasn't there anymore. That's why I wasn't able to lock the door before I went to help pick up the glass.

When I got back to the kitchen I was frantic. I ran out to look for her, but I didn't call out her name, because I was afraid that Sir Cornelius, who was in his studio upstairs, would hear me and then he would know what had happened. Sir Cornelius was a lovely man, but he was so besotted by Miss Rose that if he'd known I'd been negligent and let her run away, there's no telling what he would have done.

For several minutes I ran around like a headless chicken looking for her. Eventually it dawned on me that she might have gone to Gareth's tree house. She was always asking if she could go up there, but Sir Cornelius had strictly forbidden it. He said it was too dangerous until she was older and bigger. I always thought he was a bit overprotective of her, but she was his daughter, not mine, so I always respected his wishes. Anyway, I went over to the tree house and sure enough she was there with Gareth, playing with one of the models he'd made. You've absolutely no idea how relieved I was. Then I saw that her hands were filthy and her white dress had black marks all over it, so I had to quickly take her back to the House and get her cleaned up and changed before anyone noticed. Eventually, I took her back to the kitchen and because I was afraid she'd tell her parents what had happened and I'd be in trouble, I made it out to be a bit of a game and said we should treat her adventure as our little secret. Fortunately, she thought that sounded like fun.

Of course, she never did get a chance to tell her mother. And poor Sir Cornelius was so distraught and had so many other things to concern himself with: the inquest, the funeral and then the burglary. Even if he had found out what had happened, I'm not sure it would have mattered much anyway. After all, she'd come to no harm, had she? From that day to this I've never uttered a word about what happened, not even to Jonathan, but it's always been something I've had on my conscience." Mrs Richards paused, before asking, "What are you going to do with what I've told you, Reverend?"

"I'm going to keep it to myself, Mrs Richards and probably over time, forget about it completely," replied Brazelle. "Believe me I've had far, far worse things than what you've just told me, on my conscience, but I've managed to put them all behind me and move on and so should you."

Mrs Richards finished drying her tears and gave a faint smile. "Thank you Reverend. You're a kind and wise man. I'm sorry I lied to you."

Brazelle placed his hand on her shoulder. "You're clearly an honest woman Mrs Richards, don't think anymore about it. But you just mentioned a burglary. I didn't know about that. What exactly happened?"

"Well, I call it a burglary, but nothing was actually taken, except for a videotape. It happened at the time of Lady Justine's funeral, so there was nobody in the House because we were all at the Church. Everyone except for Gareth, that is. He was only eleven, so I know that people might condemn me for leaving him on his own, but he was very upset by Lady Justine's death and I knew the funeral would be too much for him, so I told him to stay in the tree house until I returned. When we got back we realised straightaway that someone must have been in the House whilst we were all out. The first thing we noticed was the alarm had been switched off. Jonathan and me were the last to leave the House and the first to get back. He swore blind he'd set the alarm before we left and I knew he had, because I watched him do it. Then I found some muddy footprints by the back door, and when Jonathan went to look at the videotape in the CCTV recorder, he found it was missing. He usually changed it every seven days or so, and he was fairly sure he'd loaded a new blank tape just the day before. The security system we have these days is a lot more sophisticated than the one we had then, but even the old one had an event log, so Jonathan checked it. It confirmed that the system had been switched off about ten minutes after we'd left the

House and, to our surprise, it showed it was done using Lady Justine's security code.

Lady Justine wasn't very good at handling numbers, or remembering them, so she had her alarm code written down in a little notebook that she usually kept in whichever handbag she was using. But she did leave it lying around on occasions, so I suppose someone else could have got a look at it at sometime. Anyway, we called the police, but they didn't come immediately. By the time they did arrive, we'd all had a good look around and decided that nothing had been taken, apart from the videotape. I must have searched around in every room at least twice.....well, except for Sir Cornelius' studio, he dealt with that room himself. After we told the police that it didn't look like anything apart from the videotape had been taken, they lost interest. They said it was probably the action of some disgruntled ex-employee who'd managed to get a look at Lady Justine's code. Afterwards, all the alarm codes were changed and the CCTV video recorder was moved to a more secure place."

Brazelle was puzzled. "It does seem very odd. I'm not sure it even qualifies as a burglary. It seems as if someone came in just for a look around and then took the videotape, so they wouldn't be identified. But could it have been Gareth's footprints you found in the kitchen?"

Mrs Richards shook her head. "No, I knew immediately they couldn't be Gareth's, because they were so big.

"Were the codes changed and the video recorder moved straightaway?" asked Brazelle.

"More or less, but as you know, Sir Cornelius hung himself the very next day after Lady Justine's funeral. That threw everything into even more chaos, so the video recorder didn't get moved and the codes changed until a few days later. In fact we were all in such a state of confusion, when Jonathan came to move the recorder he found there wasn't a tape in it. To begin with he said he was quite sure he'd replaced the one that had been stolen, but then he began to doubt himself. You have to remember, Reverend, it was a very stressful time for all of us."

Before Brazelle could respond, Gareth came into the kitchen. He had a cloth wrapped round his lower left arm and was in an agitated state. "I've cut myself, Mum," he said.

Mrs Richards inspected her son's arm. "I don't think it needs stitches, dear. Come with me. The first aid box is in the utility room."

A few minutes later, Gareth reappeared with a large plaster over his wound and Mrs Richards placed the bloodied cloth by the sink, before introducing Brazelle to her son. "This is Reverend Brazelle, Gareth. He's a friend of the family." Brazelle held out his hand and Gareth looked at it for a moment, before taking hold and shaking it.

"I hear you're something of a technological wizz, Gareth," said Brazelle.

Gareth pondered for a moment. "Yes, I suppose I am," he said, before turning to his mother. "What's for lunch?"

"I haven't decided yet, dear, but, whatever it is, it'll be ready for you at the usual time."

Gareth moved to the door. "I'll come back then," he said, before leaving the room without any further interaction or eye contact with Brazelle.

"My son is very special," said Mrs Richards with a smile.

Brazelle nodded and returned her smile. "Yes he is," he said, before returning to business. "I know you attend the services at the Parish Church quite regularly, because I've seen you there on a number of occasions. I was wondering if you knew very much about Reverend Caulfield's two immediate predecessors, Reverend Raynworth and Reverend Pickering, and if you could tell me something about them."

"Yes, I remember them both quite well," replied Mrs Richards, who thought the questions were becoming even more unexpected, given the event that was supposed to be being investigated. "Reverend Raynworth was here for years. He was such a lovely man, so kind and patient, and so was his wife. He had a great sense of humour and would often tell jokes from the pulpit and have us all in stitches. We were all very sad when he retired, but he must have been well into his seventies by then. His wife had angina, so it was the best thing they could have done. They'd worked very hard for the Parish over many years."

"Do you know what happened to him after he left the Parish?" Brazelle asked.

"Yes, actually I do. I still exchange Christmas cards with him and Mrs Raynworth. They bought a little cottage in Northope and still live there. I bumped into him there, just over a year ago, and asked why he never came back to the Parish for the odd visit. He said he believed that once you hand over your position of leadership to someone else it's always best to just leave that person to get on with it. But I think there was more to it than that. I think he just didn't like his successor, Reverend Pickering. In fact I'm not sure anybody did. I certainly didn't. Can I be frank with you, Reverend?"

Brazelle was intrigued. "I wouldn't want it any other way, Mrs Richards."

"Well, there were times when I actually wondered whether Reverend Pickering really was a Christian. He was a young man and wasn't married, as far as any of us knew, so I suppose he was entitled to have girlfriends, but there did seem to be quite a lot of different ones going in and out of the Vicarage. And some of them definitely stayed there overnight. You don't think I'm jumping to too many conclusions and being too judgemental, do you, Reverend?"

Brazelle wondered what Mrs Richards would make of Rose's overnight stays at Holford's Cottage and he swallowed hard as he responded in a rather hoarse voice. "No, I can see why you might draw such conclusions, but please go on."

Mrs Richards took Brazelle's comment as encouragement to continue with her character assassination of Reverend Pickering. "After he took over the Parish, the congregation quickly began to dwindle, until there were very few of us regulars left, but that never seemed to bother him. His sermons were always very short and there never seemed to be any real substance or structure to them. When they'd finished, I was usually left wondering what it had all been about. And almost every other Sunday he'd go on about the importance of tithing and giving generously to the Church, if you wanted to reserve your place in heaven. I only kept going myself because I was a member of the Ladies Group and we used to have such a lot of fun together. Reverend Raynworth used to always come and join us once a month, but Reverend Pickering couldn't ever be bothered to turn up. In fact I'm not sure he even knew we existed. Quite frankly, just about everything was too much trouble for him." Mrs Richards abruptly stopped talking and stared straight ahead, leading Brazelle to fear that she'd worked herself up so much she was in danger of having a seizure. He was just about to say something to calm the situation, when suddenly and in a much louder voice than before, she exclaimed, "Then one night he just upped and left!"

Brazelle took a few moments before responding, thinking it was probably best to give a rather unsettled Mrs Richards a little more time to regain her composure. "Well, whether it's the correct one or not, you've certainly drawn me a very clear picture, Mrs Richards. It's a picture of a money-grubbing, debauched and indolent heathen, who appears to have had no redeeming features whatsoever. And clearly a man of whom you thoroughly disapproved."

"Oh, it's a correct picture alright," said Mrs Richards, "and if I may say so, I think you've just given an excellent summing up, Reverend."

"And then you say that, quite literally, he just disappeared one night? Did he give any warning of his intentions, or tell anyone where he was going?" asked Brazelle.

Mrs Richards shook her head. "No, nothing, one day he was here and the next he was gone. Just like that. It turned out he hadn't even told the Diocese he was leaving. The first they knew he'd gone was when someone from the village contacted them and asked who was going to bury their father. It was what my mother used to call a real, 'midnight flit'. We didn't have a vicar for several weeks after he'd gone, but then Reverend Caulfield appeared. Just like a breath of fresh air. I'm not just saying this because I know she's a friend of yours Reverend, but she really is a lovely person and a truly excellent vicar, the exact opposite of Reverend Pickering."

"Yes, I can only agree with you there. I think Prinsted is lucky to have her," said Brazelle, before changing the subject. "You've been extremely helpful Mrs Richards. You probably have no idea quite how helpful, and I'm extremely grateful to you. I've got no more questions for now, but, before I leave, I would like to pay a second visit to Sir Cornelius' studio, if you wouldn't mind. There are just a couple of things I'd like to quickly take a second look at, so it shouldn't take long. But before doing that, I would very much like to have a few words with Gareth. Do you think he'd be alright with that?"

"Yes, I'm sure that will be alright," replied Mrs Richards. "He's probably in his tree house. If he's not in bed asleep or eating in here with me, he spends practically all of his free time up there."

Brazelle returned to the role of inquisitor. "You've mentioned the tree house several times. It seems to have played an important part in Gareth's life."

"Yes, it's his little private space and has been since it was built for him twenty three years ago, when he was eight. It was Sir Cornelius' idea. He was very fond of Gareth and was happy for him to have the run of the House, but he was a bit concerned when he found out that he'd gone missing on a couple of occasions and somehow found his way into the remains of the old House. We could never quite work out how he managed to get in there because, as far as we knew, the only keys to it were locked away in Sir Cornelius' studio. Anyway, that's when Sir Cornelius suggested that Jonathan should build the tree house and it seemed to work. Once it was completed, Gareth tended to spend most of his free time in it, although he may well have still paid the occasional visit to the old House remains. I think Sir Cornelius appreciated that Gareth wanted a space that he could consider his own, somewhere he could go to keep his own company. I guess Sir Cornelius understood, because he was very much the same and, of course, he had his own studio to escape to. Although there have been several changes made to it over the years, it's essentially the same now as it was when it was first built. Fortunately, building it where it is, meant I could keep an eye on him from the kitchen."

Brazelle had risen from his stool, but, having just heard something that caught his interest, he chose to sit down again. "I didn't know that any part of the old House survived. Is there very much of it?"

"Above ground, no, not much at all," replied Mrs Richards. "Practically all of what remains is below ground level. It was part of the original basement. Lady Brigitte used to refer to it as the 'dungeon' and both she and Lady Justine, at some time or other, asked Sir Cornelius to get it all filled in, but he wouldn't have it. He said it was the family's only remaining direct link with Sir Richard, the first baronet, and so it should stay. If you're interested in taking a look, ask Gareth to show you. He knows more about it than anyone else, including any member of the family. In fact, I can't remember the last time any of them went down there."

Mrs Richards looked out through the kitchen window and having confirmed she could see Gareth up in the tree house, offered to go and bring him to meet with Brazelle.

"That won't be necessary, Mrs Richards," said Brazelle. "I'll go and join him. I'd like to see inside the tree house, assuming Gareth won't object, of course."

"Oh, he won't object," responded Mrs Richards. "He knows you're helping Miss Rose. He'll do anything for her."

As Brazelle moved to the door, Mrs Richards began looking around the kitchen with a puzzled look on her face. "Is something the matter?" he asked.

Mrs Richards gave a faint shrug. "It's nothing important, but I could have sworn I put Gareth's bloodied cloth by the sink. Now it seems to have wandered off. I must have moved it whilst my mind was somewhere else, but I'm sure it'll reappear eventually."

Brazelle gave an encouraging smile. "I'm sure it will, Mrs Richards."

Access to the tree house was via a hinged ladder which Gareth always pulled up after him once he had entered. When he saw Brazelle approaching he lowered it.

Brazelle was pleased to find he was able to stand upright in the tree house and looking around, he was immediately struck at how neat and well ordered it was. Just like Sir Cornelius, Gareth was clearly methodical and well organised, the possessor of a logical mind and tidy habits. There were assorted boxes stacked neatly on the floor, each clearly labelled, and the many shelves on the walls carried a range of different items, including a number of wooden and metal models, some of which looked to Brazelle, to be incredibly complex. There was a computer on a desk standing in the centre of the tree house and Gareth was seated in front of it on the only chair. He got up, gesturing for Brazelle to take his place.

Brazelle was content to remain standing. "Thanks, Gareth, but you stay where you are. I won't be here long.

I just wanted to see inside your magnificent tree house and ask you a couple of questions, if you don't mind. Before I leave completely, though, I'd be grateful if you'd show me the remains of the old House. Your mother said you know it better than anyone else. Are you okay with that?"

Gareth gave a faint nod. "What do you want to know?" he asked, with no hint of emotion.

"It's about the medallion that you gave to Rose, when she was five years old. I wondered where you got it from."

Gareth frowned. "I didn't steal it. I found it in the basement of the old House."

Brazelle attempted a reassuring smile. "No. I never thought that you stole it. When you take me to the remains of the old House, perhaps you could show me where you found it. Is there anything else you can tell me about it? For instance, did you ever tell anyone else that you'd found it? And did you know that it was made from solid gold?"

"Yes, of course, I knew it was solid gold," replied Gareth, rather abruptly. "And it was a secret between Rose and me, so I couldn't tell anyone else about it. Has she shown it to you?"

It had already occurred to Brazelle that Gareth would be unhappy at the thought that Rose had shared the secret of the phalera with him and guessed that a simple 'yes' in response to his question would be far from sufficient. "She did show it to me, but only because I have a drawing of it and I was able to tell her some of its history. I haven't mentioned it to anyone else."

Brazelle paused, waiting for a reaction, but none came, so he continued with his questioning. "There is just one more thing, Gareth. I know it was a long time ago and you were only eleven at the time, but can you recall the day that Lady Justine died and Rose came into the tree house for the first time. Do you remember what you were doing?"

Gareth nodded. "I showed Rose a model I'd just made and let her play with it. Then Mum came and took her away."

Brazelle looked out of the tree house window through which he had seen Gareth earlier that morning. As he expected, he had a perfect view of the bridge from which Justine had fallen and drowned. "What was the model you'd made?" he asked, casually.

Gareth appeared agitated. "I can't remember," he replied.

Brazelle had deliberately taken the whole process very slowly, hoping that Gareth wouldn't feel in any way stressed, but he had clearly failed. He was enough of an amateur psychologist to know that he had hit a raw nerve and needed to calm things down. "That's okay, Gareth. I have no more questions. You've been really helpful and I'm very grateful. Now, if you're sure you don't mind, will you take me to the remains of the old House and show me where you found the medallion?"

Gareth led the way to a door in the back wall of the new House and opened it with a key which, in Brazelle's judgement, Gareth may well have made himself. The external door opened into a small windowless vestibule with a second door through the wall opposite. Gareth opened the second door with a second key, which Brazelle thought he might also have made himself, before leading the way down an unlit stone staircase. Gareth had come prepared with a powerful torch and Brazelle fortunately still had with him, the torch he had taken to the Church for examining the niche. After eight steps the staircase turned left through ninety degrees and there were thirteen steps in total, leading eventually into a large open chamber. Brazelle realised he must be standing in a basement room that lay beneath the southwest corner of the new House. The only source of natural light came from two tiny windows high up on one wall, but Gareth moved the beam from his torch slowly around the chamber, so Brazelle could get a good view of it. The walls were completely wood panelled, although understandably, the panelling was showing its age. And the only furniture was an old table, two rather ancient looking chairs and an empty wooden chest from which the lid had been removed. After giving Brazelle an opportunity to have a good look round, Gareth removed part of the panelling in one corner to reveal a hidden compartment into which he shone his torch. It contained a small wooden box, which he removed, and a second item, which Brazelle pulled out.

Gareth opened the box and showed Brazelle that it was empty. "I found the gold medallion in here," he said, before closing it up and putting it back where he got it from.

Brazelle examined the item that he himself had removed. At first glance, it appeared as an amorphous, congealed mass, however, bit by bit, gently, but firmly, Brazelle prised it apart until he could recognise it as a wide leather belt, with two pistol holsters and a dagger sheath attached. Even more surprising, although they were well rusted, the pistols and dagger were still in place. Having seen Gareth replace the box, he felt he should do the same with the belt and its attachments, although not before taking a few pictures. When he did come to replace it, he realised he had missed several smaller items on his first inspection of the compartment. Right at the back, was a collection of small lead balls and they appeared to be identical to those in Frank Weston's box that he had assumed were musket balls. Now, though, he was more inclined to think they were ammunition for the two pistols he had just found. He showed them to Gareth and asked if he knew anything about them, but Gareth became agitated once more and gave a mumbled and unintelligible reply. Brazelle decided it was probably best to let the matter rest for the time being, whilst also taking Gareth's incoherent response to be a very definite, 'YES'.

Brazelle left the old House basement and thanked a still mildly agitated Gareth for being his guide. Rejoining Mrs Richards in the kitchen, he explained that he may have inadvertently upset Gareth with some of his questions and apologised.

Mrs Richards dismissed Brazelle's concerns. "He'll be alright, Reverend. He's a creature of routine and prefers his own company. Any change from the normal and he finds it a bit of a challenge, but he'll be fine. If anything gets too much for him he'll come and see me, so don't worry about it. Now, you said you wanted to visit Sir Cornelius' studio again, Reverend."

"Yes I do, but if you wouldn't mind, before we go, Mrs Richards, there is something else that I'd like to ask you about. I know this will be unexpected and probably rather upsetting for you, but I believe it may be relevant to the enquiry that Rose has asked me to undertake. I assure you I wouldn't ask if I didn't believe that. I'd like you to tell me what you can remember about the day that Sir Cornelius died. I understand that you were the last person to have any contact with him when he was alive and the one who found him dead in his studio."

Brazelle anticipated that his request would be upsetting for Mrs Richards and reckoned it would be the case regardless of when, or, how, he made it, so decided he might as well ask the question now, in a very direct way, and get it over and done with.

Mrs Richards was indeed taken by surprise. After Rose spoke to her about Brazelle's role, she thought it likely that at some time he would ask her to recall events on the day that Lady Justine died, but she never anticipated being questioned about the death of Sir Cornelius. Not surprisingly, it took her a few minutes to gather her thoughts before responding. "Very well, Reverend, I can't for the life of me see how the two things are connected, but Miss Rose asked me to help you in any way that I can and so that is what I shall do." She cleared her throat and began her story. "As you know, Sir Cornelius took his own life the day after Lady Justine's funeral. Sir Damien was away with his work and Lady Frances took Miss Rose into town to buy some new clothes, to try and take her mind off things. All the other staff had been given the day off, including Jonathan who went to visit his mother, so there was just me and Sir Cornelius in the House, and Gareth was up in his tree house. There was some shopping needed, so at about 10 o'clock I went up to Sir Cornelius, who was in his studio, to ask if he minded if I popped out for a couple of hours. It seemed to be a good time to do it, because there were no other pressures on me with everyone else being away. I said I'd take him up some tea and sandwiches for his lunch when I got back. It was just after twelve noon when I returned and took his lunch up to him. I knocked on his studio door, but he didn't answer. I thought he might have gone out, or possibly fallen asleep, so I unlocked the door with my key and that's when I found him, just hanging there."

"I understand he left a note. Can you remember what it said?" asked Brazelle.

"It just said 'SORRY' in big capital letters and he'd signed it, just like he signs his paintings. I don't know what happened to it after the inquest. Maybe Lady Frances has it, or perhaps it got destroyed."

Brazelle had several more questions. "I'm sure you were asked these questions before, and I'm sorry for taking you through it all again, but please bear with me for just a little longer. When you left the House, were all the external doors locked and the alarm switched on? And did you notice anything unusual when you were leaving? For example, did you see anybody near the gates as you left, someone who might have got into the grounds, before the gates closed behind you?"

Mrs Richards racked her brains. "I'm pretty sure all the external doors were locked, because we have a strict night routine that includes locking them and, apart from the main front door that I locked as I was leaving, none of them had been opened that morning. I didn't put any part of the alarm on because Sir Cornelius was in the House. And I don't recall noticing anything out of the ordinary, or see anyone about, when I left."

Brazelle was now ready to see the studio. Mrs Richards led the way up the stairs, but when she came to the studio door she realised she had left her keys in the kitchen. "Not to worry," she said, "I'm not the only one who forgets their keys from time to time. That's why we keep one hidden up here." She opened an unlocked store cupboard on the landing, reached in and pulled out a key.

"Does everyone in the House know about that key?" asked Brazelle."

"Not everyone, just the family, Jonathan and me. None of the other staff have ever been allowed to enter Sir Cornelius' studio, so they wouldn't need to know about it. It's a long way up the stairs, and if you've forgotten your key and have to go back down for it, only to have to climb back up again! Well, you can imagine can't you! It was Lady Brigitte who first put it there and Lady Justine never had her own key, she only ever used this hidden one."

Mrs Richards opened the door to the studio, but before making way for Brazelle reminded him of Rose's rule about her 'Daddy's Things'. Once he had confirmed his understanding she allowed him to enter, but remained in the doorway watching, what Brazelle took to be, his every move. It was clear that Rose's instructions, first given twenty years ago when she was still an infant, were still being taken very seriously.

Brazelle's desire to take a second look at the studio wasn't just for the opportunity to see it in daylight, he had two specific objectives in mind and the first of these was easily and quickly achieved. From the large oak desk, he picked up the notebook from which pages had been ripped and made a mental note of the date of the last entry. It was the day before Frank Weston returned Justine's handbag. Any subsequent entries that Sir Cornelius may have made would have been included in the pages that had been roughly ripped out.

Brazelle's second objective would not be quite so easy to achieve. He went over to the shelf where the jars that contained the samples of Sir Cornelius' hair were kept, took out a notepad and pen and scribbled something into the pad. Then, having casually placed his pen on the shelf, he said he had seen everything he wished to see and was ready to leave.

Mrs Richards led the way out of the studio, but no sooner had she stepped over the threshold than Brazelle suddenly announced that he had left his pen and rushed back to get it. Mrs Richards didn't bother to follow, but remained just outside the studio until Brazelle returned to join her, having retrieved his pen and pocketed one of the jars.

After leaving Harfield House, Brazelle returned home to Holford and put together a small parcel before making a phone call to Major Daniel Coyte-Sherman.

After some friendly banter, Brazelle came to the reason for his call. "Danny, I'm going to give you an opportunity to repay one or two of that long list of favours you owe me. I've put together a small package containing all the details of what I'd like you to do and the stuff you'll need, but unfortunately, I've missed today's post and tomorrow's Sunday. Since I'd really like to have the results back by sometime on Tuesday, I wondered if you could get one of your couriers to come and collect it from me. Like now!"

Following some further exchanges, Coyte–Sherman eventually agreed to the request, for which Brazelle was grateful. "Thanks Danny, I'll put in a good word for you at church tomorrow, although I can't promise it will do much good in your case." He finished his call with a quick "Goodbye", and hung up, before Coyte-Sherman could give him an expletive laced response.

Despite all their feigned sarcastic and abusive banter, the bond between Brazelle and Coyte-Sherman was a strong one, so, sure enough, a couple of hours after their phonecall ended, a courier arrived and took away Brazelle's package.

Day Nine - Sunday

Rose drove into the yard at Holford's Cottage at exactly twelve thirty. Getting out of her car she looked up to see Brazelle knocking on Max's studio door. "He's not there," she called out.

Brazelle came back down the stairs. "How do you know?"

"I've just seen him going into Cromwell's Treasure."

Brazelle began to look worried. "Oh, this may not end well. Can you give me a ride over there, straightaway?"

Rose was puzzled by Brazelle's reaction. "Sure, but what's the problem? Is he an alcoholic?"

Brazelle shook his head. "No, he's a drunk."

The car pulled up in front of the tavern and had barely stopped before Brazelle leapt out and moved quickly towards the entrance. Inside he found Max sitting alone at a corner table and went over to join him.

"What brings you here, boss?" Max asked in his Glaswegian accent. "Just passing were you?"

Brazelle ignored Max's questions, sat down next to him and asked one of his own. "Bad day is it, Max?"

"I've known better," Max replied.

A few moments later, Rose arrived and took a third seat at the table.

"I believe you two have already met," said Brazelle.

Max stared at Rose. "I remember. You're the Yank who crashed into the field the other day."

"She's the one who crashed into the field, but she's not a Yank," explained Brazelle, before formally introducing the pair.

Max held out his right hand to Rose. "I'm sorry about the other day. You caught me at a bad time, but if I'd known you were a friend of the boss, I'd have helped you out."

"We weren't friends then," said Rose. "In fact we hadn't even met and if you had helped me, perhaps we never would have."

There were two almost empty glasses on the table in front of Max, one beer, the other whisky. "How many of these have you had already?" Brazelle asked.

"Not enough," Max replied. "In fact I was just about to get a couple of refills when you arrived. And have a friendly chat with three of England's finest scumbags sitting over there, whilst I was about it."

Brazelle and Rose both turned to see who he was referring to and saw three undesirable looking male twenty somethings at a table directly opposite a few metres away, staring back at them.

"They've been sitting there pulling faces and laughing at me ever since I came in," said Max, before turning to face Rose. "But since you arrived they've lost interest in me."

Rose turned to take a second, slightly longer look at the three men and saw that two of them were making obscene gestures, whilst the third, with his lips pursed, was blowing her a kiss.

Max began to stand up. "Right that's it! I'll just go over and explain the facts of life to 'em."

Brazelle pulled Max back into his seat. "No, leave it Max. We'll be gone in a minute."

"That's right, leave it Max," echoed Rose, before taking a band out of her bag, pulling back her long jet-black hair and forming it into a ponytail. She then stood up and, smiling at the three undesirables, walked over to their table.

"What on earth is she doing?" Brazelle whispered to Max, whilst at the same time rising from his seat.

Max, beginning to smile for the first time, grabbed Brazelle's arm and pulled him back. "Don't worry boss, she won't come to any harm while we're here. Just relax."

Rose was wearing a short skirt, but when she got to the men's table she hitched it up even higher, before raising her left leg onto a vacant stool. Still with her eyes fixed firmly on the three men and a smile on her face, she stuck out her tongue and ran it seductively over the palm and fingers of her left hand, before running them slowly up her left leg. Her actions had the intended effect, she had the undivided attention of all three men and the one nearest could not resist reaching out to touch her. His hand, however, had barely made contact as Rose brought her right fist up under his chin rendering him senseless and sending him backwards until the back of his head hit the floor with such a loud thud, that it prompted a collective "Owwwww......." from the other customers in the tavern. Rose's punch though, was only the prelude to a series of further movements she performed, all coming together in one smooth flowing motion, at the end of which, the second man found himself in a neck lock applied from behind and the third lay flat on his back with the sharp heel of Rose's left stiletto pressing firmly into his throat.

"If you resist, I will rupture your windpipe and you will either suffocate or drown in your own blood," Rose whispered to the man under her heel. And to the man in the neck lock, she said, "And if you resist I will break your neck." Then speaking a little louder so that both men could hear, "In a moment I will release you, but if either of you does anything that displeases me I will inflict excruciating pain on you and do serious and permanent damage to your spinal column. Once released, you will pick up your friend, thank the nice barman and then leave quietly. If you complain to the police I will say that you touched me indecently and I had to defend my virtue. And, if you tell anyone else...... well....... they'll just think you're a bunch of pussies, won't they. Oh......... and if I ever see you in here again? But we'll cross that bridge if we come to it, shall we?"

Rose released the two men and took a step back, but remained vigilant, just in case she had failed to convince them of her sincerity. By this time, the first man was beginning to regain consciousness, though probably not his senses, and his two companions helped him to his feet and towards the door, pausing only momentarily, to say a quick 'thank you' to the barman.

Rose went over to the window and watched the men get into a car and drive away, before turning her attention to the lone barman who had still not fully recovered from the shock of what he had just witnessed. "Do you know who I am?" she asked. The barman said nothing, but simply nodded. Rose acknowledged his response with a smile, before going to rejoin her two companions where Max proffered a high-five, which she accepted.

Brazelle was shocked and in a state of near disbelief. What he had just witnessed had not been an adrenaline fuelled defensive reaction to some clearly defined threat, but a deliberate and offensive act performed in the coldest of blood. It brought back memories of his former self and he found it rather unnerving. "How did you learn to do all that stuff?" he asked.

Rose removed the band from her hair to release her ponytail. "When I hit thirteen, Damien said it was time I learnt how to take care of myself, so he sent me to a martial arts school in downtown Manhattan. It was run by a couple of gay guys called Jerry and Perry. Jerry was ex-military - he'd served in the Green Berets; and Perry was a ballet dancer and part time movie stuntman. It was called the Vixen School of Self Defence and Focussed Aggression and only taught females. And they had a really neat advertising slogan – '*Ladies - Learn How To Ruin Some Asshole's Day – In Six Easy Lessons*'. They'd developed their own form of martial art, which they called *Tu-kul-di*. They said it was ancient Sumerian for 'Weapon of Justice' and that *Tu-kul-di* was to Karate what Dirty Dancing was to Swan Lake. Their philosophy was that attack is always the best form of defence, and they believed in inflicting as much pain and damage as possible on any aggressor. 'A slap across the face is one thing.' they used to say, 'but when it comes to discouraging an indecent assault, few things work better than a ruptured spleen'. They also believed that a woman's intuition is rarely wrong, so if she felt under threat then she probably was and, in such circumstances, taking pre-emptive action was an acceptable thing to do. And that's what I just did!"

Brazelle shook his head. "I'm not sure I approve of all that."

Max beamed. "I do! It sounds fucking brilliant."

"But you didn't learn all that in just six easy lessons," observed Brazelle.

"No, I didn't," confirmed Rose. "From the age of thirteen I was a pupil at the school for the next eight years, until Jerry and Perry decided to retire and sell the business..............to me."

Brazelle again shook his head. "You really are full of surprises."

Rose responded in a self-satisfied sort of way. "Well, I guess that makes two of us then, doesn't it."

"Fair comment," said Brazelle. "But do you still own the business?"

"Yes I do. And I've worked hard to build it up since I took it over nearly four years ago. I now have twenty instructors working for me and we have many hundreds of trainees. And I've had to move into much bigger premises. Fundamentally though, I still run things the way that Jerry and Perry did, like we still only train women and girls, but I have made a few minor changes. For example, I've changed the school's advertising slogan."

"Well I'm glad to hear that," commented Brazelle.

"Yes, it now reads, *'Ladies - Learn How To REALLY Ruin Some Asshole's Day - In Six Easy Lessons'.*"

"That's even better," said Max, gleefully. "I can see you have a way with words."

Brazelle shook his head once more and decided to change the subject. "So what are your plans now, Max? Can we give you a ride home?"

"Yes, I guess so," Max replied, before turning to face Rose. "I feel a lot better after all that. You've just made ma' day, lassie."

Having arrived back at Holford, Max got out of the car and began walking towards the staircase leading up to his studio, but he suddenly remembered something, stopped and looked back at Rose. "Why did you ask the barman if he knew who you were?" he asked.

"Because my sister and I own the place," Rose replied.

Max beamed and looked Rose up and down in an exaggerated fashion. "You're a fortunate man, boss." And as he mounted his staircase, but without looking back, he shouted, "AND SHE OWNS A PUB!"

Rose turned to face Brazelle, "Are you Chris? Are you a fortunate man?"

Brazelle's face broke into a broad smile. "Yes, I am a VERY fortunate man." Handing his car keys over to Rose, he added, "And I have the Ferrari to prove it!"

Brazelle had reserved a table at Alberto's in Northope for one o'clock, but because of their unplanned visit to Cromwell's Treasure, it was after one thirty by the time he arrived with Rose. Fortunately, despite it being the most popular and oversubscribed restaurant in the town, Alberto had held their table for them.

Alberto greeted them effusively, with what Rose thought to be a French accent. "It's lovely to see you again Reverend and very nice to meet you also, mademoiselle."

Brazelle apologised for turning up late, but Alberto merely waved his hand with a flourish, insisting that it was not a problem and that he was happy to hold the table for one of his most valued patrons.

Once the couple were seated, Alberto made a few comments regarding the day's specialities and left them to peruse the menu.

"You must be a regular here," said Rose.

Brazelle corrected her. "Not at all, but Gerald and Jenny are and I've been here a few times with them. Gerald introduced me to Alberto on my first visit, which is how he knows me. A couple of years ago, the Caulfields were in here one evening when Alberto's wife had a heart attack. Gerald saved her life and ever since, Alberto can't do enough for them. And since Gerald told him I'm an old friend, I've also been getting the five-star treatment."

"Well, that can't hurt, can it?" responded Rose. "But one thing's puzzling me. His name's Alberto, which is Italian, just like most of what's on the menu, but he spoke with a French accent and called me mademoiselle. So, which is it? Is he Italian or French?"

"Neither," replied Brazelle. "He's from Essex and his real name is Albert Burns. He confessed it once to Gerald. Apparently, he didn't think his real name conjured up the image of an up-market restaurateur, especially one who specialises in Italian cuisine, so he changed it to Alberto Brucia. Why he uses a fake French accent, though, I couldn't say."

Brazelle always enjoyed being with Rose, but he also planned on using their lunch date as an opportunity to get some more information, so, after placing their order, he began working through the list of questions he had on his mind. "I expect you know that I spoke with Mrs Richards and Gareth, yesterday."

Rose nodded. "Yes. Mrs Richards told me. She said you'd asked a lot of questions about the day my mother died. And she said you also asked about the day my father died. I was a bit puzzled why you did that, but assumed you must have a good reason. Tell me though, did you ask Gareth about the..... what did you call it?......the....."

"Phalera," said Brazelle, finishing Rose's sentence. "Yes I did, and he showed me exactly where he'd found it, in the basement of the old House. I didn't know there was anything of the old Harfield House remaining until Mrs Richards mentioned it. She told me that Gareth occasionally disappeared down there when he was a child and that was why your father asked Jonathan to get the tree house built for him. Your father was clearly very fond of Gareth."

"Yes he was," agreed Rose. "We all were...I mean.....are. People who don't know Gareth can easily misunderstand him. They don't realise that he's incredibly bright. It's just that he has some emotional issues. He can easily be unnerved in some social situations and he gets anxious if there's too sudden a change from what he's used to. He likes making things, especially things he's designed or invented himself. And he likes technology, the more complicated the better. My father was always buying him stuff to feed his interests and help him develop new skills. It was father who bought him his first digital camera, when he was only nine years old. Gareth quickly learnt how to use it and transfer his pictures onto his computer, which my father had also given him. But what about the phalera! You told me how valuable it is, so why would anyone leave it in the basement of the old House?"

"Gareth found it in a hidden compartment behind the wood panelling," Brazelle explained. "Perhaps the person who put it there died before they could retrieve it. If they hadn't told anyone about it, then it would stay there until someone came along to rediscover it. Since it was Gareth who seems to have been the one who most often went down there, I suppose it's no great surprise that he's the one who found it. And then it became his secret, a secret that he eventually shared with you. I understand you also shared a secret with Mrs Richards, on the morning of the day that your mother died. Do you remember that?"

"Yes, I remember it very well," said Rose. "It was the first time I managed to get inside the tree house. I'd always wanted to go in there, but was never allowed to, so when I saw my opportunity, I took it. Mrs Richards was really cross when she found me especially since my white dress was so dirty, but she stopped being angry when I agreed it would be our secret. I used to like that kind of thing. Sharing a secret used to make me feel special, I suppose. I remember doing the same thing with my mother, just a few days before she died. I'd hidden under the bed in her bedroom intending to jump out and surprise her. It was something I'd done a couple of times before and my mother always pretended that I'd frightened her. I thought it was great fun, but this time was different. She came into the bedroom in a hurry, unlocked one of her cabinets and took out a box which she also unlocked. But then whilst she was putting something in the box, she dropped her key ring without noticing, so I was able to reach out and take it. Once she realised she didn't have her keys she ran around the bedroom frantically looking for them. I just stayed quiet and watched, thinking it was great fun, until eventually she got on her hands and knees and looked under the bed. That's when she saw me and when she realised I had her key ring she became so angry. I'd never seen her like that before and she scared me so much, I started to cry. When she saw how distressed I was she started to calm down and said she was sorry for upsetting me. Then she said that what had happened would be our secret and neither of us should tell anyone else about it. And I never have, until now."

Once again, Brazelle found himself intrigued by something which, to most people, would simply have appeared as just an insignificant remark. Remembering what he had been told about how much of a doting mother Justine was, he was puzzled why such a seemingly inconsequential matter would make her so angry that she would reduce Rose to tears and then be so keen to keep it secret. He recalled the dream he had, just a few nights before, the dream in which Justine appeared and placed some keys on his mantelpiece. He didn't believe in messages coming from the dead, so concluded that, for a reason he was yet to consciously appreciate, his subconscious had decided the keys were in some way important. And if they were, then for Justine, in thinking she may have lost them, it might well have become a far from inconsequential matter.

The couple were coming to the end of their meal and most of the other diners had left when Rose brought up the subject of her birthday. "I've decided to have a party at Harfield House on Wednesday evening and, of course, I want you to be there. I'm also going to invite Jenny and Gerald, but there won't be too many other guests, apart from Damien and Frankie and a couple of their friends, because I don't know many people over here. It's a bit short notice and a long way to come for any of my friends back in the States."

"Sounds good to me," said Brazelle. "When did you decide on it?"

"Just now," Rose replied. "Do you think Max would come if I invited him, now that we're more or less friends?"

"Oh, you've become friends alright," agreed Brazelle. "And, of course, you can invite him, but I'm quite certain what he'll say."

Brazelle leaned forward and lowered his voice. "I told you that Max was an intensely private person who had little interaction with other people and wouldn't appreciate me talking about him, not even to you, who is now his friend. Well I'm going to tell you something about him Rose, but you must promise never to repeat it to anyone and certainly never tell Max that I told you. Do you promise?"

Rose nodded. "Yes, I promise."

"Max suffers from Post Traumatic Stress Disorder. Not the PTSD that some people claim after breaking a fingernail, but the real deal. A few years ago he was involved in something that left not just the physical scars that you can see on his face, but some really serious and deep mental ones as well. He has treatment of various forms, but there's been very slow progress and quite a few regressions. He finds interaction with other people stressful and difficult and he suffers from bouts of paranoia. I'm one of only a very small number of people he trusts, or has any influence with him. That's why I offered him the studio when I moved here, so he'd have someone to lean on when it was needed and I could keep an eye on him. It's obvious he likes you and feels he can communicate with you, so you've now become a member of a very exclusive group, although I'd rather it had happened in, well...... perhaps a less eventful way."

"Was he a soldier?" asked Rose. "And I've been wondering why he calls you boss."

"I've already told you more than I would have told anyone else," responded Brazelle. "Please don't ask any questions. Perhaps one day I'll feel it's possible to tell you more, but, for the moment, can we just leave it there..........and finish our meals, before Alberto comes to throw us out?"

"I suppose I wouldn't be human if I wasn't curious," said Rose. "But, like I said before, it really isn't any of my business. Thanks for trusting me enough to tell me what you have done. I promise to keep it to myself. Over the past few days you've found out how good I am at keeping secrets, haven't you? Anyway, I have something else to tell you. Unfortunately, I won't be around for a couple of days. Will you miss me?"

Brazelle smiled. "Yes, of course I'll miss you, but we both have commitments. Where are you planning on going?"

"Damien told me this morning that he's got some tickets for the opera tomorrow night, as a birthday surprise. He knows how much I love opera. My favourite's Don Giovanni by Mozart and Lorenzo da Ponte, so that's the one we're going to see. It's in London, so we're going down tomorrow afternoon and then staying over on Monday night. I should be back by Tuesday afternoon, so I could meet up with you later if you're free and if you want to see me."

Brazelle smiled. "Of course I want to see you and I'll make sure I'm free, but isn't Don Giovanni a bit dark? It's all about a man who lives a fairly debauched and sinful life, before being dragged down to hell. But, on a lighter note, is there anything in particular you'd like to do on Tuesday evening, especially seeing as this is your birthday week?"

"I'll be happy just to come and spend some time round at your place. You still haven't given me a talk on your artwork, so maybe you could do that for a start. But you don't need to be on your own tomorrow night, while I'm away. Frankie told me to ask if you'd join her for dinner at Harfield House. She hates opera, so she's not coming to London with us. She said if you accept her invitation, I should give you a choice of either, high formality in the Long Dining Room, or complete informality in the small dining room. So what do you say?"

"I say 'yes' to everything," replied Brazelle, "your tour of my art gallery and to Frances' invitation. And as far as the choice that she's given me is concerned, I'll always choose informality over formality, whether it's eating or most other things."

"Great," said Rose. "It will give you and Frankie a chance to get to know each other. You could ask her to show you some more of the House. It's a big place and you only got to see barely half of it the other night." Then, as an afterthought, she added, "Oh! I meant to tell you something else. Frankie told me that when she met you on your first visit to Harfield House last week, she got the feeling that the two of you had met somewhere before, although she couldn't remember where or when. And she thought you recognised her as well. Do you think you've met before?"

Brazelle gave what might be seen as an ambiguous response. "Well, if we have met before, I'm sure I would remember. Your sister is a very striking woman."

The couple had been the only diners in the restaurant for at least fifteen minutes and Brazelle realised that if he was to maintain his status as one of Alberto's most valued customers, he should pay the bill, leave a reasonable tip and depart. As he reached for his wallet, Rose grabbed his arm. "I'd like to pay for this," she said.

"Absolutely not," Brazelle objected. "This is your birthday week. In any case, just like you did for Max, you've made my day."

As the couple drove back to Prinsted, Brazelle asked if Rose wanted to join him at the evening service and afterwards for the social gathering that always took place on the first Sunday of the month. Rose, however, declined his invitation, leaving Brazelle to continue to consider her, at least in so far as her spiritual development was concerned, to be 'a work in progress'.

Day Ten - Monday

Before going to see how work was progressing at the Church, Brazelle phoned Sir Andrew. He dialled the telephone number printed on the card he had been given and within three rings the phone was answered. "Who is it?" said the voice on the other end.

Brazelle sighed, before giving the password that was written on the reverse off the card. "I am a weird priest."

"Thank you, Mr Brazelle," responded the operator. "I'll just see if Sir Andrew is available."

A few moments later Sir Andrew came on the line. "Good morning, Mr Brazelle. I'm glad you remembered your password. I was going to give you a call myself later, but you've beaten me to it. Have you anything to report?"

Brazelle was sure he heard Sir Andrew chuckling, but decided to let it pass and do his best to maintain his dignity. "Not quite," he replied. "I'm beginning to formulate a plan to propose to you, but in the meantime I was hoping you might be able to use your considerable investigative powers to trace someone's whereabouts. His name is David Pickering and he is, or at least was, an ordained Anglican priest."

"Can you tell me anything else about the man?" asked Sir Andrew, no longer chuckling.

"Well, until a little over a year ago he was Vicar of Prinsted and I have it on good authority that he's a money-grubbing, debauched and indolent heathen, with absolutely no redeeming features whatsoever. Does that help?"

"Not particularly." said Sir Andrew. "The description fits many of the people I've locked up over the years and there's plenty more of them still wandering about. What's your interest in him?"

"I'm not entirely sure. It's just a hunch I have," replied Brazelle.

"A hunch eh?" said Sir Andrew. "I've had plenty of them myself over the years, although most have come to nothing. But I'll see what I can come up with and get back to you. Is there anything else?"

"I don't suppose your Inspector Jenkins has come up with much about Lady Justine yet, has he?" asked Brazelle.

"He's found a couple of things of interest, but it's early days, so I'll keep you posted." And with that, Sir Andrew hung up.

When Brazelle arrived at the Church he found Jenny in the vestry completing some paper work.

"Oh, I'm glad you're here," she said. "I've got something to tell you. Shut the door would you."

Brazelle did as he was asked and Jenny, with delight written all over her face, announced she was pregnant.

"That's wonderful news. Congratulations," said Brazelle, before moving forward to give her a hug.

Jenny beamed. "We've kept it quiet until now because of the disappointments we've had in the past, but I'm over three months on now and everything's going well, so we thought we'd let the immediate family and just a few close friends know about it. To be quite frank, Chris, I'm amazed and feeling very blessed. I'll be forty, next year, and with the problems I've had in the past and my clock ticking, I began to think it would never happen. But apart from wanting to tell you that, there's another reason I'm glad I caught you. Next Monday, I intend to inform the Bishop about the pregnancy and tell him that I want to take leave of absence from the end of this month. I was wondering if you would be happy for me to propose you as my temporary replacement. I say 'temporary', but I honestly don't know how long it might be for. I have friends whose maternal instincts have stopped them from ever returning to work, so I just can't say what I'll eventually decide. All I know is that I don't want to take any risks with this pregnancy. I may never get another chance, so I'm going to give up work early. What do you think?"

Brazelle was hesitant in his response. "I'm really pleased for you and Gerald. It really is great news, but as for me taking over the Parish for a while, I think I'll need a few days to think about it, before I can give you a clear response."

"I understand," said Jenny. "And it's what I thought you'd say. That's why I'm leaving it until next week before I tell the Bishop. It'll give you time to think about it. But keep the news to yourself until we decide to make it public will you please, Chris, although we're perfectly happy for you to tell Rose. Did she tell you that the two of us have been communicating ever since our first meeting at Harfield House? We've even met up in the village for a coffee a couple of times. And last night she rang to invite us to her birthday celebration on Wednesday night. I assume you'll be there."

Brazelle nodded. "Yes, I'll be there. I'm pleased that you and Rose are becoming good friends. And thanks for giving me permission to tell her about your good news. I'm seeing her tomorrow evening, so I'll tell her then, and I'll make sure she understands that it's privileged information."

Jenny adopted a more serious tone and expression. "Actually, there is something else I want to say to you and it's about Rose. At any point you can tell me to shut up and mind my own business, but what I've got to say, I say as your friend and also as Rose's friend. I told you on that evening at Harfield House that she was smitten with you, and everything I've seen and heard since has only confirmed that I was right. I've known you a long time now, Chris, and, since the very early days of our friendship, I've felt that you carry within you heavy and deep feelings of guilt and grief, but that you've kept them suppressed by overwhelming them with your Christian faith. Remember, Chris, I'm not just a fellow priest, but also a trained and experienced psychiatrist, and if I say so myself, quite a good one. I've seen how sometimes an individual's relationships with others can be damaged, or, even destroyed, through their failure to come to terms fully with their past. I don't want to see that happen to you, who may be left bereft, or to Rose, whose heart might get broken. There, I've said my piece and you're under no obligation to respond, but just remember that Gerald and I are always here for you, and for Rose."

Brazelle said nothing, but he had absorbed what he'd just heard and nodded an acknowledgement.

Jenny regained her smile, "Right that's it. The consultation is over. We both have work to do. You're now dismissed."

It was just coming up to seven o'clock when Brazelle entered the code to open Napoleon's Gates on his way to his dinner date with Frances.

Jonathan, dressed in his butler's garb, opened the front door and led Brazelle to a room at the back of the House where Frances was waiting. There was a dining table already laid for two people in one corner and Brazelle assumed it must be the 'small dining room' that Rose had referred to, although it also had a lounge area.

As Brazelle entered, Frances stood up to greet him and signalled to Jonathan that he was free to leave. "I'm so glad you could come, Chris, and I'm pleased you opted for this less formal setting. The Long Dining Room can be a bit overpowering, especially when there are only two people dining."

"Thank you for inviting me," replied Brazelle. "I feel very privileged and your invitation came at a time when I was hoping to have an opportunity to speak with you again. But what would you like me to call you?"

"Frankie. You must call me Frankie. Now, I seem to remember that last time you were here you asked for whisky with just one piece of ice. Is that what you'd like?"

"Yes, thank you, Frankie."

Frances passed Brazelle his whisky. "I told Jonathan that we'd start dinner in thirty minutes."

Whilst Frances was talking, Brazelle, although still listening, let his eyes wander around the room. One feature in particular struck him as unusual for Harfield House. It was a room without any paintings, although there were quite a lot of photographs. It was so unexpected he decided to ask Frances about it. "I know I haven't seen all of the rooms in the House, but I can't help noticing that this is the only one I've visited so far, that doesn't have any paintings on its walls. I noticed there were even a few paintings hanging in the kitchen, when I was in there the other day. Is there any particular reason why there aren't any in here?"

Frances smiled. "Yes, as a matter of fact, there is. Many years ago my mother, who herself was not any kind of artist, demanded that there must be at least one room in the House that didn't have any of my father's or my paintings on its walls. At first my father was resistant, but eventually he gave in and this was the room that was chosen. My father though, as he so often did, went along with the letter of his agreement, but not its spirit, so, over the next few months and years, he mounted ever more photographs on the walls."

"If you don't mind me saying so, they strike me as being rather varied in their quality," commented Brazelle. "Who took them?"

"Oh, I certainly don't mind you saying that, and in fact, I completely agree," responded Frances. "Most of those you might consider to be the more aesthetically pleasing were either taken by my father himself, or by one of his more photographically accomplished friends. Some of them, of course, look like they might have been taken by an untrained ten-year old. And there's a perfectly good reason for that. They were! Father gave Gareth his first digital camera when he was about nine. For the next couple of years he was quite obsessive about taking pictures and my father thought it would be good for Gareth's self-esteem if he praised him for his efforts and then mounted some of his photos alongside his own. I think it probably worked, because every now and again, even after all these years, we occasionally find Gareth has wondered in here to take another look at them. We wouldn't dream of taking any of them down, of course. As you're probably aware, Gareth is a sensitive soul and he'd be very upset if we did."

"Rose told me that your father introduced Gareth to photography," said Brazelle, "but she didn't tell me he was such a prolific photographer. You said he was obsessive about it for the first couple of years, so what happened to diminish his interest?"

Frances thought the question was rather odd, but nevertheless gave an answer. "We all noticed that after my father died Gareth's interest in photography seemed to wane. In fact, his interest in a number of his usual activities appeared to be reduced for a while, before eventually recovering. He still takes odd photographs from time to time, but his enthusiasm has never quite got back to what it was before my father died. In his own way, Gareth returned my father's affection and when he died I believe Gareth behaved the way he did, because of his grief."

Brazelle was clearly interested. "So, Gareth must have taken a considerable number of photographs over the years, especially in the couple of years immediately prior your father's death. Do you know what happened to them?"

Frances was still puzzled by Brazelle's apparent interest in Gareth's photography, but responded with good grace. "Not exactly, but I'm sure most of them will still exist somewhere. Gareth never discards anything. He's a hoarder. Probably a habit he learned through observing my father. As far as I can remember, he always stored his pictures digitally. Apart from the ones you see here, very few were ever printed. If you really are interested in looking at some of them, you could always ask him. Gareth is not just your normal hoarder. He's incredibly tidy and well organised, so he'll probably be able to find them, more or less straightaway. I wouldn't mind betting they're stored away in the basement. Father allocated him one of the big storage rooms down there to keep his things in and as far as I'm aware he still uses it."

"Yes I think I will ask Gareth about his photography," said Brazelle. "It's just a bit of a hunch I've got. Don't think me rude for not telling you what it is, because it really is rather a vague notion and if it doesn't work out, I'll feel a bit of an idiot for having told you about it."

"Very well," said Frances. "Obviously, Rose told me what it is that she's asked you to do for her and although I think it will come to nothing, you were good enough to agree to take it on. So, the least I can do, is help you where I can and, if you'll forgive me for putting it so bluntly, humour you. In fact one of the reasons that I wanted to spend some time with you this evening was to talk to you about Rose. And I think now is as good a time as any to bring it up."

Frances took a sip of her drink. "In strictly blood relationship terms Rose, as you know, is my much younger half sister, but in life relationship terms she's much more than that. When her mother and our father died I was a married adult woman, but she was still a very young child and was left utterly devastated. Damien and I did the best we could for her and although we knew we could never really replace her parents, over time that's exactly what we saw ourselves as having become. Unfortunately, we were unable to have children of our own, but Rose became our surrogate daughter and it isn't just a one-way feeling.

Although Rose may not fully appreciate it herself, in very many ways she sees me as her mother figure and treats me accordingly. She keeps very little from me, Chris. I think you can see where I'm going with this and although many would say that it is no business of mine, I would respectfully disagree. I've nursed Rose through two major crises in her life and I intend to do my utmost to ensure that I don't have to do it again. I like you, Chris, and based on what I've seen and heard I think you're a thoroughly decent human being, but I also have the feeling that you're a man who carries with him an awful lot of baggage. And I'm concerned that it might be enough for Rose to trip over and be very seriously hurt."

Frances paused and took another sip of her drink before continuing. "I've reached my conclusion for a couple of reasons. Obviously, there's your reluctance to speak about your past, but there's also something else that's been playing on my mind. When we met here last week, I got a strong feeling that it wasn't for the first time, although I couldn't and still can't remember where or when we might have met before. But more than that, I sensed that you had the same feeling, although you chose not to mention it. So, tell me, Chris, am I right? Have we met before?"

Brazelle took time, before eventually responding. "Yes, you're right, we have met once before, but it was quite a long time ago and such a brief event, I'm amazed you remember me. I didn't know your name and had no idea who you were, but I recognised you straightaway when we met again last week. Rose told me you thought you'd met me before, but the fact you hadn't mentioned it to me made me think you were unsure, so I thought you might soon put it out of your mind and forget about it. It seems I was wrong."

"Are you going to tell me anymore?" Frances asked.

"In time," Brazelle replied "But not yet. When I eventually tell you, you will understand."

"Very well," responded Frances. "For the moment I'll let the matter rest. As I told you when you were here last week, the Harfields are a family stocked full with mysteries. I daresay we can suffer another one for a while. And at least you've confirmed that I'm not becoming delusional."

Brazelle smiled and nodded his appreciation. "As far as my relationship with Rose is concerned, I can promise that whatever I do, it will be in what I believe is Rose's best interest."

There was a knock on the door and Jonathan and Layla entered, carrying trays.

"Your timing Jonathan is, as usual, impeccable," said Frances, before inviting Brazelle to join her at the dining table.

Over dinner the conversation touched on much lighter matters, until Brazelle suddenly asked, "Would you mind if I asked about the period between Justine's death and the death of your father?"

Frances was taken by surprise. "That's an unexpected question, but go on, what exactly do you want to know?"

"I was wondering if you noticed anything unusual about your father's behaviour during that period," said Brazelle. "Obviously he would have been shocked and upset when he was informed that his wife had been found dead in the stream, but how did he appear after that? Were there any mood swings, for example, or did he do anything that was very much out of character? Anything at all that might have struck you as odd at the time. I understand, of course, that everyone in the House would have been suffering from shock and grief to one extent or another."

"Well you're certainly right about the shock and grief," replied Frances. "For the first few days we were all living in a daze. And I was the one left with the dreadful task of having to tell Rose that her mummy wasn't coming back. It was one of the worst things I've ever had to do in my life. Then, two weeks later, I had to tell her that our father was dead. You can't imagine what Rose was like, absolutely distraught. When I told her about Justine, she began hitting me and shouted, 'It's not true. It's not true'. Then she ran into the library and knelt down sobbing in front of Justine's portrait.

As far as my father's behaviour was concerned, I suppose it was very much what you might expect of a husband, suddenly bereaved of a much-loved wife, although he did try and put a brave face on it for Rose's sake, in his effort to comfort her. Having said that though, there were a couple of episodes that I never really understood and have stuck in my mind ever since.

The first incident took place on the day the village policeman came to return Justine's handbag, about a week after she died. I went through it with my father and, as far as we could tell, there was nothing missing, but we found three keys, one that looked just like an ordinary door key and a key ring with two smaller keys on it. Neither my father nor I had ever seen any of the keys before. He asked Mrs Richards about them, but she said she'd never seen them before either. Later that day I found him in the library, kneeling in front of Justine's portrait, sobbing, just like I'd seen Rose a few days earlier. I asked him what the matter was and he just said he'd found out what the two small keys were for. Then he got up off his knees, went upstairs and locked himself in his studio. When he eventually reappeared he never mentioned the keys or the episode in the library again.

The second incident took place the very next day. I'd been out all morning and when I came back I saw Jonathan and one of the gardeners carrying off Justine's portrait. I asked them what on earth they thought they were doing and Jonathan said my father had told him to take it down and destroy it. I thought my father had gone temporarily mad because of his grief and that once he came to his senses he'd regret it, so I told Jonathan to hide the portrait somewhere in the basement. After that, my father seemed to return to sanity, although he was never quite the same as before Justine died. From then on, I would have described him more as a sad man, rather than one who was grief-stricken. Rose had always worshipped him, but she became far more-clingy with him. Perfectly understandable, given that she'd just lost one parent. He responded well to that, so I was becoming hopeful and started to think he was beginning to slowly recover, but then we had Justine's funeral and the next day he hung himself. I was shocked and saddened when I first learned of Justine's accident, but felt much worse when I was informed of my own father's death. Then I had to tell Rose that she was now an orphan and, may God forgive me, Chris, I began to feel bitterness and anger towards him. How could he do this to us? Was his grief so overwhelming that it outweighed not only his love for me, but also his love and concern for Rose? I have to admit that it took me a long time to suppress those feelings. Even today, after all these years, they occasionally resurface and I have to have a few of these." Frances raised her wine glass before emptying it in one gulp.

Brazelle waited until Frances had refilled her glass before breaking the silence. "Did it ever occur to you that your father's death wasn't suicide?"

Frances was shocked. "My goodness, you really don't shilly-shally about do you, Chris? You like to cut straight to the chase. Well, let me be equally direct. Although some people would judge what I am about to say as being unforgivable, there have been times when, quite frankly, I would have welcomed the news that my father had been murdered. It would mean he hadn't taken the decision himself to leave me, and, more importantly, to abandon Rose. But surely, you don't think that do you? Why on earth would anyone want to kill my father? He had no enemies. And how could they have done it? And what about the note he left?"

Brazelle sat back in his seat and took a sip of his drink. "Before I came here tonight, because of what I already knew or thought was highly likely, I had a strong suspicion that your father may well have been murdered. Having heard what you've just told me, I'm now convinced that he was. And I have a good idea how and why it was done, and who did it. However, to be able to prove it to the satisfaction of a coroner and a court of law, aswell as to you and the rest of your household, I'll need some hard evidence to back up the strong circumstantial evidence that I've so far uncovered. Fortunately, I think I know where I have a chance of getting some. But first, would you mind inviting Mrs Richards in here to join us for a few minutes, in order to get clarity on one or two points that I talked to her about on Saturday?"

Frances took a few moments to absorb everything she had just heard, and take a few more sips of wine, before eventually giving a response. "No, I don't mind, if you think it will help. Megan's probably in the kitchen, I'll call her and ask her to join us."

A few minutes later Mrs Richards arrived with something of a worried look on her face.

Frances reassured her. "Don't worry Megan. There's absolutely nothing for you to get concerned about. Dinner was excellent as always. I only asked you to pop in for a moment because Reverend Brazelle wants to ask you a couple of questions."

Brazelle also put on a reassuring smile. "I just want to clear up one or two things that have been on my mind since we last spoke. I'm sorry to have to bring the subject up again, but I think it's really important. I want you to cast your mind back to the morning of the day that Sir Cornelius died. In particular, I want you to think carefully about what passed between the two of you, when you went up to his studio to tell him you were planning on leaving the House for a couple of hours. Is that okay?"

Mrs Richards nodded. "Yes, of course, I want to help in any way that I can."

Brazelle moved into inquisitor mode. "Please tell me, in as much detail as possible, EXACTLY what each of you said to the other and anything else you can recall about your exchange with Sir Cornelius."

Mrs Richards took a few moments to gather her thoughts before responding. "Well, I knocked on the studio door, but got no reply, so I thought Sir Cornelius might have gone out without me noticing, or perhaps he'd fallen asleep, or maybe gone into his en-suite. I thought I'd better check, but the door was locked. I hadn't taken my own key with me and when I went to get the spare key from the landing cupboard I found it wasn't there, so I had to go all the way back downstairs again. When I got back to the studio with my key I couldn't get it in the lock, so I knew Sir Cornelius must be inside and left his key in the lock. I knocked again and called out his name. This time he answered."

"What exactly was the response that you got Mrs Richards? Did he open the door to you?" Brazelle asked.

"No, he never opened up. We just communicated through the locked studio door. After I'd knocked and called his name, he just said, 'Yes?' You know, sort of asking me what I wanted. In fact I had to make a guess that was what he'd said, because he coughed as he said it. I asked him if it was all right if I left the House for a couple of hours and then bring him some tea and sandwiches, as usual, when I returned. Again he said, 'Yes,' but, just like before, he coughed as he said it."

Brazelle frowned. "So, in fact, you never actually saw Sir Cornelius when you went upstairs to say you were going out, and the only thing you heard him say, was the word 'Yes', said twice, through a closed door and whilst he was coughing?"

Mrs Richards nodded. "Yes, I suppose that's right."

"You said you couldn't find the key to the studio when you looked for it in the landing cupboard. Did it ever turn up again?" asked Brazelle.

"Yes, oddly enough it did. When I looked in the cupboard a few days later, there it was, back on its hook. I just assumed someone must have used it and forgotten to put it back straight away."

Brazelle sat back in his chair and smiled. "Thank you, Mrs Richards, you've been really helpful. Now, on a completely different matter, I wondered how much use the door through Napoleon's Wall gets. I mean the door down by the bridge."

Each of the women gave a negative response.

"I haven't used that door myself in all the time I've worked here," said Mrs Richards. "The key for it went missing years ago and that's when a digital code lock was fixed to it. I've never even bothered finding out what the code for it is and I don't remember seeing anyone else use that door since Lady Justine died. I saw her go through on several occasions. She probably had the code written down in her notebook."

"It's been years since I used that door," added Frances, "and I've long since forgotten whatever the code is."

Brazelle looked at his watch. It was almost nine thirty. "Just one last thing, please, Mrs Richards. Will Gareth still be up and about? And if he is, do you think he'd mind giving us a few minutes of his time?" Brazelle suddenly remembered he was a guest in someone else's home. "Oh, I'm sorry Frankie, I got carried away. Would you mind if Gareth came to join us for a few minutes?"

"That's not a problem, Chris," said Frances, reassuringly. "In the past few minutes, I've learned things about the day my father died that I never knew before. If you think that speaking with Gareth might be helpful in bringing this matter to a conclusion, then that's absolutely fine by me."

"Gareth will certainly be around somewhere," said Mrs Richards. "He only ever goes out with me or Jonathan. It shouldn't take me long to find him. What shall I say you want to speak to him about, Reverend?"

"Tell him I want to talk about his photography, Mrs Richards," replied Brazelle.

Mrs Richards smiled. "He'll like that," she said, before going off to find her son.

Frances looked puzzled. "Why do you want to speak to Gareth about his photography?"

Brazelle pointed at the photographs on the walls. "I'm not particularly interested in any of these, although they're a good lead in. I want to know if he took any photographs around the time when Justine and your father died. If he did, and they still exist, I'd like to see them. You said yourself, for a couple of years up until your father's death Gareth was a fairly prolific photographer. And there's one other thing I'd like to see, assuming it still exists, your father's alleged suicide note. Do you have it, or know where it might be?"

"Yes, I do know exactly where it is," replied Frances. "It's in the safe. And quite why I've kept it all these years, I really don't know. I'll go and get it." She offered Brazelle more wine, which he declined, before refilling her own glass and carrying it off with her. A few minutes later she returned with her father's alleged suicide note, which she handed to Brazelle, and an empty wine glass, which she quickly refilled.

Brazelle studied the note for a few minutes before asking if Frances minded if he went to take a look at something in the library. Frances assured him he was free to visit any room in the House to further his research and, after topping up her glass once more, she went with him to the library.

Brazelle pointed up at Justine's portrait above the fireplace. "You told me your father completed Justine's portrait about two years before she died. Presumably he wouldn't have signed it until he'd finished it, so his signature must date from about two years before he died. Are there any paintings of his that are even more recent than this one?"

"There are two that he started, but they were a long way from being finished when he died," replied Frances. "They're the ones still standing on easels in his studio. The only one that he actually completed was a painting of the tree house that he created as a gift for Gareth. Well, I call it a painting, although really it was little more than a sketch. But Gareth was very pleased with it and hung it on the wall in his basement storeroom. Perhaps it's still there."

"Is there any particular reason why your father didn't paint so much after completing Justine's portrait?" asked Brazelle.

Frances nodded. "Yes, there is. Father had a fall and, in trying to save himself, he unfortunately sustained a Colles fracture of his right wrist and broke several bones in his hand. It was just about one of the worst things that could happen to a painter. To make things even worse he also started to suffer from arthritis in his finger joints. He managed to get Justine's portrait finished, because it was so close to completion when he had his accident, but painting was never very easy for him after his fall. I remember him saying he didn't have the same control of the brush and that painting had become painful for him. That's why those two paintings on the easels in his studio remained unfinished."

Brazelle focussed on Sir Cornelius' self-portrait. "When we were in here last week I said that your father's signature on his self-portrait, your grandfather's portrait and the portrait of the man with no face, all more or less matched his signature on Justine's portrait. However, on closer inspection, it's evident that there are some small differences between his signature on Justine's portrait and his signature on each of the other three, which, to my eyes at least, are indistinguishable. I believe you've just explained the reason for that difference. When your father signed Justine's portrait it was after he had his accident and was also suffering from arthritis in his fingers."

Frances moved between the four paintings and carried out her own inspection of the signatures. "My word, you're absolutely right. I can see the difference myself, although I've never noticed it before. The signatures on the portraits of the three men are indistinguishable, even though they were painted at different times over something like a thirty year period, but the one on Justine's portrait, on close inspection, is noticeably different."

"You told me that Justine's portrait was taken down a few days before your father died. Do you remember when it was put back?" asked Brazelle.

"It was a few weeks after my father died. Rose wasn't normally allowed in here on her own because she had a tendency to scribble in any book that she found. But, a couple of weeks after his death, she came in without anyone noticing and, when she found that Justine's portrait was missing, she started screaming and became almost hysterical. Just after that episode, I told Jonathan to get it back up as quickly as possible and it's remained there ever since."

Brazelle was now the cat that had found the cream. "So, when the investigation into your father's death was happening, Justine's portrait was still hidden away somewhere in the basement and not available for anyone to inspect the signature."

Frances was puzzled. "Yes, that's right, but why is that relevant?"

Brazelle handed the suicide note to Frances. "Take a look at the signature on this."

Frances did as she was asked, before taking a second look at the signature on each of the four paintings in the library that her father had painted and signed.

"Does anything strike you?" asked Brazelle.

"Yes," replied Frances. "The signature on the suicide note matches the signatures on the paintings of the men, but not the signature on Justine's portrait."

"I seem to remember that there are four of your father's paintings mounted on the walls of his studio. Do you know when they were painted?" asked Brazelle.

Frances nodded. "Yes. They were all painted at least twenty years before my father died."

"So, well before he had his accident, or, suffered from arthritis in his fingers." said Brazelle. "And therefore his signature on each of them should appear as it does on his self-portrait, your grandfather's portrait and the faceless portrait of Sir Richard, but definitely not as it appears on the much more recent portrait of Justine. Have you reached a conclusion yet, Frankie?"

Frances took a seat and looked again at the suicide note.
"Yes, I have. My father did not sign this note."

To be certain he was right, Brazelle, accompanied by
Frances, went up to Sir Cornelius' studio. Having first
confirmed that the two unfinished paintings had not been
signed, he checked the signature on each of the four
paintings mounted on the walls. As he had predicted, they
were all identical and essentially indistinguishable from
the one on the suicide note. "I believe that your father's
killer copied his signature from one of these paintings, and
I have to say it's a very good forgery, but it is twenty or
thirty years too early. This House is full of paintings
bearing your father's signature and they probably all look
the same, just like the ones on the walls in here, or, those in
the library, except for the one on Justine's portrait and,
most probably, the sketch of the tree house that your
father gave to Gareth. And, as for the word SORRY
written in capitals above the signature, well, quite frankly,
just about anyone could have written that. When the
police carried out their routine investigation of your
father's death they would have compared the signature on
the suicide note with that on his paintings and found that
it matched beautifully. Then, given the recent tragic death
of Justine and everything else they thought they knew
about the case, they would have very quickly dismissed the
possibility of any third party involvement, concluded that
it was another tragic suicide of a grief stricken man and
closed the file."

By the time Brazelle and Frances returned to the small
dining room, Gareth was already present, waiting patiently
with his mother. Brazelle took a few minutes to comment
on Gareth's photographs that were mounted on the walls,
before asking him if he had kept many of the other
photographs he had taken over the years. Gareth confirmed

he had kept just about every photograph he had ever taken in his life and that they were all stored on compact discs in the basement. He agreed to show them to Brazelle.

As Brazelle imagined it would be, Gareth's storeroom was a model of order and neat organisation. Not surprisingly, it took Gareth only seconds to identify the box that contained his photographic collection, before handing it to Brazelle.

The photographs were saved on a collection of just over two hundred discs, each labelled with the year and month in which the photographs saved on it had been taken. They were arranged in date order, so it took Brazelle less than a minute to identify the one CD whose contents he was keen to explore. "Would you mind if I borrowed this one until tomorrow and made a copy of it, Gareth?" he asked.

Gareth looked to his mother for a nod of approval, before agreeing to the proposal, but only on the strict understanding that Brazelle kept his promise to return the CD the next day.

Frances had been right about the whereabouts of the sketch of the tree house. It was hanging on Gareth's storeroom wall. Brazelle inspected Sir Cornelius' signature and pointed out to Frances how it differed from the one on the suicide note, in exactly the same way as did the signature on Justine's portrait. In fact, the differences were even more obvious and Brazelle assumed this was because Sir Cornelius' arthritis had worsened in the time between him signing Justine's portrait and signing the sketch of the tree house. If he had any doubts before, they were now gone completely and Brazelle was certain that the suicide note was a forgery.

As the group returned upstairs, Brazelle decided it was time to leave and thanked Frances for the evening.

"It's me who should definitely be thanking you, Chris," said Frances. "Rose certainly chose well when she asked you to be her private investigator. But where do we go to from here?"

Brazelle held up the disc Gareth had loaned him. "I'm hoping to find something helpful on this, but regardless, there are still some aspects of the puzzle that remain to be solved. I'm sure you're keen to tell your family about what we've discovered, but I'd really like to keep these things between ourselves for the time being. Will you trust me for just a little longer and say nothing to anyone else?"

Frances smiled and nodded. "Of course, if you think it best. Now go. I can tell you're eager to find out what's on that disc."

Brazelle returned to Holford and went immediately into the study, booted up his computer and loaded the contents of Gareth's CD. Every photograph was tagged with the precise date and time it was taken and they were all arranged in date order. It didn't take Brazelle long to identify the photographs taken on those days that were of particular interest to him and when he did, his face lit up. He looked up to heaven and said, "Thank you, God!"

Day Eleven - Tuesday

Brazelle was woken by the ringing of the telephone. Just before answering he turned on the light and glanced at the clock. It was just before six.

"I hope I haven't woken you," said Sir Andrew.

"No, of course not, it's well after five," responded Brazelle, with the irony obvious in his voice.

"Good," said Sir Andrew, "so you'll be alert to hear what I have to say. I'll start with the Reverend Pickering, and it seems your character witness was spot on. Just after he'd left Prinsted, the Diocese discovered he'd been cooking the books throughout his time there. They reckon he pilfered at least twenty thousand pounds. The Diocese never reported it at the time, because of concern for the Church's reputation, and they also thought it would be a kick in the teeth for his parishioners, if they found out where their money had gone. This may have started with a bit of curiosity from you, but we have an official interest in him now. Apart from embezzling from the Church, we have information suggesting he was also involved in one or two other criminal activities. A couple of days after he jumped ship at your end, he flew down to Marseille. From that point we've lost track of him for the moment, but we'll catch up with him eventually. We've passed his details to Interpol and Jenkins is still working on it.

Then there's the late Lady Justine, and this really does get interesting. She wasn't born Justine Hellyer fifty years ago, in Lewisham in Kent, as she claimed. That Justine Hellyer died just four months after she was born. We believe her real name was Rosina Fletcher and she was born in Naples, to an English father and an Italian mother, just a few days after the real Justine Hellyer was born. Rosina grew up spending lengthy periods in both Italy and the UK, which accounts for her being able to speak Italian like a native, as well as English. In a minute, I'll explain how Jenkins managed to discover all of this, so please bear with me for the time being.

It seems that at age nineteen, Rosina was cohabiting in Naples with a rather unsavoury character who was involved in money laundering for the Mafia. Whether or not she knew what he was up to I don't suppose we'll ever know, but the Italian police arrested and questioned her at the same time that they arrested her boyfriend. Eventually, in the absence of any hard evidence against her, her passport was confiscated and she was given bail while the police continued to investigate. Then something rather unexpected and, from her point of view, extremely dangerous happened: her boyfriend turned State's evidence. That instantly made him and, through association, her, a Mafia target. What could she do? On the one hand, the police were still investigating and there was no knowing what they might throw at her, especially since her boyfriend seemed to be keen on saving himself from a lengthy prison sentence. And on the other hand, the Mafia was less than amused by her boyfriend's antics. So, she jumped bail and absconded. When she was allowed bail she had to surrender her Italian passport, but she also had a British passport that the Italian police knew nothing about, so she used it to fly out of Italy and come to the UK. By the time the Italians knew she'd gone, it was too late.

She arrived in the UK, a fugitive, not just from the Italian police but very likely from the Mafia as well, so she would have been afraid to use her real name and probably just made one up. And she needed money, but she'd had very little formal education because of the disruption caused through her parents regularly moving the family between the UK and Italy. However, she did have two very marketable attributes: her beautiful looks; and, her ability to speak Italian like a native. So she approached an up-market escort agency in London, one of those that specialise in giving comfort to wealthy foreign businessmen. Naturally, they just took one look at her and she was hired. And when they found out about her language skills, well that must have been a bonus. The escort agency wasn't interested in the slightest in what she called herself and it was strictly a cash business, so there was no need for her to produce any official documentation, or a National Insurance number, for example. For a while, everything must have been going along just fine, but there was an unfortunate glitch. The Met Vice Squad got a new addition, one Chief Inspector Malcolm Hobson, a man determined to make a name and a career for himself. He got a warrant and raided the agency that she worked for, on suspicion, would you believe, that they might not be quite as virtuous and upstanding an organisation as the Salvation Army! Justine was arrested on suspicion of soliciting, tax evasion and half a dozen other misdemeanours. She was photographed and her fingerprints were taken, but that was the easy bit. Who was she? The name she initially gave to the police didn't stack up, so, at some point, she decided that she had little choice but to take the risk of telling them her real name, perhaps producing her passport to prove it. She probably thought that the offences she was facing were so low-key, she'd simply have to pay a fine and the police wouldn't bother investigating her any further. That would then be the end of the matter and she'd be free to slip back into the shadows once more. Maybe Hobson didn't dig into her past, but we'll probably never know.

I knew Malcolm Hobson. In fact, he was a friend of mine - right up until the day I arrested him and charged him with corruption. He went down for nine years, and who knows how much justice that man must have perverted. Anyway, my point is, as senior investigating officer he may or may not have investigated Rosina further, but if he did, and discovered she was wanted in Italy, he may have simply taken a bribe and forgotten about it. Who knows? Eventually, Rosina was fined and released, but she left a police record behind, filed under her real name, Rosina Fletcher.

It appears to be around that time she adopted the identity of a real person, someone who was born at about the same time she was, but was never going to turn up at any time in the future. And so she became Justine Hellyer. It's possible that Rosina Fletcher knew something about the family of Justine Hellyer. Perhaps their families had been friends and she may have thought that knowing something about the background of the person whose identity she'd adopted would reduce the chances of being found out, but we'll probably never know."

Brazelle was impressed. "Your Inspector Jenkins has uncovered a great deal in a relatively short amount of time, but how did he get all this information?

"I'm just about to come to that," said Sir Andrew. "Jenkins very quickly discovered that the woman who Sir Cornelius' married was certainly not Justine Hellyer. He identified a matching birth registration, but discovered that the child it related to never left hospital from the day she was born until her death, just four months later. So, to discover Justine's true identity, Jenkins began tracking her back from the date of her marriage to Sir Cornelius. After going back four years, he came to the time when she got a job as an interpreter with a British engineering company that did a lot of business in Italy. She translated letters and various other documents, handled phone calls and attended meetings in the UK to act as interpreter. It was all very straightforward stuff and fortunately for her, the job didn't involve her ever having to travel to Italy. When she first went to work for the company they couldn't have been too painstaking in checking her out, but, in any case, I'm sure if she flashed a smile at some young buck of an HR executive, he probably wouldn't have asked too many questions. Prior to her getting that particular job there's no trace of her using the name Justine Hellyer.

At that point Jenkins was still unaware of Justine's real name, but he knew the most common reason for someone choosing to adopt a new identity was their wish to hide a criminal record, so, armed with Justine's picture and an approximate age, not to mention the fact that she may have had some Italian connections, he set to work to discover who she really was. He fed everything he knew about her into our central database and worked backwards, from the earliest date that he had for her using her assumed identity. And bingo, less than four months before she started work at the engineering company, he had a match between Lady Justine and Rosina Fletcher, the Anglo-Italian with a British criminal record in connection with prostitution and tax evasion. But he didn't stop there. After Rosina Fletcher jumped bail in Italy, the Italians put out her details through Interpol and they were still there, so Jenkins contacted the Italian police in Naples to get more information and then filled in the dots."

"Well done, Jenkins!" said Brazelle. "But something is still puzzling me. When Justine and Sir Cornelius met for the first time it was at a conference for which all participants, including Justine, who was acting as an interpreter, required security clearance. She would certainly have undergone vetting by the Security Service and even the most inexperienced and incompetent MI5 officer would have quickly discovered she was an imposter."

"You're absolutely right, of course," said Sir Andrew. "She would have been very quickly detected, but what happened after that would depend on who did the vetting, wouldn't it, Mr Brazelle?"

Brazelle's face began to break into a smile. "It was Gant, wasn't it? He carried out the vetting."

"Yes, and now you know how he got the material to blackmail her," said Sir Andrew. "Justine underwent vetting whilst she was still working for the engineering company. The company had a division that took on contracts from both the British and the Italian military and Justine was offered the opportunity of moving to work there, with an increase in salary, which she accepted. What she almost certainly didn't realise, was that before she could take up her new position, her details would be passed to the Security Service as a matter of routine and she would be checked out by them. That's almost certainly when Gant identified her as a potential recruit."

"Or more accurately, a victim," interrupted Brazelle.

Sir Andrew nodded and continued. "At that time she was still working primarily for the engineering company, but, because she'd supposedly been vetted and given clearance by the Security Service, she was occasionally asked to undertake work where an English - Italian interpreter was required at conferences and meetings, where confidential material was discussed. Quite when Justine was approached and told that her cover was blown and the blackmail began, it's impossible to be sure. And the chances are that, at first, the demands her blackmailers made were fairly low-key, to draw her in deeper, so that escape became ever more difficult. She might even have thought that the first task she was given would also be the last, but the longer it went on, the more she was trapped."

"How did you find out about Gant's connection to Justine?" asked Brazelle. "It's important we don't inadvertently alert him to our interest in him."

"I don't think you need to worry," replied Sir Andrew. "After the Philby affair and then Burgess and Maclean, MI5 created a master database of everyone who has ever been positively vetted. It gives very little other information, apart from the identity of the person who had overall responsibility for carrying it out. There are very few Security Service databases that Special Branch has direct access to, but fortunately this is one of them, so I was able to take a look. I didn't need to ask for access to Justine's file. In fact, I wouldn't mind betting that Gant made sure it went missing after she died and probably kept a close eye on it whilst she was alive. And he probably had it so well doctored, that it wouldn't have told anyone very much of interest in any case. I don't usually feel pity for criminals, Mr Brazelle, but, when I'd finished reading Jenkins' report, I did feel some sympathy for Justine. It's the same sad old story. A young innocent, without realising it, naively gets involved with some bad people and then fairly soon afterwards, their life gets shredded.

But now I've just realised the time and this phone call has taken longer than I'd intended. Unfortunately, I have another pressing engagement, so we will have to leave anything else until next time. I have one more matter to inform you about and we still have to agree on a plan for dealing with Gant. I think it would be best if our next discussion takes place face to face, but not at your home, or here at Scotland Yard. Can you suggest somewhere suitably discreet, not too far away from Prinsted? Thursday morning at ten o'clock would suit me best?"

Brazelle proposed that they meet at a small coffee shop, The Meeting Place, just off the High Street in Northope. "It's never very busy and the coffee's quite drinkable," he said.

"Sounds ideal," said Sir Andrew. "I'll see you there at ten o'clock on Thursday morning."

A short time later, a courier arrived from Coyte-Sherman, returning Brazelle's package and delivering the results of the research that Brazelle had asked to be carried out. There were no surprises. The results confirmed something that Brazelle had strongly suspected.

Brazelle headed over to Harfield House to return Gareth's photo CD, but made a slight detour on the way and paid a second trip to the bridge from which Justine had fallen. This time, though, it wasn't actually the bridge he was interested in visiting, but the nearby door in Napoleon's Wall. He had with him a photocopy that Frank Weston had made of one of the pages in Justine's notebook. On it was written: *Bridge door 113048.* Brazelle entered the code into the lock and the door opened. With a feeling of great satisfaction, he relocked the door and completed his journey to Harfield House, entering the grounds through Napoleon's Gates.

Mrs Richards answered the door and invited Brazelle to follow her into the kitchen where Gareth was drinking tea.

Brazelle handed over the CD. "Thanks for letting me borrow it and make a copy. I've already looked through the photos and three in particular caught my interest."

Gareth made no response, but finished his tea, before telling his mother he would put the CD back in his basement storeroom and return later for his lunch at the usual time.

"I saw that Gareth had taken a number of photographs of wooden models he'd made and then tagged them with their name and description," said Brazelle. "He seems to have had a partricular interest in Roman weapons of war and enjoyed reconstructing some of them on a small scale. Quite amazing, and what makes it even more amazing is that he was only aged ten or eleven when he first started creating them. He obviously has an outstanding brain and quite exceptional creative skills, just like his father."

"Oh, I don't think so, Reverend," said Mrs Richards. "Jonathan is an intelligent and resourceful man, but he'd be the first to tell you that Gareth is in a different league."

"No, I didn't mean your husband, Mrs Richards," said Brazelle. "I meant Gareth's father."

Mrs Richards froze and Brazelle sought to reassure her. "Please, don't worry. I have no intention of telling anyone else." From his pocket he took out the tiny jar that he had taken from Sir Cornelius' studio and placed it on the table. "This jar contains a sample of Sir Cornelius' hair and only the tiniest amount was needed to show the DNA match between him and Gareth." He then took out the blood stained cloth that he had taken from the kitchen the previous Saturday and placed it on the table beside the jar.

Mrs Richards picked up the cloth and the jar and sat looking at them for a moment. "I suppose I always knew that some day it would come out. I'm surprised it took this long. Gareth is just like Sir Cornelius in so many ways. It was just one of those inexplicable things. It happened shortly after Lady Brigitte died when Sir Cornelius and I were the only ones in the House. Lady Frances was away with friends and Jonathan had gone to stay with his mother for a couple of days. I took Sir Cornelius some supper in the drawing room and he asked me to sit and talk with him a while. He must have been so lonely after Lady Brigitte died. Well, we just sat and talked and we both drank quite a bit of brandy. Then one thing led to another and .... well, there you are, Reverend. A few weeks later I realised I was pregnant and I knew. Women do you know, Reverend. Whether or not Jonathan has ever suspected, I really don't know, but then he's such a good man I don't think he'd ever say anything. And he's certainly been the best possible father to Gareth, even though it will have been hard for him at times."

"Did you ever think of telling Sir Cornelius?" asked Brazelle.

Mrs Richards sighed. "Well, there were one or two occasions when it crossed my mind. And there were times when I thought he'd probably guessed, and that was why he treated Gareth the way he did. I doubt he could have given him any more attention. But if I had said something, what would it have achieved, apart from a lot of heartache and upset for so many people. Life doesn't always throw up easy choices, does it, Reverend?"

"No, Mrs Richards, it most certainly doesn't," agreed Brazelle.

"So now you know, Reverend, what are you going to do?"

Brazelle shook his head. "Nothing, and probably in time I shall forget all about it."

Mrs Richards was clearly puzzled. "But Reverend, if you don't intend to do anything with this information, why did you bother to find out. And why did you tell me?"

"I have two reasons," replied Brazelle. "The first is a purely selfish one, I suppose. I don't like having unanswered questions buzzing around in my head, however unimportant they may appear to some people. Or even, if they appear to be none of my business. I suspected that Gareth might well be Sir Cornelius' son and I wanted to know one way or the other, just to satisfy my own curiosity. But had that been the only reason, I would never have raised the subject with you and you would never have known that I knew. However, there is a second reason, and it's why I have raised the matter with you. Tomorrow, the trust that was set up when Sir Cornelius died will be dissolved and his estate will be distributed according to his stated wishes. I believe that when that happens, at the very least, suspicions will be raised and there is a possibility that questions will be asked. I wanted to give you fair warning, so you could prepare to face them."

Mrs Richards' face took on a worried look. "What sort of questions?" she asked.

"I believe Sir Cornelius knew that Gareth was his son," answered Brazelle. "He may even have done what I've done, just to be sure, but, whether or not he had a DNA test carried out, there is very little doubt in my mind, that he knew. After his Will is read tomorrow, I think there is a good chance that, at the very least, a number of people will suspect it and, if I'm right, all kinds of questions could follow."

"I don't know what to say, Reverend. Perhaps I should thank you for forewarning me, but then I hope and pray that you're wrong."

"Perhaps I am," said Brazelle, "but tomorrow we will find out one way or the other. I shall now leave, but with the reassurance, for what it's worth, that if you need my help or support in any way, you need only ask."

After leaving Harfield House, Brazelle spent the rest of the day at the Church and later in the afternoon, as he stood chatting to Fred Simpson, he saw Rose enter the churchyard carrying a bouquet of flowers.

"Are those for me?" he asked jokingly.

"Of course not," replied Rose. "I picked them up from a roadside seller on the way back from London. I've brought them to put on my parents' grave. They're buried in the family plot."

Brazelle walked with Rose to an area of the churchyard that was bounded by a low iron railing. He counted just over forty headstones within the enclosure and since there appeared to be always a minimum of two names on each of them and frequently more, he guessed there were probably well in excess of a hundred people buried within the precinct.

Rose's parents and Sir Cornelius' first wife, Brigitte, were all buried in the same grave, sited towards the northern edge of the family plot. Rose began replacing some old, now withered flowers, with the fresh ones she had brought and Brazelle wandered around the Harfield family plot, examining the headstones. They came in various styles and sizes, but the Harfield family crest always appeared, prominently placed at the top. The Harfield surname was the only one to appear on the vast majority of the monuments, but in the few cases where a different surname did make an appearance, it was invariably a woman's Christian name that preceded it. Brazelle presumed these were Harfield women who had married and acquired a new surname, but been brought back into the family fold, so to speak, after their death. When Rose came over to join him, Brazelle was standing in the very centre of the plot staring at the headstone of the founders of the Harfield dynasty in Prinsted, *Sir Richard, 1st Baronet Harfield (1642 – 1722) and his wife, Lady Adeline (1659 – 1758)*.

"They both lived to a ripe old age," commented Brazelle, "quite amazingly so, by the standards of their time."

"Yes, they certainly did, especially Adeline," said Rose. "It's such a pity we know so little about them. I would really love to know so much more. Anyway, I'd better get back. I said I'd go through tomorrow night's menu with Mrs Richards. She wants to start preparations this afternoon. I'll see you later, sometime after six." She kissed him and walked back to her car.

Brazelle continued with his stroll around the churchyard, but amongst the headstones that lay outside the Harfield family plot. Very soon he found himself in a part of the churchyard that he had never wandered through before and he was struck by how old some of the headstones and monuments appeared to be. Fortunately the stone used to create them was a particularly hard stone, so, despite many years of weathering, the text carved on them was, in most cases, still legible. They came in all shapes and sizes, with most of them appearing very modest when compared with those that he had seen within the Harfield family plot. However, there was one that struck Brazelle as being significantly more impressive than all of the others that stood immediately around it. He went over and read the inscription that was written on it: *William Wellings (1616 – 1642) and his wife, Mary (1617-1642)*. A closer look at the dates of death showed that, in fact, both husband and wife had died on the very same day. There were some markings towards the top of the headstone, partially obscured by moss. Brazelle removed the moss and was astonished to find that he had just uncovered the Harfield family crest. He was puzzled. How on earth had the Harfield family crest come to be on the headstone of the grave of two people who had died forty-three years before Sir Richard Harfield made his first appearance in Prinsted? Brazelle made a note of all the details that appeared on the mysterious headstone before returning to the Church. He found Jenny completing some paperwork in the vestry and asked her where the Prinsted parish records were kept.

"Well, that depends which ones you're interested in," she said. "The most recent ones, covering the last twenty years or so are kept in the cabinet in here, but any older ones are in the Diocesan office archives. I have to tell you though, if you want to take a look at the records from Reverend Pickering's time, you may be disappointed. I'm afraid he seems to have been less than diligent in keeping them up to date."

"It's actually some very old records that I'd like to take a look at. Those from around 1642," said Brazelle. "Do you know whether the records still exist from that time?"

Jenny gave a facial shrug. "Off the top of my head I couldn't say. 1642 was the year the English Civil War started and because of the chaos that followed a lot of church records got destroyed, or weren't even kept in the first place. I honestly don't know if Prinsted was one of the parishes affected. You'll just have to take a look. But you don't have to go all the way to the Diocesan office. Some years ago, all of the old records were digitised and put online by the county family history society. They even went to the trouble of transcribing and indexing them all. I'll show you." Jenny booted up her laptop, logged on to the website of the county family history society and called up the Prinsted parish records. "It's your lucky day, Chris. It seems that Prinsted's parish records do exist for 1642 and for many years either side. And fortunately, the online digitised copy is quite legible." Jenny passed her laptop over to Brazelle.

An hour later Brazelle had completed his family history research and returned Jenny's laptop. She asked if he had found what he had been looking for.

"Yes, I believe I have," he said. "When I was wandering through the graveyard earlier, I came across the headstone of a married couple, William and Mary Wellings. They both died on the same day in 1642 and I've just found their burial record. It says they were paupers who both died of the fever. They died young. Their ages at death are given in the parish records as twenty-six for William and twenty-five for Mary, so I guessed they probably hadn't been married very long and it turns out I was right. I found the record of a marriage that took place in 1638, between William Wellings, aged twenty-two, and Mary Buttery, aged twenty-one. I can't find any other William Wellings in the records, so it must be beyond reasonable doubt that it's the same couple that are buried out there."

"Why are you so interested in this particular couple?" Jenny asked

"I'm puzzled by something on their headstone. They both died in 1642, which is forty-three years before the founding of the Harfield dynasty here in Prinsted, and their grave lies well away from the Harfield family plot, yet the Harfield crest appears on their headstone. Having just consulted the parish records, the matter gets even more curious, because the couple are recorded as being paupers who were given a paupers burial. So, where did the relatively expensive headstone come from? Who paid for that? But I didn't stop there. I checked the christening records from the time of their marriage until the time of their death and it appears they had a son, Adam Wellings, who was born on the 1st of March 1642, just four months before they died. I wonder what ever happened to him."

Until that moment Jenny had been only half listening to what Brazelle had to say, but when she heard him mention the name Adam Wellings she put down her pen, closed her notebook and gave him her full attention. "Well, I can't tell you what happened to Adam Wellings, but I can show you what he looked like," she said, pointing to the portrait of a boy, hanging on the vestry wall.

Brazelle went to take a closer look. A small badge attached to the portrait's frame read, 'Adam Wellings aged 10'. The initials R.S. appeared in the portrait's bottom right hand corner, with the year 1652 written underneath.

"That painting was hanging there when I first came to the parish," said Jenny. "If you look around the walls here you'll see there are three more paintings with the initials R.S. on them, and I think I know who R.S. was. Between the years 1638 and 1658 the vicar here in Prinsted was a bachelor called Richard Shuttleworth. Since all the paintings that are signed R.S. have dates between those years, it seems too much of a coincidence for it not to have been him who painted them, doesn't it?"

"Yes it does," agreed Brazelle.

Jenny's curiosity was now well caught. "What else of interest have you found in your rummage through the parish records?" she asked.

"Just one more thing," replied Brazelle. "It seems pretty obvious to me that someone with money to spare must have paid for the Wellings' headstone. Since it bears the Harfield family crest, a symbol that doesn't seem to have had a connection with Prinsted until the arrival of Sir Richard, in 1685, I jumped forwards in the parish records to that year. I know things are organised differently now, but at that time there was a financial reckoning recorded in the parish register at the end of each season of the liturgical year. At the end of Advent in 1685 I found an entry in the 'Season's Reckonings' for a payment of two shillings, received from 'Anon', for the erection of a carved headstone upon the grave of William and Mary Wellings. It was to be accompanied by the saying of prayers, for which a further one shilling was received from 'Anon'. If the headstone was being erected for a fee of only two shillings, I think we can safely assume that it was paid for separately and delivered to the Church already inscribed and ready for erection. Whoever made and inscribed the headstone probably never realised the significance of the Harfield family crest and probably neither did the vicar. I doubt that anyone would have made a connection between the paupers in the grave and the recently arrived and seemingly very wealthy, Sir Richard Harfield. So, Jenny, what do you think of all this?"

Jenny smiled. "I think that Sir Richard was honouring his parents, because the wealthy baronet, Sir Richard Harfield and the son of paupers, Adam Wellings, were one and the same person!"

"Bullseye," said Brazelle. "I really can't think of any other explanation that fits all the facts."

"But why would Adam Wellings have adopted another identity?" asked Jenny.

Brazelle gave a faint shrug. "The precise reason, we may never know, but, as a very senior policeman recently told me, most people do it because they have something to hide, usually a criminal record. Perhaps Adam carried out some misdemeanour in the village before disappearing to join the army under an assumed name, but when his army service came to an end he was home sick for the place of his birth, so he returned. By then he was much older and it would have been doubtful that any of the villagers would have recognised him. Indeed, many of those who knew him as a boy or as a very young man would have been dead when he returned. He also appears to have been something of a recluse, so he probably thought that after such a long time, and with a different identity, he was safe to return. However, Jenny, do you think we could keep this discovery to ourselves for a little while?"

"Yes, okay, if that's what you want, but can I tell Gerald. After all he is a doctor and keeping other people's secrets goes with the job."

"Sure. You can tell Gerald," said Brazelle. "But I'd like to have a few more days before we tell the Harfields just who we think their founding father really was."

Brazelle took a closer look at the other three paintings on the vestry walls that were initialled R.S. The first two were representations of Biblical scenes: a painting of Christ on the Cross; and, a painting of Moses holding the tablets bearing the Ten Commandments. The third, however, was very different. It was the painting of an elderly man standing in what appeared to be the Prinsted Church graveyard, with his right hand resting on one of the gravestones. Brazelle moved closer and saw that the man was wearing a leather belt that carried two holsters, each holding a pistol, and a sheath containing a dagger. He took out his phone and compared the belt in the painting with the one he had discovered and photographed in the underground chamber of the old Harfield House. They were identical and as far as Brazelle was concerned, one and the same. He then turned his attention to the inscription on the gravestone that the man's hand was resting on. It simply read, 'Abigail Pringle RIP'.

It was almost seven o'clock as Rose's car swept into Holford's yard and she got out carrying two pizza boxes.

"I was going to whip something up for us," said Brazelle. "Why the pizzas? Didn't I impress you with my culinary skills the other night?"

"Of course you did," replied Rose. "Just about everything you do impresses me, but I thought I'd save you the effort. And since you took me to an Italian restaurant for lunch on Sunday, I assumed you were a fan of Italian food. I just picked them up at the new place in the village, so I've no idea what they taste like, but they smell good."

"I'm sure they'll be absolutely delicious," said Brazelle, taking his first slice and continuing speaking with his mouth full. "Have you sent out all your birthday party invitations?"

Rose shook her head. "No, there was no need, because I don't have anyone to send them to. Like I said on Sunday, here in the UK I don't really know anyone, apart from you and Jenny and Gerald and of course, now Max. I did call on him earlier to invite him, but you were right about his reaction. He was very nice about it, but said he had a jigsaw puzzle he was desperate to finish. Anyway, Jenny and Gerald are coming. Damien and Frankie will be there, of course, and they've invited a couple of old friends of the family to stay for a few days, so they'll be there as well. And that's it."

"As long as you're happy," said Brazelle. "So, how was the opera?"

"It was great. I really enjoyed it. I've seen it on stage a couple of times before and always loved the singing, the music and the sets and everything, but I never really understood the storyline, because unlike my mother, I don't speak Italian. What you said the other day was right though, about it being very dark. I hadn't appreciated just how dark, until seeing it this time. Fortunately, I had Damien with me, so he could translate the dialogue and tell me exactly what was going on. Damien is really quite brilliant. He's a poly-linguist. Frankie says he's fluent in so many languages that he can dream in at least three of them and frequently snores in French." She laughed. "And he's a really experienced diplomat. At the moment he's number two at the Foreign Office, but he's tipped to become the number one later this year. Oops! I think that might be confidential, so perhaps you ought to forget that I told you. Actually, I don't know why I'm singing Damien's praises, because he really upset me and made me quite angry when we were on the way back from London. He told me he'd made some enquiries about you and that there appeared to be no trace of you before you started training to be a priest. He said he thought you must have something to hide from your past and that worried him. I told him he had no business prying and that he should stick to minding his own affairs. When he saw how angry I was he started to backtrack. He said he was only doing what any caring father would do and since he was the nearest thing I had to a father, that's why he did it. Anyway, when I told him I didn't care whatever he thought he'd found out about you he eventually dropped it. When we got back home this afternoon I told Frankie what he'd said and she really went for him. I've never seen her like that before. I even began to feel sorry for him, despite how he'd made me feel earlier. After what Frankie said to him, I don't think he'll be bringing you up as the subject of conversation any time soon. It's obvious that Frankie really likes you. I don't know what you did last night but you've certainly charmed her. She said she really enjoyed the evening and was already looking forward to seeing you again tomorrow night."

"Well I can assure you that the feeling's mutual. I think your sister is a remarkable woman," said Brazelle. "And don't be too hard on Damien. I'm sure that whatever he did, he did because he cares about you. Anyway, did Frankie say anything else about last night?"

"Only that you showed an interest in Gareth's photography and ended up borrowing one of his picture CDs," replied Rose. "Oh, and she said she may have over imbibed slightly and got a bit tipsy, but that's not unusual for Frankie. She said she hoped you hadn't noticed. But did you Chris? Did you notice that she got a bit tipsy?"

Brazelle put on a fake look of astonishment. "Rose! Only a crass oaf with no sense of chivalry would even notice that a lady was tipsy, let alone mention it." He paused before adding, "Of course, I noticed."

For a moment Rose didn't know how to react, but then burst out laughing and so did Brazelle.

Rose then adopted a more serious tone. "You know, Chris, I really don't know what I would have done without Frankie. Throughout my life she's always been there for me, always stood up for me. Whatever I needed at the time, whether it was a friend, a sister or a mother figure that's what she became. But there was a time when I thought I might have lost her forever. It was something that happened eleven years ago when I was fourteen. Perhaps you remember it. Some armed gangsters went into a hotel restaurant in Belmopan, in Belize, intending to rob the diners who were mostly wealthy guests of the hotel. When some police arrived, the gangsters took a group of hostages and Frankie was one of them. She'd gone to Belmopan with Damien when he was sent there on Foreign Office business. It was the hotel where they were staying that was attacked, but Damien wasn't there at the time, so he wasn't one of the hostages. The siege went on for four days until eventually some soldiers went in and shot all the gangsters. They managed to save all except one of the hostages and, thankfully, Frankie was one of those rescued. Do you remember it? In the States it was on TV all the time whilst it was happening. I guess it was probably the same over here, because most of the hostages were British."

Brazelle nodded. "Yes, I remember it very well. It must have been a terrible experience for the hostages to have endured those four days and I'm sure the rescuers must have felt really bad about the one hostage who they failed to save."

"It always makes me sad to think about it, because I remember how I felt whilst it was all going on," said Rose. "But whilst I'm in that frame of mind maybe I ought to mention something else that makes me sad when I think about it. I was wondering if you'd made much progress looking into my mother's death. I know you've spoken to several people about it, but I don't want you to think I'm pressuring you though. I know you've got lots of other things to deal with."

"You don't need to feel you're pressuring me," replied Brazelle. "I have made some progress, although there are a few more things I want to find out, before I give you my final conclusion. What I can say though, is that so far, everything I've seen and heard keeps pointing to the same conclusion. Your mother's death was a tragic accident and nothing more."

"Thanks for doing all this, Chris. You've no idea how grateful I am, but it's probably not a good idea to dwell on any of this for too long, it always makes me terribly sad. Let's choose a different topic and talk about a happier subject."

"I agree," said Brazelle. "And as it happens there is something I can tell you that will bring a smile to your face. Jenny's pregnant and as you can imagine, she's over the moon about it."

Rose beamed. "That's great news, but I wonder why she didn't tell me herself when I saw her yesterday. Do you remember I told you on Sunday that I'd had a lot of contact with her since I first met her at Harfield House that evening? Well, I met her again yesterday morning in the village coffee shop." Rose paused before continuing. "I told her how I feel about you and she said that on that first night at Harfield House she guessed that I was smitten. I didn't know what smitten meant and she had to explain it to me. She said she knew exactly how I felt because she felt the same way when she first met Gerald. Well, she was right, Chris, I am smitten and I want to know how you feel about me."

That explains why Jenny chose yesterday to give me her pep talk, thought Brazelle. "I thought you knew how I felt about you, Rose. I'm your loyal and adoring friend," he said.

"Is that all you are, Chris........just my friend? Well, I don't believe you."

Brazelle sighed heavily. "Rose, you're twenty-five tomorrow and I'll be thirty-nine next month. And Damien was right, there are things about me that I would prefer to keep hidden. I'm far from being proud of everything I've ever done in my life. Believe me Rose, you can do a lot better than me.

"Do you really think I care about any of that?" Rose objected. "And I think you feel the same about me, as I feel about you. I've wanted you to make love to me every day since we first met, but I know you're a priest and, well, I know it's difficult, so I've kept it to myself......until now."

Rose moved forward, put her arms around him and kissed him on the lips. Brazelle did not resist.

Day Twelve - Wednesday

Brazelle and Rose had just finished breakfast when Gearald appeared at the front door. As was his usual habit, he didn't wait for an invitation before walking straight in, and he feigned surprise at seeing Rose. "Good morning, Rose. I didn't expect to find you here."

"Yes you did," said Brazelle. "Her car's parked outside."

Gerald looked out of the window. "Oh yes, so it is. Anyway, I was just passing and thought I'd pop in and ask if you want a lift over to Harfield House later, Chris. Obviously Jenny's not drinking, and unfortunately I won't be able to either, I'm on emergency call out tonight."

Brazelle dropped the sarcasm. "That's a kind offer, Gerald, which I shall gratefully accept."

"And whether you expected to find me here or not, Gerald, congratulations," said Rose. "Chris told me your wonderful news. I'm so pleased for you both."

Gerald thanked Rose for her good wishes. "As you can imagine we're both delighted and looking forward to the joys of parenting. You know, the disturbed nights, the dirty nappy changing, tantrums and, of course, the sheer expense of it all. We really can't wait to get started."

Rose giggled. "Very funny, but I know you don't mean any of that. You'll love every minute of it. But I'm afraid I can't offer you any breakfast this time, we've just finished."

"That's alright," said Gerald. "I've already eaten. I fixed us a slap up grill for two at some unearthly hour this morning. Jenny woke me at five o'clock and said she was hungry and fancied something fattening and greasy. So much for early morning sickness! As a village doctor, I've been involved in scores of pregnancies over the years.........oh, hang on, that doesn't sound right, does it? Anyway, you know what I mean. But somehow, I think this is going to be the most difficult one I've ever had to deal with. In the past, when a pregnant woman told me she had some peculiar desire, like an overwhelming urge to chew coal, blow up a frog, or do something equally ridiculous, I would reassure her that strange impulses during pregnancy were perfectly normal, although she certainly shouldn't actually respond to any of them. But now..... well.... I'm not so sure. Was it in fact normal to have such weird urges? And what happens if Jenny gets one? Do I indulge her? Her desire for greasy food at five o'clock in the morning is certainly unusual. I sincerely hope it isn't just the thin end of a rather thick wedge."

"Now I know why you're really here," said Brazelle. "Your self-confidence has begun to fail you and you felt the need for some reassurance that everything will be okay. Like the priest who feels the need to confess, just whom does he turn to for absolution? Well let me reassure you Gerald, things will be just fine and you'll turn out to be a model father. I'm sure of it. Now why don't you put your omniscient doctor front back on and go and patronise some of your patients."

Gerald responded with irony. "As always, Chris, you get straight to the heart of the problem and come up with the definitive solution. I shall now leave a much wiser man."

At the front door, with Rose out of earshot, Gerald whispered to Brazelle, "I was just wondering if you wanted to give me any more of that twaddle about Rose's presence here not being what it looked like?"

"Not that it's any of your business one way or the other, but on this occasion, no, I don't," replied Brazelle.

Gerald smiled, gave Brazelle a wink and left.

Just before leaving Holford, Rose explained that the family solicitor would be arriving at Harfield House at eleven o'clock, to provide details of the dissolution of the Trust that was set up when her father died. She asked if Brazelle would be there with her when it happened and he agreed.

Mr George Parnaby Snr. of Parnaby and Parnaby LLP had been the Harfield family solicitor for over forty years. Although he had relinquished his role as lead partner in the business ten years earlier, when he went into semi retirement, he continued to work part time, taking an interest in the affairs of a small number of his most favoured clients. These days the position of lead partner was occupied by his son, Mr George Parnaby Jnr. Both men arrived at Harfield House at exactly eleven o'clock. In advance of the meeting, George Snr. had written to Frances asking for six named people to be present: Frances herself; Rose; Damien, and, the three members of the Richards family.

After the usual greetings and handshakes had been exchanged and Rose had introduced Brazelle to the Parnabys, George Snr. took control of proceedings and began by reminding everyone of the reason for the gathering. "A few days before his death, Sir Cornelius contacted me and instructed that his previous Last Will and Testament should be destroyed. In its place he asked if I would make the necessary arrangements, such that immediately upon the occasion of his death, his entire estate would be placed into a Trust, which, from here on, I shall refer to simply as, 'The Trust'. The Trust was to receive all payments due to the Harfield Estate and remain fully in place until the date of the twenty-fifth birthday of his youngest child, Rose, which as we all know, is today."

George Snr. paused, looked over to Rose and, with a broad smile, wished her a happy birthday.

Rose returned the old man's smile and graciously nodded her acknowledgement of his good wishes, whilst at the same time, and not quite so graciously, thinking, 'For God's sake, get on with it old man!'

George Snr. continued. "During its existence, The Trust was to pay all the running costs of Harfield House and provide a monthly allowance to each of Sir Cornelius' two daughters, Frances and Rose."

For a second time, the old man paused with a broad smile on his face, nodded to each of the two daughters in turn and waited for a gracious response from each, before continuing.

"Sir Cornelius instructed that on the occasion of the dissolution of The Trust, various itemised cash bequests were to be made to a number of individuals, mostly employees or former employees of the Harfield Estate. I can confirm that those bequests were all authorised for payment by me and my fellow trustees earlier today and that in the few cases where the beneficiary is deceased, the payment will be made to their estate. We now arrive at the main specifications that follow from the dissolution of The Trust. And I have to say I have no idea what they are. Sir Cornelius instructed that they should remain sealed in the envelope that I have here, until this very morning. He did, however, confirm that they had been properly witnessed as required by law, although, at the moment, I am unaware of the identity of his witnesses. Sir Cornelius also instructed, in anticipation of this meeting, that the current value of the Harfield Estate should be calculated and expressed in two parts. Firstly, there is the total value of cash and other liquid assets, which, net of all taxes, fees and the smaller bequests that I referred to earlier, stands at just over sixty million pounds. Then there is the total value of the balance of the Estate, which includes land, property, chattels and patent rights etc. The current value of this portion is much harder to assess, however, having taken expert advice, my fellow trustees and I have agreed that a figure of approximately one hundred million pounds is our best estimate. Sir Cornelius also stated that his sealed instructions only had implications for the people present here today. Mr Brazelle excepted, of course."

The old man opened the envelope and began reading its contents. "Firstly, to Mr and Mrs Richards, my loyal household stewards. Each is to receive a cash sum equivalent to five years salary at the time of The Trust's dissolution, or, if they are no longer under employment by the Harfield Estate, five times the salary that they earned in their last full year of employment. Mr and Mrs Richards are also to receive a pension equivalent to half that salary from the age of sixty-five, for life."

George Snr. paused once more, this time casting his smile at Jonathan and Megan who returned his smile, before hugging and kissing each other.

"Secondly, the balance of the cash and other liquid assets to be divided into three equal portions, with one portion going to each of my two daughters, Frances and Rose, and the third portion going to......" George Snr. suddenly fell silent and showed his script to his son. Following some whispering between the two, George Jnr. took over and completed the reading, "......and the third portion going to Gareth Richards."

Brazelle and Gareth were the only people in the room who made no sound of astonishment. Mrs Richards glanced over at Brazelle who gave her a faint smile and a gentle nod.

"Well, young man," said George Snr. "Whether or not you were before, you would definitely appear to be a most eligible bachelor now."

Gareth continued to sit in silence, but was beginning to show some unease at the amount of attention that was being directed towards him and his mother went to put her arm around him.

George Jnr. eventually returned to reading out Sir Cornelius' instructions. "Finally, ownership of the balance of The Trust is to be shared equally between each of my children."

George Snr. took control of the proceedings once more. "You may be interested to know that the expected Harfield Estate net income, accruing from investments, rents, patent royalties and the like, is currently of the order of four hundred thousand pounds per annum."

The few questions that followed were easily dealt with by the Parnabys and shortly before noon, after confirming he would personally ensure all legal requirements would be efficiently dealt with, George Snr. declared the morning's proceedings at an end.

The Parnabys packed up their papers and moved off to the front door, escorted by the Harfield sisters. Damien, Jonathan and Gareth also withdrew, leaving just Mrs Richards and Brazelle in the drawing room.

"You were right," said Mrs Richards. "He knew didn't he?"

"Yes, I'm sure he did," replied Brazelle. "And I believe he chose his words carefully, when he instructed that ownership of the balance of his Estate should be divided equally between each of his children. He left it for you to decide whether or not to claim Gareth's one third share."

Mrs Richards nodded. "Yes, I realise that. It's one of those awful choices that life throws up from time to time, isn't it? But on this occasion, maybe it isn't too difficult a choice to have to make. Gareth has been given almost twenty million pounds, which is far more than he will ever need. And we have our relationships in tact. I think we should leave it like that don't you, Reverend?"

Brazelle's response was non-committal. "Your decision, whatever it is, will be the right one."

Mrs Richards said nothing more, but cast a faint smile at Brazelle and left the room.

Brazelle arrived at the front door just in time to see the Parnabys driving off, watched by Frances and Rose. "I'm going to head off myself now," he announced. "I look forward to seeing you all again this evening."

Rose walked out to his car with him. "Well I'm certainly worth knowing now, aren't I?" she said.

"If you were poor as a church mouse you'd be worth knowing," Brazelle replied.

Rose smiled. "I was surprised at how much my father left Gareth though. Weren't you? I knew he was fond of Gareth, but, twenty million! As much cash as he left Frankie and me."

If only she knew the half of it, thought Brazelle.

It was shortly after six when Gerald drove up to Napoleon's Gates and Brazelle demonstrated his privileged status by opening them using the security code he had been given. Gerald parked his BMW at the front of the House next to a rather grand-looking Bentley. Brazelle assumed it belonged to the other party guests.

Jonathan, dressed in his butler's garb, greeted them at the front door and led them into the drawing room where the other guests were already enjoying drinks and canapés being offered round by Layla. Rose and Frances immediately went to welcome them, with handshakes, hugs, and kisses, distributed appropriately. They were quickly joined by Damien who, following the verbal thrashing he had been given by Frances, clearly felt he needed to make some very obvious gesture of contrition. Consequently, his greeting of Brazelle was quite effusive and, for the first time, addressed him as, 'Chris'.

Brazelle thought Damien had gone a bit over the top, but responded with good grace, as he introduced him to Jenny and Gerald. Damien completed the introductions by presenting the new arrivals to the house guests, who he identified as, "Lady Helen and Sir Ted Gant."

Having a strong constitution, it is extremely rare for Brazelle to feel nauseous, but for a brief moment he thought he might be in danger of throwing up. Fortunately, he managed to keep himself together as the inevitable handshakes followed and after a few minutes of small talk, he drew Rose to one side. "Where exactly does Sir Ted Gant fit into your family history?" he asked.

"He was a long standing friend of my father's and the man who first introduced him to my mother," Rose replied. "Frankie said he was involved in the organisation of an international conference that my father attended and appointed my mother to work as father's Italian interpreter. Frankie reckons he was with MI5, but I'm not sure I'm supposed to know that, so probably best keep it to yourself."

"I will. Your secret is safe with me," responded Brazelle. "So, that's why they've been invited, because Sir Ted's the man who introduced your parents? And as a result here YOU are."

"Well, yes, but there's more to it than that. They're my godparents," replied Rose.

Brazelle's feeling of nausea returned.

"I had no idea they were coming," continued Rose. "Damien and Frankie only told me they'd invited a couple of their old friends. They wanted it to be a surprise, so I suppose I should show them some attention."

A few minutes later, with his feeling of nausea easing, and in the hope there were no more shocks to come, Brazelle struck up a conversation with Gant. "Rose tells me you were a very close friend of her parents, Sir Ted, and that it was you who first introduced them to each other. I was wondering how you first came to know them."

"I'd known Cornelius quite some time before Justine came on the scene," replied Sir Ted. "In those days I worked at the Home Office and was involved in the organisation of quite a few conferences at which Cornelius was a major contributor. He was a brilliant man, as you probably know, and his input on a whole range of subjects was much sought after and very highly valued. It was at one of those conferences that I first put Cornelius and Justine together. Quite a few of those attending were Italian and not all had particularly good English, so I paired up Cornelius with Justine. She could handle Italian just like a native. Quite amazing, and the rest, as they say, is history."

"You put your reference to working at the Home Office in the past tense, I noticed, Sir Ted," commented Brazelle. "Are you still involved in any of the arms of government?"

Damien interrupted. "Ted works at the Foreign Office, these days, so in a way we're colleagues, although we work in entirely different sections. But now Jonathan's gesturing that it's time to go into dinner."

As the group moved off to the dining room a sudden thought came to Brazelle. He realised he had been presented with an exceptional opportunity. His feelings of nausea now disappeared entirely and a faint smile began to play on his lips.

For the rest of the evening, Brazelle was hoping for a chance to have a few private words with Sir Ted and as the group began to move back to the drawing room the opportunity arose. Gant was standing alone in a corner of the room, studying one of Sir Cornelius' paintings. Brazelle came alongside and struck up a conversation. "Sir Cornelius was a brilliant artist, was he not, and a man with so many other outstanding talents? It was a complete tragedy that his life was cut short."

Sir Ted responded, but without taking his eyes off the painting. "Indeed it was. His death came as a great shock to all of us who knew him."

Brazelle continued. "Yes I'm sure it did. A man like Sir Cornelius, who, despite the sad passing of his wife, had so much to live for. Especially to someone like you, who knew him so well, his apparent suicide must have seemed not just shocking, but also quite puzzling."

For the first time in their conversation, Gant turned to face Brazelle. "That's an odd thing to say, Mr Brazelle. Why on earth do you refer to Cornelius' suicide as, 'apparent'?"

Brazelle began to feel like an angler who had just hooked a fish. The challenge now was to land it. "I first became interested in the matter on my first visit to Harfield House, just over a week ago. Very quickly, I realised there was a great deal that didn't add up, well not to me anyway, so I decided to make some further enquiries. I've now reached the point where, although I accept there are still one or two minor gaps in my understanding, I'm fairly convinced that Sir Cornelius was murdered. And what's more, I believe I know how it was done and who did it."

Sir Ted displayed obvious concern. "Good Lord! Have you mentioned this to anyone else?"

Brazelle crossed his fingers and lied. "No. You're the first person I've told. There are still some small details I want to clear up, before I say anything to the family and then go public with the evidence I've gathered."

"And why are you telling me?" asked Sir Ted.

"Because I've reached the point where I need to tell someone," replied Brazelle, "ideally someone who knew Sir Cornelius, as well as someone who may be able to help me sort out the few remaining details. I believe that you may well be that person, Sir Ted. It was indeed fortunate that we met here tonight."

"I think we need to discuss this further," said Gant.

Brazelle scribbled his address and phone number on a scrap of paper and handed it to Gant.

"I'll call you tomorrow to continue our conversation Mr Brazelle," said Gant. "But, in the meantime, please don't mention any of this, including our conversation, to anyone else."

Nothing more was said about the matter and the evening was eventually brought to an end when Jenny said she felt she needed to go home and get some rest.

"Are you coming with us Chris, or staying on?" Gerald asked.

Rose lifted her half empty glass. "It wasn't non-alcoholic tonight, Chris, so I won't be able to give you a lift," she said, before whispering in his ear, "I'd love to come home with you, but I think I ought to spend a bit of time with my godparents. But they'll be gone on Saturday morning."

Brazelle smiled and kissed her, before accepting Gerald's offer of a ride home.

Rose and Frances accompanied their three departing guests to the front door. Watching them drive off, Frances put her arm around Rose. "He really is a most amazing man, your Reverend Brazelle," she said.

Rose corrected her, "THE most amazing, Frankie; THE most amazing."

Day Thirteen – Thursday

There were several tasks that Brazelle intended to complete before going over to Northope to meet with Sir Andrew. First on the list was the reorganisation of Frank Weston's box. Having replaced all the items he had previously taken out, he added a photocopy of Sir Cornelius' forged suicide note and a copy of Gareth's CD, before placing an A4 sheet on top, with the name ORLANDO written on it in large capital letters, so it would be the first thing seen when the box lid was removed. Next, he telephoned Daniel Coyte-Sherman and offered him an opportunity to play a part in the plot he was hatching, which Coyte-Sherman readily accepted. Finally, he took a few minutes to write some notes in preparation for his meeting with Sir Andrew. So much had happened over the past few days there was a lot to remember and he wanted to be sure he didn't miss out any part of it.

The Meeting Place is a small coffee shop tucked away in a quiet side street, just off the main road through Northope. It is a remnant from an earlier time, where one can simply order coffee, without the need for further elaboration. And despite the image its name might conjure up, it is not, in fact, a particularly popular place for the good folk of Northope to choose to meet. Consequently, the establishment's footfall is quite low, which was the main reason why Brazelle chose it as the place to meet with Sir Andrew. He was confident there would be little chance of being overheard, or being in any way disturbed.

Brazelle arrived shortly before ten o'clock, ordered a coffee and took a seat at a corner table. Sir Andrew, dressed in civilian clothes, arrived a few minutes later, but he was not alone. He was accompanied by a much taller and younger man who was also dressed in civilian clothes. Sir Andrew bought himself and his companion a drink, before both men went over to join Brazelle and Sir Andrew performed the introductions. "This is Inspector Jenkins, Mr Brazelle. He's my aide that I mentioned to you, and someone I felt it necessary to take into my confidence. I've told him everything, so you can speak freely, but before we begin our discussion, Jenkins has something to say, which, I believe, will explain his prescence." Sir Andrew gestured for Jenkins to take over.

"Sir Andrew has asked me to stress that he had no part in what I'm about to tell you, Mr Brazelle." Jenkins paused for a moment and looked to Sir Andrew for a nod of approval, before continuing. "As you know, Reverend, just before you and Sir Andrew met for the first time, last week, he asked me to look into your background. I believe you also know that my investigations were fruitless and Sir Andrew instructed me to stop my research. However, whilst making those original enquiries, I came across an army officer with whom I believe you're acquainted, Major Daniel Coyte-Sherman. Now, I think you should know, Mr Brazelle, I'm a fairly liberal minded and reasonably easygoing copper, and over the years I've suffered being called all sorts of unpleasant things. It's an occupational hazard, unfortunately. But I draw the line at being called a 'fucking Welsh prick', so, without saying anything to Sir Andrew, I decided to track down the Major and have a few words with him about his overuse of the Anglo-Saxon vernacular. As I think you'll agree, the surname Coyte-Sherman isn't a particularly common one, so, during my enquiries to identify and locate the Major,

I was surprised to discover yet another army officer with the same surname, a Captain Martin Coyte-Sherman. As my enquiries progressed, I discovered these two Coyte-Shermans were born on the same day, in the same place and to the same parents. It turned out that they are twins, or, more correctly, they were twins, because Captain Martin Coyte-Sherman is dead. According to army records, he died on active service, along with six others, about five and a half years ago. At that point I had temporarily drawn a blank on the Major, because my contacts in the military were either unable, or unwilling, to tell me where I could contact him. So, I decided to come at the situation from a different direction. A few months before his death, Martin Coyte-Sherman got married, so I located his widow, in the hope that she might be able to help me discover her brother-in-law's whereabouts. Accompanied by a locally based female PC who is an experienced family liaison officer, I went to see Mrs Coyte-Sherman, on the pretext of giving advice on matters of home security to young women living alone, following one or two burglaries in the area. Fortunately, we managed to quickly put Mrs Coyte-Sherman at her ease and she was soon talking about her late husband. She even went so far as to bring out her wedding photos and that's when I got a surprise...........when she showed me this picture." Jenkins took out his phone and showed Brazelle an image of the original photograph he was referring to. "Mrs Coyte-Sherman identified the bearded man standing on the left in the photo as her husband's commanding officer, who had died along with him and five others, five and a half years ago. Although you are currently clean-shaven and clearly not dead Mr Brazelle, there is little doubt in my mind that the man in the photo is you. I asked for the man's name and Mrs. Coyte-Sherman called him Chris, but gave an entirely different surname to the one you use these days. Unfortunately, Mrs. Coyte-Sherman was unable to provide any information concerning the current whereabouts of her brother-in-law, the true purpose for my call on her, but I didn't consider my visit to be a complete waste of time."

Very early on, Brazelle had guessed what was coming. "Who else knows about this?" he asked.

"Nobody," answered Sir Andrew. "The WPC who accompanied Jenkins hadn't got the faintest idea what the real reason for the visit was, and she certainly knows nothing about you. The three people sitting at this table are the only ones who know anything. You can see now why it was necessary for me to take Inspector Jenkins into my confidence."

Brazelle sat back and stared silently into the distance for a few moments, before eventually responding to Jenkins' revelation. "As you said yourself Sir Andrew, there are many reasons why someone seeks to abandon the identity they were born with. I'll let you decide what mine is. I was twenty-eight, been in the army for just over ten years and recently promoted to the rank of major, when I was approached by General Michaels, who was a brigadier in those days. He said the military chiefs and some of the country's top politicians had become tired of fighting the same enemies in different places and watching some very evil people, quite literally, get away with mass murder. And they'd decided to do something about it. Two highly specialised and top-secret units were being created to go after these people and he wanted me to lead one of them. The only people who knew who we were and what we were doing were a handful of the army top brass, a very few members of the Cabinet and a small operational support team headed by Daniel Coyte-Sherman from military intelligence. I put together my own seven-man team, choosing Martin Coyte-Sherman as my second in command and Max, the man you saw with the shotgun, Sir Andrew, as my senior NCO. The other four members of the team were all junior NCOs and we were all experienced special-forces operatives. For five years we went after the bad guys, but these weren't the sorts of people that you two gentlemen deal with. These were the people who the law never reaches. The untouchables. Illegal arms traders, warlords, terrorist leaders, international drug smugglers and the sorts of corrupt politicians who destroy nations and cause death by the thousands. Coming close to them, I found myself looking the Devil in the eye on more than one occasion.

We believed in what we were doing and thought we were making the world a better, safer place. We thought of ourselves as the other Magnificent Seven, bounty hunters, but strictly not for profit. For five years we hunted those embodiments of evil and, one by one, we removed them. And for those five years we were lucky, my team never suffered any casualties. Apart from a few minor scratches we were completely untouched, until, on the one and only occasion we involved another organisation in any part of our operations, we were more or less wiped out. Our target was an illegal arms trader who specialised in supplying terrorist groups. He had many aliases, but his real name was Jan Van Dyke, who, no doubt for the most obvious of reasons, gloried in the nickname, 'the artist'. He moved around the world constantly, but he had a base in Johannesburg, to which he occasionally returned, so we decided to take him down there. To do this we needed a safe house and, as you probably know, MI6 has many of these spread around the world, so they were asked for the use of one they had in Johannesburg. Once everything was in place, all seven of us travelled independently to South Africa to rendezvous there. It would have been too risky to try and take weapons with us into the country, so they were supplied to the safe house through MI6's connections. On arrival, the first thing we did was check them and realised immediately they'd been deactivated and were all useless. It was obvious straightaway that we'd been betrayed and needed to quickly leave. But it was too late. The place was raided by at least twenty heavily armed men and we didn't stand a chance. It was a complete bloodbath, I took three bullets and Max took four, including one in the face. As I lay slowly bleeding to death I saw Orlando for the first time. He was wandering amongst the bodies, checking that everyone was dead. The first one he came to who wasn't was Martin and he put a bullet in his head. I couldn't move and knew that in a few moments he'd get to me and simply finish me off, but one thing saved Max and me. At least some of the gunmen were not professionals, probably just local gangsters hired to do a job against seven unarmed men. They'd made so much noise that the neighbours had called the police and the sound of half a dozen police sirens panicked them. The last thing I heard before I passed out was a voice shouting at Orlando to leave, as we were obviously all dead and he needed to get out before the police arrived. That's when I heard his name 'Orlando' used for the first time. Fortunately, just before we were attacked, we'd managed to send a signal to the operations support team, just a single code word that told them we'd been betrayed and needed help. They'd immediately sent a message to the military attaché in the British Embassy in Johannesburg, ordering him to find out what had happened to us and to do whatever was necessary. By the time he got to the safe house the police had already removed the bodies of the dead and were just about to take Max and me, barely still alive, to the local hospital.

As I'm sure you both know, all too well, every police service in the world has its corrupt elements and South

Africa is no exception. Fortunately for us, the attaché had come into contact with one of them. With the help of a large bribe, he persuaded the police commander to report that seven corpses had been taken to the morgue, before arranging for Max and me to be taken, unidentified, to a private hospital on the outskirts of the city.

We were both there for about a week while we were stabilised, before being brought back to the UK and kept in a military hospital for several more weeks, still incognito. In the meantime some more money changed hands in South Africa and the bodies of my five men were repatriated.

Once we'd started to recover, General Michaels told Max and me that the deaths of all seven of us had been reported as having happened during routine military actions in the Middle East, but with no further details given. He said our funerals had already taken place with full military honours and handed me a copy of the eulogy that he'd given as my commanding officer. I read it, told him how touched I was and how I wished I'd been there to hear him give it.

When I'd recovered sufficiently to be debriefed I could remember the name Orlando, the red hair and the big feet. It didn't take Military Intelligence long to identify him as someone already on their database as a suspected freelance assassin. They had a name, almost certainly not his real one, and a description, but no photograph.

There was an investigation, of course, but the source of the leak was never identified, although General Michaels always reckoned it came from somewhere within MI6.

Because we never found the source of the leak it was decided best that Max and I stayed dead and changed our identities. By then, in any case, we'd both decided, although for different reasons, that our soldiering days were over."

"What happened to Van Dyke, the man you'd been sent to South Africa to remove?" asked Jenkins.

"Oh, he didn't survive long," said Brazelle. "I told you my team was one of two that were created. A couple of months after our betrayal, the other team went and took him out, but this time without the help of MI6."

"And what about you becoming a priest?" asked Sir Andrew. "How did that come about?"

"Whilst I was recovering in the military hospital I only ever had two visitors, General Michaels, and an army chaplain called, very appropriately, Padre Monk. The Padre gave me a Bible and we talked together a lot. It was the only book I read whilst I was in the hospital and at some point something happened to me. It was my Damoscene moment, if you like. My epiphany. I can remember it just as if it was just minutes ago. And in that second I was changed."

"How did you come to choose your new name?" asked Jenkins.

"I decided to keep my original Christian name, but the surname I took from a man I once met in a bar in Beirut. He was a wealthy Lebanese diamond trader and I won his Ferrari from him playing poker. I guess I thought it might bring me luck."

"And has it?" asked Jenkins.

Brazelle smiled and nodded. "Yes, I believe it has."

"Thank you for trusting us with that information, Mr Brazelle. You can be confident that it will go no further," said Sir Andrew, looking at Jenkins to receive his nod of agreement. "But, before we get to the subject of Gant, I thought you might like to know about Reverend Pickering. He's been living in a small French town, St-Étienne-du-Grès, about an hour's drive from Marseille, using an assumed name and passing himself off as a prosperous olive grower. We've also identified the source of his apparent wealth. He was involved in a series of mortgage scams, which we believe may have netted upto ten million pounds, not to mention the twenty thousand or so that he pilfered from the Church of England and the good folk of Prinsted. He's currently under arrest in Marseille and should be back in Britain within the next few days to stand trial. I've already alerted the Diocese, because when this goes public, the press will probably be all over it. You might want to keep a low profile until it all dies down."

"Thanks for the warning," responded Brazelle. "For a while I thought Pickering might have pilfered rather more than a few thousand from the Church, but it seems I was wrong."

Brazelle moved to the subject of Gant and Orlando. He started by recounting a great deal of what he had discovered over the past few days, but made no reference to anything that was irrelevant to the matter under discussion, such as the phalera, the parentage of Gareth, or what happened during the time that Mrs Richards was looking after Rose on the day her mother died. To begin with, he also omitted mentioning the relationship between Gant and the Harfield family.

Having laid out the facts, he intended to give details of what he believed had happened during the period between the death of Justine and the death of Sir Cornelius, but first explained how The Agency communicated with Justine. "Frank Weston had asked Mrs Richards, the housekeeper of Harfield House, which newspaper Justine had been reading just before she went out on the morning she died. She told him it was a local newspaper, The Morning Chronicle, the one that Justine read every morning. My first thought was that it was an odd question for Weston to have asked, but then it occurred to me that he might be looking for a reason why Justine should suddenly, at very short notice, decide to leave the House, especially without taking Rose with her. Was it because of something she'd just read in the paper? He'd put a copy of that day's Morning Chronicle in the box he gave me, so I went through it Fortunately, I started with the personal ads, because very quickly, I came to one written in Italian:

'Bella, andare al ponte alle 12:00. Amore Marco'.

Or, in English:

'Bella, go to the bridge at 12 noon. Love Marco'.

I then visited the office of the Morning Chronicle and they were kind enough to let me explore their archives. I was particularly interested in the edition of the day before Justine died, which was the last time she took Rose to the playground. And guess what? In the personal ads there was another message for Bella from Marco, again written in Italian.

'Bella, venire a giocare alle 14:00. Io sventolano a voi. Amore Marco'.

Or, in English:

> 'Bella, come to play at 2pm. I will wave to you.
> Love Marco'.

Going back through earlier editions of The Morning Chronicle, I found a number of other communications from Marco to Bella, although not a single one from Bella to Marco and, apart from the one I've just mentioned, none suggesting that any actual meeting was going to take place. This is how The Agency communicated with Justine, through placing messages in the Personal Ads column of The Morning Chronicle and the use of two drop-points. The first drop-point was close to one of the bridges over the stream that Justine drowned in, although not the one she fell from, and the second was at the playground, where she often took Rose. They were both places where Justine could pick up her instructions and also put her response, ready for collection. The ads in the Morning Chronicle informed her which drop-point to use and when she should go. There was no need for any regular face-to-face contact. Mrs Richards saw Justine leave the House grounds through the door in Napoleon's Wall a number of times. I think it's likely she was going to a drop-point on those occasions and, very probably, on numerous other occasions when she wasn't observed. She also had plenty of opportunities to either make a drop, or collect instructions, at the drop-point at the playground.

We may never know when Justine was first approached by The Agency and told her cover was blown, so the blackmail could begin. It might have been some time after she married Sir Cornelius. Perhaps it was after Rose was born, when she had so much more to lose if she refused to cooperate. I have little doubt, though, if she had refused to cooperate, she would have been disposed of. Had she gone to the authorities, then the trail back to Gant might have been uncovered and he would have been exposed as the man who had vetted her and declared her clean, when she most certainly was not. No doubt country living with a wealthy reclusive baronet and a child she adored must have suited Justine right down to the ground, especially after some of the things she'd had to endure in her earlier life. She would have been very reluctant to put it all at risk. Maybe, as you suggested, Sir Andrew, the early demands were low-key to draw her in ever deeper, until she was in so far that there really was no escape. The demands could then grow, as she would have had the constant fear of losing Rose, her most treasured possession. Justine's problems began when she was a victim in Italy and, for the rest of her short life, she remained a victim."

"At what point do you think Orlando first appeared on the scene?" asked Sir Andrew.

"It's impossible to be certain," Brazelle replied. "However, the fact that Justine chose not to take Rose with her on the morning of her death suggests to me that Orlando was not her usual handler and that her meeting with him at the playground, the previous day, was very likely the first time she'd met him. And having met him, she decided she didn't want Rose anywhere near him. In fact, I believe that she had rarely, and possibly never, come face to face with anyone from The Agency until she met Orlando at the playground. Knowing what I do about Orlando, I can confirm that handling spies is not his usual practice, but killing them certainly is. And that made me wonder if he'd been brought onto the scene because The Agency was beginning to have doubts about Justine's reliability and Orlando was there to make an assessment and, if necessary, take appropriate action. After Justine returned from the playground, the day before she died, Mrs Richards said she appeared unusually agitated. I believe that was a result of meeting with Orlando, who'd unnerved her. After that, of course, Justine suffered a fatal accident and the concerns of The Agency shifted.

After Orlando had visited Prinsted with you, Sir Andrew, and satisfied himself that Justine really was dead, the only matter left to attend to was the question of whether or not she'd left any incriminating evidence behind. If she had, then The Agency needed to find it and remove it. And I believe I know how they did this, as I shall shortly explain.

As I've already told you, about a week after Justine's death, Frank Weston returned her handbag to Harfield House. Along with a few other items, the handbag contained three keys, two small ones on a key ring and a slightly larger one that looked just like a house door key. Sir Cornelius, Frances and Mrs Richards all said they'd never seen any of the keys before and had no idea what they opened. Rose told me Justine had a locked cabinet in her bedroom with a box inside which she also kept locked. She told me about an incident where her mother became quite concerned and uncharacteristically angry with her when she thought that the keys to the cabinet and the box had gone missing, and how she then insisted on keeping details of the episode secret. I believe that the keys Rose saw on that occasion were the two small keys later found in Justine's handbag. When Sir Cornelius investigated what the keys were for, the obvious place for him to start was in Justine's bedroom and I doubt it took him long to identify the cabinet and the box that they opened. Quite what the box contained I can only guess at, but it was clearly something that Justine wished to keep secret. Perhaps it held clues to her real identity, such as an old passport, or her birth certificate. Possibly there was something relating specifically to what she'd been up to on behalf of The Agency, maybe even a written confession. Whatever it was, it led Sir Cornelius to realise that his wife had deceived and betrayed him. That's almost certainly why Frances found him sobbing in front of Justine's portrait and why he instructed that it should be destroyed. It also explains why his mood changed from one of abject grief to a more tempered sadness. However, for the sake of Rose no doubt, he chose not to tell anyone in the household what he'd discovered. Would he have wanted Rose to grow up knowing that the mother she adored had deceived and betrayed her father? But, I believe he did share the details of his discovery with one other person, someone who he thought should know, and also someone he thought he could trust. Unfortunately, in doing so, he signed his own death warrant. That person was Ted Gant."

Sir Andrew was shocked. "Why on earth would he tell Ted Gant?"

"Because, and I only found this out yesterday, it turns out they were very close friends. Close enough, in fact, for Sir Cornelius and Justine to choose Gant and his wife to be Rose's godparents. It would have been perfectly normal for Gant to contact Sir Cornelius to offer his condolences on the death of his wife and, no doubt, offer his support should Sir Cornelius feel he needed it. Sir Cornelius knew, of course, that Gant was an MI5 officer and so it's not surprising that it was to him that he turned when he found out that Justine had betrayed him. In fact, it would have been surprising if he hadn't. When Sir Cornelius did eventually contact Gant to tell him about Justine, I imagine Gant urged him not to let anyone else know what he'd discovered, whilst he had a chance to work out a strategy. After that discussion, I have little doubt that the first person Gant called was Orlando and a plan to recover the incriminating evidence and remove Sir Cornelius was hatched. Whilst all members of the household were assumed to be at Justine's funeral, Orlando went through the door in Napoleon's Wall and entered the House via the kitchen, leaving some muddy footprints behind. He turned off the alarm using Justine's code, removed the CCTV video from the recorder and, using the key that's kept in the cupboard on the landing, accessed Sir Cornelius' studio. That was where Sir Cornelius had left the box containing the incriminating evidence that he'd discovered in the cabinet in Justine's bedroom. Orlando had been briefed about Sir Cornelius' habit of making a written note of just about every new thought he ever had, so knew exactly where to look for anything Sir Cornelius might have written about the matter. He inspected Sir Cornelius' most current notebook and ripped out the relevant pages.

If Orlando had been able to take the two small keys from Justine's handbag on his visit to Prinsted with you, Sir Andrew, then Sir Cornelius might never have had to die. Orlando could have retrieved Justine's box himself and probably nobody would have been any the wiser. But as it was, Sir Cornelius was a loose end that had to be dealt with.

When Mrs Richards first told me about the so called 'burglar' who took nothing more than a video tape, I was puzzled why they hadn't switched the alarm back on when they eventually left and also removed the muddy footprints they'd made on their way in. If they had, then it would probably have been several days before Jonathan noticed that the video tape was missing and, with everything else that was happening, he might simply have thought it an oversight, which is exactly what he did when he found a second tape was missing a few days later. I believe I now know the answer to these questions. Orlando was the person who entered the House through the kitchen, but he hadn't left and was still there, hidden somewhere in the studio when Cornelius returned from Justine's funeral. Very soon afterwards he killed him. Orlando is a professional killer and was a much younger man than Cornelius, who wouldn't have stood a chance. Finally, Orlando created a suicide note by writing the word SORRY on a blank sheet of paper and very carefully copying Sir Cornelius' signature as it appeared on the paintings in the studio. Part of Orlando's specialised skill set is forging other people's handwriting and I have to say he's very good at it. But, in this particular case, he was forging the wrong signature.

Orlando assumed that Sir Cornelius wouldn't be missed for a while because of his habit of locking himself away in his studio, sometimes for a couple of days. And he knew it wasn't safe to leave the House during the night, because of the household routine of setting the alarm. But he was able to monitor all the comings and goings, to and from the House, using the CCTV monitors in the studio. So he simply waited for an opportunity to leave unseen, taking all the incriminating evidence with him. When Mrs Richards went out to do some shopping, he thought his opportunity had arrived. He removed the replacement tape from the CCTV recorder, left the House by the kitchen door and exited the grounds by the door in Napoleon's Wall. He must have thought he was home and dry, but there was something he didn't know. When he entered the House at the time of Justine's funeral and, again, the next day when he was leaving, the Richards' eleven year old son, Gareth, was watching him from the tree house. Even better, Gareth was photographing him and I have copies of the photographs he took."

Sir Andrew became animated. "Good heavens, Brazelle, why didn't the boy say something and produce these photographs when Sir Cornelius' death was being investigated?"

Brazelle gave a faint shrug. "For the very simple reason, Sir Andrew, that nobody asked him. What you must understand is that Gareth was not your average eleven year old. His emotional and social responses were, and still are, generally different to the norm within his peer group. If he'd been asked if he saw anyone, or took any photographs, on the two days in question, then I'm sure he would have told what he saw and produced the photographs. But nobody did."

"Having the photographs obviously helps a great deal and the narrative you've given all fits together very plausibly," said Sir Andrew. "But where did Orlando get the key he needed to get into the House, not to mention the codes to open the door in Napoleon's Wall and turn off the alarm system? And how did he come to know so much about Sir Cornelius' habits and the layout of the House, even down to knowing where the key to the studio was hidden in the landing cupboard? I cannot believe that Justine was the source for any of this."

"You're right, of course. Justine didn't provide any of it..... well..........not knowingly, anyway," replied Brazelle. "I'll explain everything in a moment, but first I have a question for you. When we first spoke, you never mentioned Justine's handbag, the one she dropped on the bridge. Did Frank Weston show it to you?"

Sir Andrew nodded. "Yes, he did. I seem to remember he showed us the contents to confirm that it didn't look like a robbery had taken place."

"And did Orlando handle the handbag?" asked Brazelle.

Sir Andrew took a moment to think before responding. "Yes, I believe he did. Why do you ask?"

"When Orlando handled the handbag, I believe he switched the large key that was in it, for one he just happened to have with him," Brazelle replied. "It would have been a spur of the moment thing, having been presented with an opportunity to take something that he thought might later prove useful. He probably guessed it was likely to be a key to one of the external doors of Harfield House. A few days later, when he entered the House grounds through the door in Napoleon's Wall, it would have been the kitchen door that he came to first, the door that the key opened. Justine had taken it out of the kitchen door lock when she took Rose to be looked after by Mrs Richards.

I believe Orlando also took a good look at the contents of the notebook in Justine's handbag. He would have seen the code to open the door through Napoleon's Wall as well as Justine's House security alarm code, both clearly identified. Justine wasn't very good at remembering numbers, so, if there was a number she might need, she wrote it in the notebook which she usually carried in her handbag.

I was initially puzzled about the route Justine had taken back to Harfield House, but later realised it made perfect sense. She'd left Rose distraught, so would have wanted to return to her as soon as possible, and the quickest route back was through the door in Napoleon's Wall, before re-entering the House through the kitchen. That's why she'd taken the key to the kitchen door.

As for Orlando's knowledge of the layout of the House and intelligence on Sir Cornelius' habits, I have no doubt that Gant was the source. As a close friend of Sir Cornelius, he would have been a reasonably frequent visitor to the House and to Sir Cornelius' studio, so in addition to everything else, he probably also knew about the key that was kept hidden in the landing cupboard."

Brazelle told Jenkins and Sir Andrew about Gant being currently at Harfield House as a guest until Saturday and gave details of their private conversation.

Sir Andrew showed concern. "You're playing a dangerous game, Mr Brazelle. By telling Gant you have evidence that Sir Cornelius was murdered and claiming to know how it was done and who did it, you are without doubt making yourself a target."

"And that is exactly what I want to be, Sir Andrew," said Brazelle. "I think it's the only way we'll flush Gant out and, assuming he's still alive, Orlando. I want justice for my men and I'm prepared to take a risk to achieve it. But I doubt Gant will simply send an assassin to put a bullet in my head. That would be too risky and, for all he knows, I might be deluding myself. First he'll want to find out whether or not I do have any real evidence. Once he's confirmed that I do, he'll want to locate and remove it, before removing me, but he won't want it to look too obviously like murder. No doubt he'll commission Orlando, or, if he's dead, someone with similar skills. But there's something else you should know. I've already told Daniel Coyte-Sherman everything I've just told you, so, if anything does happen to me, you can be assured that Gant will never become Director of MI6, although it will be extra-judicial action that stops him."

The implication of what he had just heard caused Sir Andrew to become quite agitated. "Good grief, man. I can't condone action like that. I'm a senior police officer."

Brazelle smiled. "Well, in that case, I assume you'll be keen to help me achieve my objective by judicial means."

Sir Andrew calmed slightly. "What is it you want? And it had better be something legal."

"I understand," said Brazelle. "I want you to ensure that no police officer comes anywhere near me, or Holford, for the next few days. I think there's a very good chance I'll have unexpected visitors of one sort or another and I don't want to scare them off. Is that agreed?"

Sir Andrew looked at Jenkins and both men nodded. "Anything else?" asked Sir Andrew.

"Yes," replied Brazelle. "You can pray for me."

Brazelle returned home, convinced he wouldn't have to wait long before Gant contacted him and sure enough, just after noon, the phone rang.

"Are you alone and able to talk, Mr Brazelle," asked Gant.

"Yes, where would you like me to begin?"

"You could start by telling me what evidence you have to back up your claim that Cornelius was murdered," said Gant. "What exactly have you got?"

Brazelle smiled to himself. "Well, in addition to a substantial amount of circumstantial evidence, I have clear proof that the supposed suicide note is a forgery and photographic evidence of the comings and goings of a mysterious red-haired man. Oddly enough, it was the same red-haired man who turned up with an officer from the Met a couple of weeks earlier, ostensibly to investigate the death of Lady Justine. I have a photograph taken of him on that occasion, as well."

Brazelle was confident he had said more than enough to unnerve Gant and ensure there would be some kind of incriminating response in the very near future.

There was a relatively long pause before Gant eventually responded. "What you've just told me certainly warrants further investigation and you came to the right person to ensure that it happens. I shall ensure the appropriate people become involved, in the strictest confidence, of course, and that they contact you as soon as possible. When we spoke last night you told me that you had not discussed this matter with anyone else. I would welcome receiving your guarantee that will remain the case until we agree otherwise."

Brazelle gave Gant the assurance he was asking for and the call ended.

Day Fourteen - Friday

Brazelle was confident that at some time in the near future he would be approached, but had no idea what form the contact might take. In the meantime, he was determined to try and behave normally, trusting that he had put all possible contingencies in place, without putting his plan at risk. He thought it most likely that the initial approach would be for the purpose of finding out the detail of what he had discovered and getting him to hand over any physical evidence he possessed, although he knew this was far from guaranteed. There was a very real risk that the first approach might also be intended to be the last, but he wanted justice for Sir Cornelius and Justine, as well as, for his men who had been betrayed and he was prepared to take risks to try and achieve it.

It was just before nine in the morning and Brazelle was about to go over to the Church, when a car pulled into Holford's yard. Its two occupants introduced themselves as Inspector Rodgers and Sergeant Palmer of Special Branch and said they wished to speak to Brazelle on a highly confidential matter. Sir Andrew had assured Brazelle that no police officer would come near Holford, so he was quite sure it was the approach he had been expecting and invited them into his cottage.

Inspector Rodgers opened up the conversation. "Before I explain why we're here Reverend Brazelle, I need to stress that this meeting should be treated as strictly confidential. You must not tell anyone about it, not even that it took place. Do you understand?"

"Yes, of course," responded Brazelle. "Absolutely."

Rodgers continued. "We understand that you've been carrying out an investigation into the death of Sir Cornelius Harfield. As you will be aware, investigations carried out at the time of his death, twenty years ago, led to the conclusion that he killed himself whilst in a depressed state, following the accidental death of his wife. However, we've been informed that you claim to have uncovered evidence that points to Sir Cornelius' death being due to foul play. Since Sir Cornelius was involved in a number of highly confidential matters, some having potential implications for issues of national security, Special Branch have been alerted to your claims and we've been instructed to come and interview you. We'd like you to tell us exactly what you've discovered, but first, we'd like to know if you've mentioned your findings to anyone else."

Brazelle, not for the first time, crossed his fingers and lied. "Sir Ted Gant is the only person I've discussed this matter with. I believe it's because of that conversation that the two of you are here. He said I should expect a visit. I'll be happy to share with you everything I've discovered so far. I'll go and get it."

Brazelle brought Frank Weston's box out of the study and placed it on the table in front of his two inquisitors. "Everything I have, every last scrap of evidence I have uncovered, is in this box and there are no copies. Apart from me you'll be the only other people alive who've ever seen it."

When Brazelle removed the lid, the first thing visible, as he intended it should be, was the sheet of paper with the name ORLANDO written on it. Rodgers and Palmer looked at each other with expressions that Brazelle took to be ones of shock, tinged with amazement.

Brazelle pulled his copy of Gareth's photo CD out of the box. "This contains a number of photographs of the comings and goings at Harfield House around the time of Sir Cornelius' murder. They were taken by someone who just clicks away at anything and everything, without ever realising just what they've caught on camera. Even today the photographer doesn't realise the importance of some of the photos on this disc. Did you ever see the film, Blow Up, with Vanessa Redgrave and David Hemmings?"

Each of Rodgers and Palmer, still in shock from what they had just seen in the box, simply shook their head in response to Brazelle's irrelevant and deliberately fatuous question.

Brazelle continued. "The film was made in 1967, directed by Antoniono. It's a bit art-house and something of an acquired taste, but if you do see it you'll know exactly what I mean." Next, he pulled out the copy of The Morning Chronicle from the day that Justine died and showed his visitors the message written in Italian. "Lady Justine was spying on her husband and this is how her handlers communicated with her, through personal ads written in Italian in her morning newspaper." He then returned the CD and newspaper to Weston's box and replaced the lid. "There's a lot more in here. I imagine you'll want to take it with you, won't you?"

"Yes, we do," Rodgers replied. "I'm afraid we'll have to insist on it. Are you sure there's absolutely nothing else?"

"Well, there is just one more thing in the bedroom that I think you should see." Brazelle opened the bedroom door, but didn't enter. Instead he just stepped aside to allow Daniel Coyte-Sherman to step out, carrying a pump action shotgun.

"Couldn't you have brought something a little less powerful?" Brazelle asked. "If that thing goes off, not only will it blow these two misfits apart, it'll probably wreck my sitting room."

Coyte-Sherman gave a slight shrug. "To be honest, I'm not too worried about what happens to these two and, quite frankly, the room looks like it could do with a makeover."

The fake policemen remained silent and slowly raised their hands.

A few moments later Max arrived, handed his shotgun to Brazelle and searched the two prisoners, placing everything he found onto the table. "Since when did Special Branch start carrying Smith and Wesson's with silencers?" he asked.

"They don't," said Brazelle, handing Max back his shotgun. "But these two aren't from Special Branch. Are you gentlemen?"

The prisoners made no response.

Brazelle inspected everything Max had placed on the table before turning his attention back to his two prisoners. "Right, we'll cut to the chase then shall we. In a moment I'm going to ask you a series of questions and you are going to answer them, or you will die and I suspect, not painlessly. Your situation is hopeless and it's as simple as that. Do you understand?"

"You're a priest. Do you really think we believe you'd kill two unarmed men in cold blood," said Rodgers.

"Well, you're not wrong there," said Brazelle. "My killing days are over, but not for my two friends here. I saw your reaction to seeing the name Orlando in that box, so before I ask my questions, I think there are a couple of things you should know."

Brazelle put his hand on Coyte-Sherman's shoulder. "I watched Orlando put a bullet into the head of this man's twin brother. And the man with the shotgun over there has Orlando to thank for his scars and his eye patch. Whereas, I want justice for Cornelius and Justine Harfield and five of my friends whose deaths Orlando is responsible for, these two will settle for simple straightforward revenge. If you two are barriers to them getting it, then you are dead men and by the time you are, I strongly suspect you'll be glad of it. I shall now ask my questions and leave. What happens after that is between you two and these two. Where is Orlando? What is your means of communication with him? And what were you planning to do after you'd got my evidence? That's it. I shall now go for a walk."

Brazelle opened the front door and was about to step outside as Max pointed his shotgun at Rodgers' left leg. "I'll start by blowing a leg off each of them with this. That should give them some encouragement," he said.

Both prisoners immediately called out to Brazelle, "Wait!"

Brazelle closed the door and re-entered his sitting room. "I'm listening," he said.

"We don't know where Orlando is," said Rodgers. "We were just told to find out what you know, take away any physical evidence that you had and then report back to him."

Brazelle nodded and smiled. "And presumably, after you'd removed whatever evidence I had, he'd turn up at some point and remove me. No doubt making it look like an accident, or that my desire to get ever closer to God had overwhelmed me?"

"We don't know what he planned to do," said Rodgers. "We were to contact him after we left and that was it. Then he was going to contact us later, so he could collect whatever we'd taken off you. We don't know any more."

"What are you going to do with us now?" Palmer asked nervously.

"We're going to hand you over to the police," Brazelle replied. "And since every word you've spoken here today has been recorded, I imagine you'll be going to jail for a long time.........although only if you're lucky! You'd better hope we get to Orlando before he finds out what's just happened. If we don't, I seriously doubt you'll ever get to start a prison sentence."

Brazelle made a brief phone call and a short while later six police officers in plain clothes arrived in three unmarked police cars. Inspector Jenkins was the only one of the six to enter the cottage where he handcuffed each of the prisoners before passing them out to his men. He asked Brazelle what he intended to do next.

"I'm going to send a message to Orlando, confirming phase one of his plan has been successfully completed and then I'll wait here with Max. I doubt it'll be long before Orlando arrives, he'll want to minimise the risk of me talking to anyone. In the meantime, Danny will come with you and brief you on everything that's just happened. He's got the fake policemen's weapons and a recording of everything they said, including their admission of what they intended to do."

Jenkins stepped out into the yard and as Coyte-Sherman went to follow him, Brazelle grabbed his arm and whispered in his ear. "Don't worry about the death threats I made, Danny, I didn't record any of that."

Outside, Jenkins introduced himself to Coyte-Sherman. "Just so you know, Major, I'm the man you called a fucking Welsh prick when we spoke on the phone a few days ago. I was hoping we might meet up sometime. I wanted to give you a chance to repeat it to my face. Seems it's my lucky day all round."

Coyte-Sherman looked up at the much taller Jenkins. "Are you sure it was me?" he asked

Jenkins opened the car door, grinned broadly and gestured for Coyte-Sherman to get in. "Oh yes, it was definitely you. We'll discuss it later, shall we?"

Brazelle drove into the village where he could get a good phone signal and sent a message to Orlando using Rodgers' phone. A reply quickly came confirming its receipt and Brazelle returned home. Less than an hour later, a tall man with red hair and big feet walked into the yard and approached the cottage.

Brazelle opened the front door. "Can I help you?" he asked.

"Well, I was hoping you could," replied Orlando. "My car's just broken down about fifty yards up the road. Unfortunately I can't get a signal on my phone to call the breakdown service, so I was hoping you'd be good enough to let me use your landline. I noticed the telephone wires connected up to your cottage."

Brazelle gritted his teeth and smiled. "Sure. Not a problem. Come on in."

Orlando took a good look around the sitting room assessing his best plan of attack. If he was to make Brazelle's death look like anything but murder, he knew it was important to take his intended victim by surprise and leave no trace of a struggle.

With his eyes fixed firmly on Orlando, Brazelle pointed to the study door. "The phone is in there on the desk. Go in and help yourself."

Orlando was a man in his mid fifties, but he still had the reflexes of a man half his age. Pushing open the study door to see Max's shotgun pointing straight at him, he moved out of the line of fire and lunged at Brazelle, pulling out a dagger as he did.

The struggle lasted for several minutes and Max could only watch and wait, hoping for an opportunity to take a shot at Orlando without also endangering Brazelle. Eventually, a split-second opportunity appeared and Max took it. The blast, especially at such close range, was so powerful it blew Orlando backwards onto the bedroom door which was knocked clean off its hinges by the impact. With one barrel of his shotgun still loaded, Max went to take a closer look at the body.

"Is he dead?" asked Brazelle.

"Well if he isn't he will be in a second," replied Max, before, moments later, shaking his head and declaring him well and truly dead. "So, what now, boss?" he asked.

"Well, your part is complete, but I'm beginning to think that for me only the easy bit is over. Later today I'm going to have to tell Rose that for the past two days she's been entertaining the man who is ultimately responsible for the death of her father. But first I'd better let Sir Andrew know what's happened."

Brazelle went into the study, dialled Sir Andrew's private number and within three rings it was answered. "Who is it?" asked the operator.

Max was standing in the study's open doorway, so privacy was impossible. Brazelle sighed, gritted his teeth and gave his password. "I am a weird priest."

"You can say that again," said a grinning Max.

Before Brazelle could respond with something unbecoming of a priest, Sir Andrew came on the line. "Are you alright, Brazelle? Is everything working out?"

Brazelle gave his report. "I expect Inspector Jenkins has already told you about the phoney Special Branch officers, well, phase two has now also been completed. Orlando paid me a visit, but it didn't end well for him, or for much of my home. Other than that, everything's fine. I guess it's now over to you to decide the next steps?"

"By 'didn't end well for him', I assume you mean he's dead," said Sir Andrew.

"As a door nail," Brazelle replied.

"Well, in that case I'd like you to step away from your cottage," said Sir Andrew. "I anticipated something like this might happen, so I've had a specialist team on stand-by, not far away from you. I'll send them over to your place to pick up Orlando's body and carry out the necessaries. They know what to do. Why don't you go over to Harfield House and pay Gant and the Harfields a visit. Take Frank Weston's box with you, I don't want that to go missing." Sir Andrew paused for a moment before continuing. "I assume Orlando was killed…….in…… self defence?"

"That's what I'd call it," said Brazelle. "Orlando came here intending to kill me and, like I said, it didn't end well for him."

"We can discuss that later, if necessary," replied Sir Andrew. "I'm going to head up there myself as soon as we've finished this call. I want to be the one to arrest Gant. I'll let Jenkins know what's happened and rendezvous with both of you at Harfield House in a couple of hours. In the meantime, please don't mention anything of what has happened today to anyone else, anyone at all. And make sure your Glaswegian friend understands that as well."

Brazelle patted Max on the shoulder. "You earned your stripes today, old friend and, not for the first time, you saved my life. I owe you one."

"We owe each other. And more than one," replied Max.

Brazelle nodded. "I guess that's true. But tell me honestly, would you really have blown their legs off?"

Max smiled. "Would you have let me?"

It was now Brazelle who smiled, but he gave no reply.

Brazelle had already downloaded the contents of the phones belonging to the two bogus police officers. It didn't take him long to determine which of Orlando's fingers was the one with the print needed to gain access to his phone. Through exploring the call logs of all three phones, he was able to draw a number of conclusions about the sequence of events that occurred after his first conversation with Gant. In particular, he believed he had identified Gant's phone number. After driving over to the Church, using Orlando's phone, he sent Gant the message, 'Job completed'. A short while later he drove over to Harfield House.

When Jonathan showed Brazelle into the drawing room it was a few minutes past two o'clock and the family and their two guests had just returned from the dining room having finished lunch. Rose immediately jumped up to greet him. "This is a pleasant surprise," she said, "and you're just in time to join us for some tea."

Brazelle doubted that Rose was the only one who was surprised to see him, as he glanced over at an ashen-faced Sir Ted Gant.

"Are you alright, Sir Ted?" he asked. "I hope you don't mind me mentioning it, but I can't help noticing that you look rather paler than when we last met."

"Yes, thank you. I'm perfectly fine," replied Sir Ted. "It must be the fact that it's now daylight and the last time we met it was in artificial light. However, if you'll all excuse me, I would just like to pop out for a moment."

"Actually Ted's colour had changed a little," said Frances. "Do you think you should go after him Damien and make sure he's alright?"

Damien went to do as Frances suggested, but Lady Helen caught his sleeve. "No, really, he'll be fine, Damien.

Don't worry yourself. He's probably eaten too much and got a little indigestion. I'm sure he'll be back and right as rain in just a few minutes. I expect he's gone to get an antacid tablet."

Brazelle thought he knew exactly what Sir Ted had gone off to do and it had nothing to do with antacid tablets. Orlando's phone was in his jacket pocket and when he felt it begin to silently vibrate, he knew he was right.

A few minutes later Sir Ted returned, still pale faced and appearing agitated.

"Are you sure you're alright, dear?" Lady Helen asked.

Sir Ted was rather abrupt in his response. "Yes. Yes, absolutely fine........but I'm afraid I've got some bad news. I know we were planning to leave some time tomorrow, but I've just had a message from the office. They want me to return to London, more or less straight away, so it looks like we'll have to get packed up and leave. It's been really lovely seeing you all again and we must get together again very soon.......Come along Helen, we'd better get our things together and head off."

Lady Helen was used to having to cope with sudden changes of plan by her husband, so meekly followed orders and accompanied him up to their room.

"Well, that was a bit unexpected," said Damien. "Something important must have come up. I hope we're not in for yet another major crisis in government."

"I suppose we'd better go and make sure they don't forget anything," said Frances.

"Or steal the towels!" Damien joked, as he followed his wife out of the drawing room.

"I'd better go and see them off as well," said Rose, "but you don't have to, if you don't want, Chris. I get the feeling you're not too keen on my Godfather and that the feeling might be mutual. I saw the way he looked at you when you first arrived....... if looks could kill!"

If only she knew how right she was, thought Brazelle. "Oh, I'll come along as well," he said, thinking he might have to improvise some stalling tactic, having got his timing wrong. As he followed Rose into the entrance hall, however, he was relieved to discover he had got it just right. Sir Ted and Lady Helen were descending the stairs just as Jonathan was opening the front door to Sir Andrew, Inspector Jenkins, and four other uniformed police officers.

Sir Ted was in shock. "Good Lord! What on earth are you doing here, Andrew?"

Sir Andrew was in no mood for discussion. "Oh, come on Gant, you know it's all over," he said, before turning to Brazelle. "Do you want to explain things, Reverend?"

Brazelle knew this would be the tricky bit. What he had to divulge would come as a shock to the entire household and be especially upsetting for the Harfield sisters, but he could think of no painless way to reveal it. "I have something unexpected to disclose," he said. "It's something that Rose and Frances, in particular, will find distressing, but there is no easy way to explain it to you." He took Orlando's phone out of his pocket. "This phone belonged to the man who murdered Sir Cornelius. I'm going to press the call button and, when I do, the phone of the man who sent him to do it will ring." Within seconds, a ringing tone was heard coming from Gant's jacket pocket.

A look of horror developed on Frances' face, but she remained silent. Rose, though, burst into tears, and as Brazelle moved to comfort her she pushed him away and ran upstairs.

Sir Andrew stepped forward and initiated the legal formalities. "Sir Ted Gant, I'm arresting you on suspicion of conspiracy to murder, contravening the Official Secrets Act and Treason."

One of the other officers completed proceedings by reading Gant his rights and the crowd that had formed in the hallway began to disperse. Jonathan went off to tell his wife what had just happened, Damien and Frances returned to the drawing room and the four officers who had arrived with Sir Andrew and Jenkins removed Gant and his wife.

Brazelle went out to his car with Jenkins and Sir Andrew, handed them Frank Weston's box and the three phones he had collected before asking what would happen to Gant's wife.

"Oh, she'll be questioned as a potential accomplice," said Sir Andrew. "It's going to be hard for her to argue that she knew nothing, after being married to the chap for the past thirty years, but in the end it comes down to what we can prove. Gant himself, on the other hand, is going to go down for life. The evidence we've already got is pretty damning, and was easily enough to convince a judge to give me some search warrants. As we speak, teams are searching his house, his villa in Spain, his boat and his office, so I think it's highly likely we'll turn up more evidence. I briefed the Home Secretary, Foreign Secretary and the PM earlier.

Understandably they were shocked, especially since they really did have Gant pencilled in for the number one spot at MI6 early next year. I'll let them know what's happened while I'm on the way back to London and meet up with them later. At the moment, they can say they inherited Gant as Deputy Director of MI6 and take the credit for exposing him, so it's hearts and flowers all round. But, if they were the people who promoted him, they'd be political toast. They'll probably want to give you some kind of reward, if only for saving their political skins, although it won't involve any kind of public recognition, which I assume you wouldn't want in any case. Whilst we're on the subject of public recognition, there's something I need to stress on you. Don't talk to anyone about what happened at your place earlier today. Not to anyone at all, about any part of it. Can I assume you are content to comply?"

"That suits me just fine," replied Brazelle, "and you can tell the PM I have no need of a reward. I've got the people responsible for the death of my men and as I told you before, I'm strictly not for profit."

"I understand," said Sir Andrew. "And there are no rewards from me, but if there's anything I can do for you in the future, providing it's legal, I'll do my best to help."

"That's very kind, Sir Andrew," said Brazelle. "As it happens there is something I could use your help with straightaway and perhaps you'll find the support of the PM might prove useful."

Brazelle pulled two sheets of paper out of his inside pocket. "It's all explained in fine detail here."

Sir Andrew took the papers and quickly read through them, before passing them to Jenkins and giving an ironic response. "My God, you don't want much for your money. Do you, Reverend? And just when do you want this done by?"

"Well, I know it's a bit of a tall order and you've got a lot of far more important matters to deal with, so how about some time tomorrow?" Brazelle replied, with equal irony.

Jenkins burst out laughing and even Sir Andrew managed a hint of a smile before responding. "I think you're right, I probably will need the PM to lend a hand on this one, but I'll see what I can do. Now though, we're leaving. I want to know what the search teams have come up with and I've also got some anxious politicians to deal with. On a more personal note though, I hope things work out between you and Rose. She's now aware that for the past few days you knowingly left her in the company of the man who ordered her father's murder. But don't worry about issues around her mother. I don't think there'll be any need for that to come out and you can be sure Gant's trial won't be a public affair. In fact, when all this gets out, there'll be a lot of angry and vengeful people out there and we'll probably have to work hard just to keep him alive until he gets to court. Maybe we'd all be saved a lot of pain and grief if somebody did just........."

Brazelle interrupted. "Steady, Sir Andrew, you're beginning to sound like I used to and look how that turned out."

Sir Andrew held out his hand. "Goodbye, Reverend."

"And good luck," added Jenkins.

Just before getting into his car Sir Andrew paused and turned to face Brazelle. "One last thing, Mr Brazelle, it's something that's been puzzling me ever since our first meeting. Were you bluffing when you threatened to go to the press?"

Brazelle smiled. "Have a safe journey back to London, Sir Andrew."

As they drove away, Sir Andrew also had a question for Jenkins. "Have you learnt anything from this case, Jenkins, something to bear in mind in the future?"

"I most certainly have, Sir," Jenkins replied.

"And what is it?"

"Don't mess with the Church of England," said Jenkins.

Sir Andrew grinned. "You're a fast learner and clearly set to go far, CHIEF Inspector."

After saying his goodbyes to Jenkins and Sir Andrew, Brazelle joined Frances and Damien in the drawing room.

"I've just finished telling Damien what we discovered on Monday evening," said Frances. "It's been difficult, keeping it to myself until now, but I did as we agreed. But, for God's sake, Chris, why on earth would Ted Gant of all people, want to have my father killed?"

Brazelle knew this question would be asked of him at some point, so had a well rehearsed response ready. "Your father stumbled across evidence of treachery, although precisely what that evidence was, I don't know. He knew, of course, that Ted Gant was an MI5 officer, so decided to tell him what he'd found. Given the apparent closeness of their relationship, I suppose it would have been surprising if he hadn't gone to him first. Unfortunately, your father was completely unaware that the evidence he'd uncovered was the end of a trail that led back to Gant himself. After your father told him what he'd discovered, Gant plotted to take possession of the evidence and remove your father as its only witness. He is a treacherous, evil man and his highest priority was saving his own skin, regardless of the cost to others.

I'm unable to give you the full details of the investigation that led to Gant's arrest, but I'll tell you what I can. It was whilst I was enquiring into the death of Justine, as Rose had asked, that I first became suspicious about the death of your father. There were a number of things that concerned me, although at that stage they were all fairly circumstantial issues. I approached Sir Andrew Carpenter after discovering he'd visited Prinsted to assist the local police at the time of Justine's death. Fortunately I was able to persuade him to become involved in my own investigation and working together, we uncovered a significant amount of further evidence that pointed to Gant as the person who ordered your father's murder. Gant's appearance here at Harfield House was entirely unexpected, but it provided an opportunity to set a trap, which he fell into. I don't believe there was a threat to any of you whilst Gant was here in the House, but, if there ever was, the threat has now been removed and you're all perfectly safe."

Frances suddenly sat bolt upright with a look of surprise on her face. "What did you just say......at the end there?"

"....... the threat has now been removed and you're all perfectly safe," Brazelle repeated.

"So I did hear you right," said Frances, sitting back in her chair. "What are your plans now?"

Brazelle sighed. "Well, it's clear that Rose is very angry with me and I can't say I blame her. She'll be aware that I must have known about Gant when I first met him here two days ago, but never told her. Instead, I let her and you, Frankie, entertain the man who ordered the murder of your father. She probably feels physically sick and I'm surprised that you're still talking to me. Unfortunately, it was the only way I could see to trap him. Had he been alerted in some way, or, become suspicious, not only would we probably not have neutralised the man who actually murdered your father, but Gant, the man who sent him to do it, might have escaped justice."

"I assume that by 'neutralised' you mean 'killed'," said Damien. "Who was he?"

"Yes, he's dead," confirmed Brazelle, "but, for the time being, at least, I can't tell you anything more."

Damien did not pursue the matter. As a senior diplomat in the United Kingdom Foreign Office he appreciated that a question should only be answered at the appropriate time. In some instances, that might be after anyone who was ever interested in knowing the answer is dead or, in some cases, perhaps never.

Frances went over to the drinks cabinet and poured herself a whisky. "I'm still talking to you, Chris, because having to entertain Ted Gant for a couple of days, is a small price to pay for what you've achieved for us. And although knowing that my father was murdered doesn't make me feel any less sad at his passing, it does mean I don't have to spend the rest of my life thinking that he abandoned Rose and me, especially just when Rose needed him most. In future I look forward to not suffering my occasional episodes of anger and bitterness towards him." She raised her whisky glass. "And who knows, maybe I'll find less use for this stuff.

As for Rose, yes, of course, she's angry and upset. It would be a miracle if she wasn't. She's just learned that her father was murdered and that it was her godfather who ordered it done. What's more, she's discovered that the man she loves knew all of it and never told her. But nobody knows her like I do. In a moment I'm going to talk with her. Things will be different tomorrow, believe me." Frances hugged and kissed Brazelle before going up to her sister, leaving her untouched whisky behind.

Damien walked with Brazelle to the front door and shook his hand. "I was wrong about you, Chris, and I'm sorry. You're a good man and Rose chose well. Take care of yourself."

Brazelle drove back to Holford wondering what awaited him. His home had been the scene of a violent death and he assumed he would be banned from entering for the next few days, whilst a rigorous examination was carried out by a highly skilled team of crime scene investigators. He was, therefore, surprised to find there was no police tape marking off the site and that the cottage was deserted, except for Max, sitting alone on the sofa.

"Where is everybody?" Brazelle asked.

"Gone," replied Max. "There were only four of them and they were here for less than an hour. It didn't look to me like they'd come to search for evidence, either. They just cleaned the place up, and the way they went about it made me think they'd done this sort of thing before."

Brazelle took a look around. Orlando's body had been removed and so had all the pieces of the shattered bedroom door and the bloodstained bedroom carpet. Everything else appeared to be back in its usual place. In fact it struck Brazelle that his cottage was looking cleaner and tidier than it had done in a while.

"Did they take a statement from you, or your fingerprints?" asked Brazelle.

Max shook his head. "No, they didn't take anything........ except my shotgun......the bastards........and they wiped it clean before they took it away. They didn't say much either, except to tell me not to say anything to anybody about what happened here today and that someone will come round tomorrow morning to fit you a new bedroom door and carpet."

Brazelle was puzzled. Despite his cottage being the scene of a violent death and somewhere that two imposters had masqueraded as police officers, the team sent by Sir Andrew had clearly been more concerned to remove or destroy evidence, rather than gather and secure it. It was all very intriguing. He doubted that the British police service employed a specialist team of 'cleaners', but he was aware of a few organisations that did.

"Did you tell anyone at Harfield House what went on here?" asked Max.

"No. I didn't," Brazelle replied. "I kept quiet about it. Just as the Commissioner demanded I should. Now I understand why he did. Officially, nothing happened here today."

Day Fifteen - Saturday

Just after nine o'clock, a small team of workmen turned up at Holford and by shortly after eleven, when the men departed, not only did the cottage have a new bedroom door and carpet fitted, but quite a bit of the woodwork had been touched up aswell. Brazelle was pleased with the result. His home hadn't looked quite so good at any time since he moved in.

He was contemplating paying a visit to Harfield House to see if Rose would speak to him, when the phone rang in the study. It was Jenny. "Chris, can you come to the Church right away? Something's happening that I think you should see. The place has gone mad."

"Yes, of course, I'll......." Before Brazelle could finish his reply, Jenny had hung up.

There were several vehicles, including two police cars, parked on the road outside the Church and at least twenty villagers were gathered, clearly interested in some fairly noisy activity that was taking place in the churchyard. Brazelle approached the lichgate, but was stopped from going through by two police officers. "Who's in charge?" he asked.

"That would be me," said a familiar voice from behind. Brazelle turned to see newly promoted Chief Inspector Jenkins approaching.

"You can let him through," Jenkins instructed, and the gatekeepers immediately made way.

Jenny was already inside the churchyard and Brazelle and Jenkins went over to join her. "Thanks for coming, Chris. I really don't know what's going on," she said. "Well, that is, I do know what's going on, they're digging up one of the graves, but I haven't got the faintest idea why. About half an hour ago these people turned up and handed me this." She waved a bundle of papers she was holding. "They said they'd been instructed to exhume the body of...." She paused for a moment to consult the bundle of papers. ".....Abigail Pringle. She was buried on the thirty-first of August, 1651. I asked the Chief Inspector here, what it was all about, but he said he wasn't at liberty to say anymore than what was written on here." Again she waved the bundle of papers.

"Oh, so it's CHIEF Inspector now, is it Jenkins? Congratulations." commented Brazelle.

Jenny looked surprised. "You two know each other, do you?"

Brazelle and Jenkins both nodded and Jenny continued. "What was just as surprising, they knew exactly where to go to find Abigail Pringle's grave. They went straight to it."

"Well, that would be down to me," said Brazelle. "I drew a sketch of the graveyard and marked her grave clearly on it."

Jenny's mouth fell open. "You knew about this, Chris? Why didn't you talk to me about it?"

"Please, believe me. I was going to explain it all to you later today," replied Brazelle. "It was only yesterday afternoon that I asked for it to happen. It's true I asked if it could be done sometime today, but I wasn't serious. I thought it would take at least a week and probably a lot longer for it to be authorised and organised. I honestly thought I had plenty of time to explain and prepare you. I'm truly sorry you had to find out like this."

Jenkins interrupted. "What Mr Brazelle says is true. Like he said, he only asked yesterday afternoon, and to get an exhumation authorised and organised this quickly would normally be impossible. But, if you look at the signatures at the bottom of that document you're holding, you'll see why it could happen so soon after it was asked for."

Jenny turned to the bottom of the last page of her bundle of papers to see the signatures of the PM, the Home Secretary and the Lord Chief Justice.

Brazelle was about to take Jenny off to the vestry and explain what was happening, when one of the police gatekeepers called out to Jenkins. Frances was standing by the lichgate and Jenkins gestured for her to be allowed through.

Frances was surprised at the level of activity in the churchyard. "I came hoping to have a private word with you, Chris," she said, "but, if you're busy, I can wait."

"That's alright, Frances. You can have him," said Jenny. "I'll wait for you in the vestry, Chris. Perhaps when you're finished you can come and explain to me exactly what's going on out here."

Jenkins walked back to the lichgate leaving Brazelle and Frances alone.

"I rang your cottage, but when I didn't get an answer I guessed you'd probably be here, although I wasn't expecting any of this." Frances made a sweeping arm gesture. "What on earth is going on?"

"It's a long story. I'll tell you later," said Brazelle. "How's Rose? Do you know if she's forgiven me yet?"

"Yes, she's forgiven you and she's the reason I'm here," replied Frances. "She's so dreadfully sorry about how she reacted to you yesterday. She said she was in a state of shock and confusion and wasn't thinking straight. All very understandable, of course. What she found out in just a matter of seconds must have absolutely overwhelmed her. At least I knew some of it, but she was completely in the dark about everything until that moment. I explained what I knew and she now understands why it was necessary for you to do what you did. But she's concerned that you might be angry with her, so she asked me to come and try to smooth things over. And here I am."

"You know I'm not angry with her," said Brazelle. "I intended to come to the House later today, in the hope I could see her, after she'd had time to talk with you and think things through."

Frances took out her phone. "I'll call her straightaway. I imagine she'll want to come and see you, but I'm wondering if that's a good idea, with everything that's going on here at the moment."

"Actually, it's a very good idea," said Brazelle. "I'll explain when Rose arrives."

Brazelle left Frances to make her call and went to talk to the man who appeared to be in charge of the exhumation squad. "Have you done many of these before?" he asked.

"We've done about half a dozen over the past few years, so not many," replied the man, "but then again, there isn't that many that need doing. And we certainly haven't been called in to do one with less than twenty four hours notice before. Lord knows what the urgency is, but when duty calls. You have to have a special licence for this kind of work, you know, because you're dealing with human remains. It isn't just a matter of hacking away with a digger or a spade. It's got to be done with skill and lots of patience. We don't know how far down the old lady is, so we have to take it slowly. Families can take it very badly if you end up decapitating their relatives through going at it too vigorously, even if they have been dead for.....what is it? .....the best part of four hundred years. You're not related, are you?"

Brazelle shook his head.

The man pointed to the ever growing crowd of villagers lined up along the other side of the churchyard wall. "Well, you might not be, but I reckon some of them are. I'll bet there's been quite a lot of inbreeding in this village over the years. Anyway, unless she's buried somewhere near China we should get to her some time in the next hour or so."

Brazelle stepped away and went to rejoin Frances.

"I've called Rose and she's on her way over," said Frances. "Omnia vincit amor."

"Love conquers all," Brazelle translated, before adding, "Quid enem non vinceret ille."

"For what could love not conquer?" It was Frances' turn to translate. "You know your Virgil I see, Chris."

"Just a few bits of Ciris and the Aeneid," responded Brazelle. "I did them at school nearly twenty five years ago, with most of it long forgotten."

Frances put on a more serious face. "Before Rose arrives, Chris, there is one other thing I think I should tell you. I've remembered where we first met. It was something you said yesterday that brought it back to me. You said *'now the threat has been removed and you're all perfectly safe'*. It was exactly what you said to me the first time we met, when you saved my life. Those few days when I was held hostage were the most traumatic I've ever experienced and I have you to thank for bringing my ordeal to an end."

"I wasn't the only one," said Brazelle. "But how did you recognise me? My face was covered."

"Yes, it was, but your eyes weren't and of course you spoke to me," replied Frances. "When we met again last week, and I saw your eyes and heard your voice, I got a strong sense that it wasn't for the first time. I felt sure we must have met before, and then yesterday, when you repeated those same words, I realised where and when it was. Memories of experiences like that always remain with you. It just takes the right trigger to call them to mind."

"Have you told anyone else?" asked Brazelle.

Frances shook her head. "No. I wanted to tell you first. I will tell Damien, but I won't tell anyone else, if that's what you want. And I think you should tell Rose. In fact, if you're going to have any kind of ongoing relationship, I think you should tell her everything, whatever it is."

"I intend to," said Brazelle. "And it will be soon, very soon."

Frances smiled. "Good. I'm glad that's out of the way. Trying to remember where we first met has been driving me mad, ever since your first visit to Harfield House."

A few minutes later Brazelle heard his name being called and he turned to see Jenkins opening the lichgate, allowing Rose to pass through. She put her arms around him and kissed him. "I'm sorry about how I reacted," she said.

"You have absolutely nothing to be sorry about. I'm glad you've forgiven me," responded Brazelle. "All the bad stuff is now over, but there's still a lot to reveal to both of you. Come with me and I'll explain."

Brazelle led the two sisters into the vestry to join Jenny and after indicating there were implications for all three of them in what he was about to divulge, he began his explanation.

"Several months ago, just after Jenny took over here as parish priest, the Bishop of the Diocese commissioned a contractor based in Northope, to carry out a building survey of St Catherine's and produce a report highlighting any matters needing attention. Although the report identified a number of issues of concern, unfortunately for the Parish, the Bishop decided that nothing was sufficiently serious to warrant money being spent on it. And that might have been the end of the matter, except that a couple of months later a small wooden box was sent anonymously to the Archbishop of Canterbury. It was accompanied only by a brief note that simply read, '*Found hidden in the wall of Prinsted Church*'. The box, which was clearly very old, contained several equally ancient parchments, but, not surprisingly given their age, much of what was written on them was extremely faded and difficult to interpret, and there were occasional lacunas where the parchment had simply disintegrated. However, with some careful restoration work, the story the parchments told was eventually reconstructed. The first of the parchments to be restored carried the sketch of a medallion, or more correctly, a phalera. It had been awarded by King Charles the First, to Captain John Hadlington, a soldier who fought on the Royalist side during the English Civil War and a man of significance in the history of Prinsted. He was the officer commanding a Royalist patrol that carried out an ambush of a group of Cromwell's men who were on their way to London, transporting loot that had been seized in the north of England. There were no survivors on either side of the conflict, and everyone who fought and died, including Captain Hadlington himself, is buried out there in St Catherine's graveyard. And the loot was never found, although it hasn't been entirely forgotten. In fact, it became the stuff of legend, and is still remembered and referred to locally, as Cromwell's Treasure."

Brazelle held up a collection of papers. "The parchment with the sketch of the phalera, though, was only the first to be understood and restoration of all the others soon followed. These are photocopies of all the parchments that were in the box, together with their transcripts. The originals were created by Reverend Richard Shuttleworth, the vicar here in Prinsted, at the time of the ambush. They tell the story of how he and his adopted son, Adam, stumbled across its aftermath and how the dying Hadlington asked him to hide the treasure until King Charles was restored to his throne. He also gifted his phalera to Adam."

"When I first arrived in Prinsted, I knew neither precisely where the box had been found, nor the identity of the person who'd found it and sent it to the Archbishop. But that all changed a few days ago, after we opened up a void and I found a button..........this button." Brazelle held up the button he had found in the niche a few days earlier. "Once I'd discounted the possibility that it had come off the overalls of any of Fred Simpson's team, I took it to show to the manager of the Northope contractor that carried out the initial survey of the Church. He was able to confirm that it is identical to those on the company's standard issue overalls and, after I told him where I'd found it, he suggested how it got there. One of the areas explored during the initial survey of the Church, although never actually referred to in the report, was a void that had been created at some time in the past by partitioning off one of the Church's several niches. The survey manager suspected that a void existed, because of a comparison he'd made between the internal and external dimensions of the Church walls and through considerations of its internal symmetry. Thinking it might be contributing to some of the damp issues in that area of the Church, he had one of his men open it up and take a look inside. Fortunately for me, he remembered which of his men it was, so I went to speak with him. After I gave him my word I'd keep his identity secret, he admitted to being the person who'd sent the box to the Archbishop and agreed to explain how he'd come by it. He said he removed just enough of the partition to be able to inspect the void's interior with a torch and inspection camera. He found no evidence of damp, just the small wooden box, but thinking it might have some monetary value, he chose not to report it. The hole he'd created in the partition wall was big enough for him to pull the box out of the void, but not without knocking a loose button off the sleeve of his overall.....this button." Brazelle again held up the button he'd found in the niche a few days earlier.

"After the survey manager had carried out his own inspection of the void, confirming no issue of concern existed, the void was resealed and its existence considered unnecessary to mention in the survey report. A couple of months later the man who'd purloined the box had still not mentioned it to anyone, but had begun to have feelings of guilt about stealing from a church, so he decided to return it. Not wishing to expose himself as a thief, though, he chose to send it anonymously to the Archbishop of Canterbury."

Rose thought it was a good time to interrupt. "Maybe I should tell Frankie and Jenny that I have Captain Hadlington's phalera, Chris, and that I've had it since Gareth gave it to me twenty years ago."

"Good Lord," said Frances, "I didn't know that. But where on earth did Gareth get it from?"

Brazelle answered. "He found it in a compartment hidden behind the wood panelling in the remains of the basement of the original Harfield House."

Frances was growing increasingly perplexed. "This is one shock after another. How did this phalera thing find its way into the old Harfield House?"

Until just a few minutes ago, Jenny knew nothing about the phalera, but she did know the true identity of Sir Richard, so, putting two and two together, she was confident she had the answer to Frances' question. "For the very simple reason that Adam, the adopted son of Reverend Shuttleworth, and Sir Richard, first Baronet Harfield, are one and the same person," she said.

"So, you're in on it aswell, are you?" said Frances. "You all seem to know much more than I do about the Harfield family. And I'm its senior member! Have you anything else to reveal?"

Jenny pointed to the portrait of the young Adam Wellings. "Yes. I have. That's Sir Richard up there."

Frances and Rose immediately went to take a closer look at the portrait. "I wish our father was here to see this," said Frances. "It would have made him so happy to finally be able to put a face on that portrait in the library."

"Even if it is the face of a ten year old boy," added Rose.

"Well it may be too late for Sir Cornelius," said Jenny, "but I'm sure we can sort something for posterity."

Brazelle again waved his collection of papers. "Do you want to hear the rest of this?" he asked. The three members of his audience returned to their seats and he continued. "Reverend Shuttleworth put a lot of detail into his account, but left out one critical piece of information. Where, exactly, he'd hidden the treasure. He claimed that nobody else, not even Adam, knew where he'd concealed it. He intended to do as Hadlington had asked and keep the secret of the treasure and its hiding place until the monarchy was restored. But he was an old man and understandably concerned that the Restoration might not come soon enough. Increasingly aware of his own mortality, he wrote down his story and, together with the drawing of the phalera to give it more credibility, put it in a box and sealed it up in the void. Presumably, he was hoping that if he died before he could declare it to the restored King Charles, which sadly he did, the right person would find it one day and be able to recover the treasure."

Jenny interrupted. "Surely, Reverend Shuttleworth didn't create that void just to hide a small box!"

Brazelle shook his head. "No. I'm sure he didn't. During any war, but especially civil wars, there is always a break down of law and order. The English Civil War was no exception. Churches in particular were targets for robbery, because they were major repositories of valuable items, just like mini treasuries in fact. Reverend Shuttleworth understood this and, resourceful man that he was, took steps to protect the property of his Church by placing its most precious possessions into the niche before sealing it up. Although he may have disapproved of Cromwell's rule, it at least offered the promise of a return to some semblance of law and order, so, at some point during Cromwell's Commonwealth, Shuttleworth partially uncovered the void, brought out his Church's valuables and restored them to their place of prominence. It was probably at that time he placed the box in the void, before once more sealing it up. There it stayed, undisturbed, until just a few months ago."

"And what do you think happened to Prinsted Church's most precious possessions after Reverend Shuttleworth removed them from the void?" asked Jenny. "I can assure you I found nothing that fits that description when I arrived here. Well, nothing that a potential robber might describe as precious."

"Over the centuries, some things were probably sold to help pay the bills and, sadly, no doubt some items were unfortunately stolen," replied Brazelle. "But, in any case, I think we can be fairly certain that if there was anything of value still left in the Church when your predecessor, Reverend Pickering, arrived on the scene, it wouldn't have remained for very long. In fact, when I heard from Mrs Richards and others about the kind of man that Pickering was, and how he disappeared overnight without even informing the Bishop, I began to wonder if perhaps he'd discovered the treasure and taken off with it. After receiving information about him from the police, however, I quickly concluded that was not the case."

"You really have done your homework on all this, haven't you, Chris," said Jenny. "Until now, I believed that the Archbishop of Canterbury suddenly coming up with a pile of cash and telling the Diocese to spend it on our Church was an answer to prayer. But it isn't as straightforward as that, is it, Chris? You were sent here to find the treasure, weren't you?"

Brazelle raised his hands in a metaphorical mea culpa. "It's true that my initial reason for being here was to see if I could locate the treasure, but, as we both know, Jenny, The Lord works in mysterious ways. So it can still be seen as an answer to prayer, although maybe not just yours. And I can assure you, I've taken very seriously my responsibility to ensure the renovation and repair work to the Church has been carried out properly."

"Perhaps we should discuss that later?" said Jenny, with just a hint of menace. "Please finish your story."

Brazelle gave Jenny a gentle nod and continued. "As well as the phalera, Shuttleworth sketched several items he found amongst the treasure and all of these have been identified as precious artefacts that were taken from churches in the north of England. Rightfully, they are treasures belonging to the Church of England, so, isn't it reasonable that the Church of England sends someone to find and retrieve them?"

"Perhaps it is," said Jenny, "but I wish you'd discussed all this with me a bit sooner. Just like I wish you'd forewarned me about what's going on outside. In fact, perhaps you could tell all three of us just what is happening out there."

"Of course," said Brazelle. "And if I'm right, then it's the final chapter in the story. When I was in here with you a few days ago, Jenny, and we realised that Adam Wellings and Sir Richard Harfield were one and the same person, I took a close look at another of Reverend Shuttleworth's paintings, that one up there." Brazelle pointed to the portrait of the old man in the churchyard. "It has several features that I found intriguing. Firstly, the belt the old man is wearing is identical to one I found hidden in the same secret compartment as the phalera. Secondly, just below his initials, in the bottom right of the painting, Shuttleworth wrote '1656', presumably the year he painted it. The same year that appears on the parchments he placed in the box. Thirdly, and perhaps most importantly, the old man in the painting appears to be of a similar age to that which Shuttleworth would have been in 1656 and he's standing in the graveyard of Prinsted Church where Shuttleworth was the vicar. Putting all this together, I began to consider the possibility that the old man in the portrait is Shuttleworth himself and that his purpose in painting it was to provide a further clue to the whereabouts of the treasure.

With those thoughts in mind I took another look at the original parchments and compared them with their transcriptions. On one line Shuttleworth wrote, *'the treasure is hidden in the Church'*. It was the line that brought me here to Prinsted in the first place. There is a tiny lacuna, where the parchment has disintegrated, immediately following the word, *'Church'*, but I can well understand why the transcriber would assume that the missing fragment had not caused any text to be lost. It was very small and a new sentence began immediately following it, on the next line. To have inferred that a word was missing would not have made much sense, but suppose that some text was missing. Not a separate word, but the continuation of the word *'Church'*, so the phrase should actually read, *'the treasure is hidden in the ChurchYARD'*.

My mind then went back to something I noticed last Tuesday, when I was looking through the Prinsted parish records. I recalled that a burial took place on the day immediately after the day when the ambush took place and Reverend Shuttleworth stumbled across it and removed the treasure.

In those days it was common practice to carry out burials quite early in the morning, the grave having been dug and prepared the day before. If that was the case with this particular burial, then when Shuttleworth returned to Prinsted with the treasure he would have had a ready-made hiding place. That night, under cover of darkness and when everyone in the village, including Adam, was asleep, he could deposit the two treasure chests in the ready dug grave and cover them over with some soil. In the morning, the coffin of the deceased would be placed on top and nobody would be any the wiser. The name of the person being buried that day was Abigail Pringle and, in the painting, the name on the gravestone on which the old man is resting his arm is ...... Abigail Pringle."

"And that grave is the one being dug up right now!" observed Jenny. "Brilliant!"

"Or just lucky....... and only if I'm right," said Brazelle. "But if I'm wrong, I stand to end up with a lot of egg on my face, not to mention having to explain myself to those people whose signatures appear on that document you were given this morning, Jenny."

Jenny began to have second thoughts. "Hang on a minute! Wouldn't someone at the burial have noticed that the grave appeared to be rather shallower than when it was originally dug?"

Brazelle had anticipated the question. "That's a good question, Jenny, but one to which I believe the answer is..... No. According to the parish records, there had been five graves dug during that particular Church Season and the Season's Reckonings state that the Verger, Thomas Evans, was paid for digging all five of them, but only paid for filling in four. The one he didn't get paid for filling in was Abigail Pringle's. As the man who actually dug Abigail's grave, Thomas Evans was probably the only person who knew its original depth and I believe that the ever resourceful Shuttleworth made sure he wasn't present at the time of Abigail's burial to see how less deep it had become. There would have been a number of tasks the old priest could have given him to make sure of that. And since there is no record of anyone else being paid for filling in Abigail's grave, I believe that Shuttleworth himself did the job, perhaps aided by his son, Adam."

Jenny walked over to the vestry door. "All very plausible, Chris, but I guess we'll know if you're right, soon enough. They can't be far off finishing. I'm going to take a look."

The other three followed her out into the churchyard and Brazelle once more approached the workman in charge. "How far have you got?" he asked.

The workman pointed to a new coffin that was placed near the open grave. "We've removed the deceased's remains and put them in there. As you might imagine, there wasn't much left of the original coffin after all this time. The skeleton was in pretty good nick though.

It seems a shame to have to rebury it. Some Medical School could probably make good use of it."

Brazelle resisted the temptation to get into a discussion about body snatchers. "What details were you given about what you were looking for?" he asked.

"We were told there might be something of value buried a short distance below the deceased and we needed to find it if there was. One of my lads is down in the hole taking a look."

Brazelle rejoined the three women and after a time that seemed to him like ages, but was, in fact, barely five minutes, he heard a cry come from the man in the grave. "Found something!"

Given where he was and the fact that the circumstances involved digging up a near four hundred year old corpse, Brazelle resisted the urge to let out a cheer, settling for a clenched fist.

Understandably, after such a long time in the ground, there was very little left of the wooden chests themselves, but the treasure they had contained remained and the workmen set about recovering it. One item at a time, it was handed up out of the grave and placed into a collection of wooden boxes watched over by Chief Inspector Jenkins and two other policemen.

"Well done, Chris. It seems you were right after all," said Jenny. "Is it finders keepers, do you think?"

"I'm pretty sure it isn't," replied Brazelle. "But at least you've had some money spent on the Church."

Frances also congratulated Brazelle, before making a confession. "I've always had a bit of a sneaky suspicion that the source of Sir Richard Harfield's wealth and the disappearance of Cromwell's Treasure were in some way related," she said. "It seems I was completely off the mark. But, we now know who Sir Richard really was and what he looked like, at least as a young boy, so two of our family mysteries have been solved."

Chief Inspector Jenkins came over and drew Brazelle to one side. "I've just called the Chief and told him what's happened. He asked me to give you his congratulations and say he had every confidence in you. He'll let the signatories to the Vicar's document know what's happened. I expect the politicians will find some way of claiming a bit of the credit." He was about to return to monitoring the recovery of the treasure, but remembered something. "I almost forgot, the Chief asked me to give you this, just in case you ever need it." Jenkins handed Brazelle a business card with Sir Andrew's confidential telephone number on it.

"I've already got one of these," said Brazelle.

Jenkins grinned and shook his head. "Not exactly like that one you haven't. Your password's changed."

Brazelle turned the card over and smiled.

"What are you smiling about?" asked Rose, "What does that say?"

"It says, '**I am a lucky priest**'," replied Brazelle.

"Well, I don't think there can be much doubt about that?" said Rose. "Ferrari, Cromwell's Treasure.......Me!"

"I can't argue with any of that," said Brazelle. "But there's still one thing I want to do today. How would you like to meet the Archbishop of Canterbury?"

"Sure, sounds cool. I've never met an Archbishop. When?"

"The Archbishop returns from Canada today and should land at Heathrow in about three hours. I'd like to be there and be the first to give out the good news."

Jenny overheard Brazelle's invitation to Rose. "Come and join Gerald and me at the Vicarage when you get back," she said. "There are things to explain and also things to celebrate."

"There certainly are," Brazelle agreed.

"Are we going in the Ferrari?" asked Rose.

"Sure, if you want to," replied Brazelle.

"Can I drive?" she asked.

Brazelle stared at Rose for a few seconds and gave the matter some thought. "Okay, you can drive some of the way, but you must stick to the speed limit."

Rose smiled. "What's a speed limit?"

As Brazelle and Rose waited just outside the VIP Arrivals area at Heathrow, Rose decided there was something she needed to know. "What do I call an Archbishop?" she asked, "Your Reverence? Your Holiness?"

Brazelle shook his head. "Neither of those things. The correct form of address is, 'Your Grace', unless the Archbishop tells you otherwise."

Rose had posed her question just in time, as a tall white man wearing a dog collar, accompanied by a slightly shorter black woman approached. Brazelle waved and the man returned his wave with a smile. Rose stepped forward holding out her hand to the tall man. "I'm very pleased to meet you, Your Grace," she said.

The man took the hand that was offered. "I'm very pleased to meet you too, my dear, but I'm not the Archbishop."

"No, he isn't," said the woman standing next to him. "That would be me. He's my personal assistant, Reverend Burdock. And if you call me Dandelion I shall have to break the sixth commandment."

The Archbishop hugged Brazelle who kissed her on both cheeks. "To what do I owe this pleasant surprise, Chris? Did you miss me so much? And who is this beautiful creature you've brought along with you?"

"I always miss you, Your Grace. You know that," replied Brazelle. "And this is Rose, a very dear friend of mine. But I'm afraid your very English joke might be wasted on her, she's been living in the States for the past twenty years."

"Twenty years in the States! Oh, you poor thing," said the Archbishop with a grin. "Did you commit some heinous crime as a young child?" Then looking Rose up and down, she added, "'*Very dear friend*', you say? Always one for the understatement, aren't you, Chris. Tell me Rose, has he taken you for a ride in his Ferrari yet?"

"Oh, he's done more than that. He let me drive it some of the way here this afternoon to meet you," replied Rose.

The Archbishop winked at Rose. "Well in that case, Rose, you're a lot more than just his '*very dear friend*'."

As the group walked out of the terminal building, and towards the Archbishop's waiting car, Brazelle explained exactly why he had turned up to meet her, and gave her the good news about the treasure.

"I knew you were the one for the job," said the Archbishop, "but, what now? What would you like to do next?"

"I do have something in mind and was hoping I could call you on Monday to discuss it," replied Brazelle.

"Fine. Call me around ten," said the Archbishop. Then, taking a last look at Rose, she added, "you are very blessed, Reverend Brazelle. Goodbye and God bless both of you."

As the Archbishop's car drove off, Rose turned to Brazelle, "Are you Chris? Are you very blessed?

Brazelle smiled, "I think you know the answer to that."

It was almost eight o'clock when Brazelle and Rose arrived back in Prinsted. On their way to the Vicarage they passed the Church and saw that the workmen, police officers and the village crowd had all departed. The treasure had been removed and Abigail Pringle had been re-interred, with her grave carefully returned to its former state.

"I'll leave you here for a few minutes if you don't mind," said Rose as they pulled up outside the Vicarage. "I've been in these same clothes all day and I'd like to pop home and get changed. I won't be long."

Jenny opened the door to Brazelle. "Where's Rose off to?" she asked, seeing her drive away.

"She said she wants to get changed," replied Brazelle. "But I think she just wants to spend a few more minutes driving the Ferrari. She'll be back very soon. So, what's happened to the treasure?"

"The police took it away," Jenny replied. "It has to be dealt with by the coroner, but that should be a formality. I suppose most of it will eventually be handed over to the Church at national level, seeing as how it's mostly made up of valuable items taken from churches."

Gerald interrupted. "You know, Chris, you've given Prinsted more excitement in the last twenty four hours than it's had in the last three hundred years. And the last time anything exciting happened here it inspired the naming of a pub. Prinsted is a lot bigger now than it was all those years ago, maybe it's time we had a second pub and perhaps we should call it........... The Lucky Priest."

Brazelle smiled. "I'm glad you said 'lucky'. I've been called a lot worse recently.

"So, you've helped locate the very naughty Reverend Pickering, solved a murder and found some treasure, but what about the original brief that Rose gave you?" asked Gerald. "Have you come up with a conclusion concerning Lady Justine's death?"

Brazelle nodded. "Yes, I have. And it seems Frank Weston was right."

Gerald was surprised. "So, it wasn't an accident? Justine was murdered?"

Brazelle shook his head. "No. It was definitely an accident. But what Frank said was: *Lady Justine's death was not an accident caused by her simply slipping on a wet wooden bridge. Someone helped her on her way to the great hereafter*'. And he was right. A third party was involved in causing her death, but there was absolutely no intent involved and no blame can be attached to them. To this day, the person concerned has no idea that they played any part in Justine's death. And that, by the way, is how it's going to stay."

"Do you know who this third party is?" asked Jenny.

Brazelle nodded. "Yes I do."

Gerald passed Brazelle a drink. "Does anybody else know?" he asked.

"There is just one other person who knows. In fact, they saw everything, but just like me, they'll never divulge the identity of the third person, or even own up to being a witness."

"You seem very confident about all this, Chris," commented Jenny. "But what do you intend telling Rose?"

"I shall tell her the truth. Her mother's death was a tragic accident with absolutely nobody else to blame. I hope you'll treat what I've told you as strictly confidential. Please believe me, there would be no benefit served to anyone if you were to divulge any of it, just a great deal of heartache and pain."

"Yes, of course we will," said Gerald. "When are you going to tell Rose that you've now reached your final conclusion on the matter?"

"I shall tell her later tonight, along with a whole lot of other things," replied Brazelle.

Jenny changed the subject. She had a question for Brazelle on a different matter. "Why didn't you tell me what your true purpose for being here was?" she asked.

"For the simple reason that I'd been given very clear instructions by the Archbishop that I must tell absolutely no one, not even you, Jenny. Believe me, I wanted to tell you, but the Archbishop was adamant that nobody should know until the exercise was over, one way or the other. I did think it was a bit unfair leaving you out, but since then, of course, I've found out about your predecessor, Pickering. Somebody, I now realise the Archbishop knew all about. Maybe that influenced her decision about not telling you. As for not telling anyone else... well.... if word had got out that there was treasure hidden somewhere in the Church, lord knows who might have turned up with their sledge hammers and pickaxes to try and get to it first."

"I guess you're right," agreed Jenny. "And I have to say, I also agree with your earlier comment about Reverend Shuttleworth being a resourceful man. After we talked about him the other day I contacted the Diocesan office to find out if they had any information about him. Fortunately they did, and it made very interesting reading. Apparently before he became a priest he'd been a soldier............just like you."

Brazelle was taken by surprise. "What makes you think I was a soldier?"

"Oh come on, Chris," said Jenny. "I spotted it soon after we first met, five years ago. And Gerald twigged soon after, without me ever saying anything to him. It was your punctuality, your self discipline, not to mention your well polished shoes!" She laughed.

"And let's not forget your military bearing," added Gerald with a giggle. Do you remember the old Spike Milligan joke? *'A man walked in with a military bearing, which he tossed in the air and caught'.*"

Jenny ignored Gerald's attempt at humour and went back to interrogating Brazelle. "Was the fact that you were once a soldier, one of those *'whole lot of other things'* you said you intended to tell Rose later?"

Brazelle nodded. "Yes it is."

Jenny heard a car pulling onto the drive and looked out of the window. "It's your Ferrari. I'll go and let Rose in."

Jenny left the room and Gerald took over the questioning.

"Tell me, Chris, was there some key pivotal moment during your investigation, when a light bulb switched on in your brain and a solution to all this started to form?" he asked.

"Well, oddly enough, your choice of the word 'key' is highly appropriate," replied Brazelle. "It was something that Frank Weston mentioned, about some keys that were in Justine's handbag. At the time it didn't have a conscious impact on me, but later that night I had an incredibly vivid dream, in which Justine appeared in the cottage and placed some keys on the mantelpiece. I don't believe in messages coming from the dead, so I can only assume that what Frank said had an impact in my subconscious. However it came about, though, it certainly influenced my thinking and it turned out that the keys made an important contribution to solving the case."

Gerald may well have continued with more questions but Jenny and Rose came into the room.

"Have you come to a conclusion about that matter I raised with you the other day, Chris?" asked Jenny.

"Yes, I have," said Brazelle. "I want to accept your offer and, if the Bishop agrees, look after the parish until you decide to return. In fact, I have a call booked with the Archbishop of Canterbury for Monday morning and I was going to discuss it with her then."

"Well, sounds to me like it'll be a foregone conclusion if you've got the big guns out," said Jenny. "You certainly don't do anything by halves do you, Chris?"

"There is one potential hiccup, though," said Brazelle. "My lease on the cottage is up in a couple of months' time and I haven't sorted out an extension with my landladies yet."

"Oh, I don't think you need to worry about that," said Rose.

"And what about you, Rose?" asked Jenny. "What are your plans? Do you still intend to return to the States soon?"

"Well, for the time being I'm certainly going to have to stay ....because I have a work in progress," Rose replied.

"A work in progress?" said Jenny quizzically. "What's that exactly?"

Rose pointed at Brazelle. "Him."

Brazelle smiled, "And you, my darling, are mine!"

TWENTY YEARS EARLIER

Rose was banned from going into Gareth's tree house, but she had always yearned to take a look inside.

There was the sound of breaking glass, Mrs Richards went to investigate and Rose saw her chance. Through the kitchen window she had seen Gareth enter the tree house and knowing that the kitchen door was unlocked she decided to go and join him. As she approached, Gareth saw her coming and lowered the ladder for her to climb up.

"I thought you weren't allowed to come up here," said Gareth.

Rose put on a mischievous grin. "I'm not, but nobody knows I'm here. What are you doing?"

Gareth pointed to a wooden model standing on his table. "I've just finished making an arcuballista."

Rose was puzzled. "What's an akka......? What you said?"

"It's a big catapult that the Romans used to send big rocks long distances to hit their enemies," Gareth explained.

Rose picked up some small round balls that lay on the table beside the arcuballista. "And what are these?" she asked.

"They're made from lead. I think they're what people used to shoot out of guns many years ago. I found them in the old part of the House," replied Gareth.

"They're very dirty," said Rose, wiping her hands on her pretty white dress. "What do you do with them?"

Gareth loaded up the already primed arcuballista. "You put one in here, like this. And when you push that lever, it flies out and goes a long way."

"What? Like this?" said Rose, as she pushed the lever.

"No!" shouted Gareth. But it was too late. The lead ball had already shot through the open window and was hurtling through space. Gareth moved quickly to see where it might land and caught site of a lone female figure coming over the bridge that crossed the stream. He recognised her immediately, but before he could call out a warning he saw the lead ball hit her on the side of her face. The shock of the impact was sufficient to make her react with a sudden lurch, take her hand off the guardrail and drop her handbag. In that split second, she lost her footing on the slippery wet bridge and fell headlong into the stream, hitting her head on a rock as she did. Gareth stood silent at the open window, stunned by what he had just witnessed, until he was jolted back to consciousness by the sound of his mother's voice.

"Rose!" shouted Mrs Richards. "I've been looking everywhere for you. Come down here at once. And look at the state of you. Your lovely white dress is filthy. If your mother and father find out what you've been up to they're going to be very cross with both of us. Best keep it to ourselves I think, don't you? Now come along, we'd best get you cleaned up and changed before your mother gets back."

Gareth watched Rose and his mother go back into the kitchen before breaking up his arcuballista and placing the pieces in the bin.

CPSIA information can be obtained
at www.ICGtesting.com
Printed in the USA
BVHW081330150921
616792BV00006B/37